AGAINST
THE ODDS

SUE MILLARD

Jackdaw E Books, 2018

Cover and text Copyright © Susan Millard 2018

First published in Great Britain by J A Allen, 1995

This edition 2018

JACKDAW E BOOKS

Daw Bank, Greenholme, Tebay

Penrith, Cumbria

CA10 3TA

England

http://www.jackdawebooks.co.uk

ONE

"All right. Take her away."

Steven Pickering turned back for a final word with the horsebox driver, and Siân Davies took the halter rope to lead her new charge up the yard towards the empty box. The little black mare, clean and neat in blue rug and bandages, stepped out with a free and jaunty stride. Smelling the other horses, she gave a shrill whinny, then shook her head, jiggled sideways and snuffled excitedly. Siân stroked her neck.

"Settle down. Nothing to get excited about."

The mare whinnied again but the other horses were shut in for the afternoon rest and too used to the sound of hooves to bother to reply. Pickering's took very few mares to train for steeplechasing, preferring the less-emotional geldings. There was no response from any of

3

the thirty boxes, and the mare, discouraged, remained silent.

Down the yard, the old horsebox had done a three-point turn and grumbled away down the drive. It hooted. Siân glanced round; the driver waved cheerily. Siân was tempted to wave back but seeing the Guv'nor's annoyance, she didn't. His call floated up the yard: "Don't forget the top door!" She made plain her understanding and walked on, the mare following willingly. In the loosebox, Siân took off the travelling gear, deftly unwinding bandages from the slender legs, sliding off the tail bandage and concluding the job with a kindly pat. Then, reluctantly, she went out, closed the bottom door, unhooked the top door, swung it round and bolted it shut. A wild whinny and an unhappy clatter of feet announced the dismay of the little mare at being thus deprived of view and scent, but Siân hardened her heart and, gathering up the rug and bandages, left her.

It was useless to protest. All the horses here, powerful though they might be on the gallops or racecourse, were imprisoned for most of the day, seeing nothing of the outside world except when they went racing. In the afternoons and at night all doors were closed. Siân's instinct would have been to allow the horses access to freedom and fresh air without ever closing a top door but here at Green Bank what you were told to do, you did. Closed doors saved warmth, feed, rugs and expense. The horses had to get used to it.

Siân was off duty now. Her presence to receive her new horse had been necessary but she was not expected to prolong the encounter; more, it would have been looked on as suspect, a foolish waste of free time. Siân was still getting used to the boarding-school atmosphere of the hostel and the studied indifference of the lads to any sentimental demonstration. Although many of them, especially the girls, were passionately attached to their horses, they all seemed to find it necessary to pretend they weren't, while there were some who regarded them solely as a means of earning money. Frankie, Siân's room-mate, mucked out perfunctorily, rode barely adequately and made no secret of the fact that she appreciated Siân solely for the lightening of her workload. Until Siân's arrival, Frankie had been "doing" five horses.

Siân turned into the tackroom. These items of horse clothing would have to be stored until the owner came to collect them, since Pickering's made a small show by always travelling their runners in their own green rugs with the family initials on the corners. Sweet-sour smells met her: sweat, mucky concrete and mingled English and foreign leather. As part of her breaking-in, Siân had been set to clean all the items which, technically, belonged to no one in particular: work saddles, work bridles, martingales, saddle pads, boots to protect the horses' legs when they went schooling over the hurdles or the tall birch-brush fences. They had been filthy. She would not have time to clean them again now her third horse had arrived.

She looked for an empty cupboard, put away the headcollar and the rug, and began to roll up the bandages, sighing a little. She had thought herself fit when she came here, but keeping up with the work rate of the other nineteen-year-olds had exhausted her in the past month. She remembered how she had boggled at the amount of starchy food her hostel got through in a day, and the fact that when she arrived there had been nothing left to eat, but now her appetite had grown to match her fellow lads', and still she was hungry, while her jodhpurs had begun to slide down over her thinning hips. She was aware that what she wanted most was sleep. The hostel wouldn't be quiet when she went back but that wouldn't matter. She was so tired, she could nod off anywhere; given a bed, even Frankie's ghetto blaster would not keep her awake.

The tail bandage was dirty, so, mechanically, she went to the sink and drew hot water to wash it. A face peered in at the window and she jumped. Justin always made her heart thud uncomfortably. She couldn't decide whether to be flattered by the attentions of the trainer's son, or frightened of him. Granted, he was good-looking and she couldn't help watching him, but he did trade on his position and his good looks, and he seemed to enjoy her confusion. From the sidelong glances the other girls gave her, they knew quite well the struggle she was having not to succumb. Knowing the lads in the male hostel, they probably ran a book on Justin's success with each new girl. Torn between excitement and fright, she rubbed the bandage in the soapy water and waited for him.

"Busy again, eh?" he said, wandering in. He planted himself against the draining board so he could see her face but she didn't look at him. She already knew too well the brilliantly blue eyes, much brighter than her own, the tough, bony frame of his face, the fashionable cut of his hair. Even without looking she could see the brightness of its gold.

"Come on, Shannie. Don't you ever stop? Come down the Crown and I'll give you a better feed than old Coxie can dish up."

"I've got this to do," she said, not looking up, but her cheeks reddened. She knew he was watching her. She rinsed the bandage and found pegs, and he followed her out to the washing line.

"You know your way round all right," he said. She glanced at him, but he only smiled lazily back at her. "Enjoying yourself?"

"It's a job," she said, snapping the pegs on to the line.

"Such as it is," he agreed. She rubbed her wet hands to dry them, then huddled inside her thin jacket against the brisk September wind. Steven Pickering had promised to get her a waxed jacket, for which he would take payment out of her wages, but somehow it had not yet arrived and she had not dared enquire about it. The Pickering family was a daunting one, not least its charmingly arrogant son.

"Bit of a thin wind, eh? Let's go somewhere warmer. Lasagne and chips all right with you?"

"I haven't said I'm coming," she mumbled.

"Oh, Shannie!" he laughed. "You're saying yes all over. You lads are always starving."

"I wish you wouldn't call me Shannie," she said, with a sudden burst of spirit.

"Shaan, then," he said. "Are you coming or not?" She shook her head, reluctantly unwilling to admit that in the warmth of the Crown she would probably fall asleep.

"Come out and have a meal with me tonight then."

"Tonight?"

"Yeah, why not? I didn't come over just to watch you washing grotty bandages."

"I'll think about it."

"You're not thinking about it now?"

"I've got a new horse to think about," she reminded him. "You know, this place is weird! I don't even know her name."

He shrugged. "So what? Did she come in that old blue Bedford? That was Chris Rogers. The horse'll be his mothers. Probably won't be much use; she got it for two thou at Slater's dispersal sale."

Since this represented nearly six months' living-in wages, Siân opened her mouth and shut it again rather quickly before Justin could comment. She managed to say, "Well, she looks nice."

He pulled a face. "Hope she'll stand up to this job. She looks weedy. All that breed are. They're sort of related to the Northern Dancer line, but they're a long way short of his quality."

"What's this one called?" she asked, too interested now to be shy.

9

"Oh, something daft, I suppose. Something to do with dancing, Jump, something — Double Jump, would that be it? Something like that."

"That's a nice name," said Siân tentatively. She already felt defensive about the little mare and held back from asking Justin how old Double Jump might be, not wanting him to realise how inexperienced she was with horses. But he wasn't pursuing her thoughts about the mare.

"I think Siân's a better name than Double Jump," he said, grinning at her. "And if you teach me I can probably say it right, too."

She blushed. "You said it all right that time."

"There you are then! I'll call for you this evening, shall I? If you don't fancy the Crown we can go somewhere else, you know. Maybe you'd rather not have the rest of the staff earwigging."

Siân hesitated. Going elsewhere meant putting herself entirely in his hands, because there were no other pubs within walking distance of Green Bank, but neither did she want to sit on display with the boss's son, in front of the other lads. She'd only just got over the rough testing they had given her on the yards among the horses, making sure she got the mucksack with the hole in it so that the sweeping-up made her late, watching her lead out Smokey Ash and wonder how to get on board while the yard milled with fresh-tempered horses and nobody offered her a leg up. She didn't want to set herself up for them to throw jests at once again, but the thought of being alone with Justin with his strong hands and wickedly knowing eyes, was both tempting and a bit scary.

"Where else could we go?" she asked, and realised with a thump of the heart that she'd accepted his invitation.

TWO

Justin took her to the Stirrup, a brash, designer-planned pub on the Preston road. He drove fast. His car was a top of the range Ford with its own personalised plates, JII5TIN, and as he drove he delighted in showing her all its tricks. Siân felt out of her depth and decidedly outclassed, despite her clean jeans and blouse. It was just lucky that she had been able to borrow some make-up, and that her brown hair curled naturally so she didn't look too much like a stablehand, grubby, lank and poverty-stricken.

As she had guessed, the other inhabitants of the hostel took no notice when Justin came to pick her up. He too was scrubbed and shiny but his leather trousers and jacket were carelessly scuffed, as though he knew his attraction had nothing to do with clothes. It occurred to her with unsettling force that he might be younger than she was — younger in age but years older in experience.

At the Stirrup she allowed him to usher her in and choose their table. He was very quick and the service was good. She had been half afraid that he would choose somewhere secluded for their meal and that she would find there was nothing to talk about, but here they were in the middle of a busy pub and he was making her laugh. He seemed to know everybody and which were the regulars, and if he didn't actually like them Siân hardly noticed, so dazzled was she by his glamour. She ate hungrily, feeling much better for having slept that afternoon and much braver about going out with Justin.

"You're not so ladylike tonight," he said at last, watching her scrape her pudding plate.

"Mm?"

"Well, on the yards you'd think butter wouldn't melt in your mouth."

"I'm afraid I've proved that wrong at least," she said, putting down her spoon.

"Cheese and biscuits?" he suggested. "Charlotte'll bring us some." And at the click of his fingers, she did.

Siân wondered at the ease of it all. This was quite unlike cooking for her father or waiting patiently in cheap cafés until the waitress noticed. Charlotte had a very nice smile. Siân wondered, too, whether she only imagined it or did the smile become a smirk when Charlotte turned it on her?

"You look a lot better for that grub," Justin went on. "A bonny lass like you shouldn't be frozen-faced all the time."

She shook her head slightly, refusing the compliment. People in the greengrocer's shop had only called her a bonny lass when they wanted a favour doing, and neither her father nor her mother — before she left — had lavished praise upon her, in fact, the opposite. She bent her head over her biscuits and said nothing.

"I'll have to bring you here again, I can see you like it." Then he waved his empty glass towards her Perrier. "Are you going to have something a bit stronger now?"

"No, just another the same please."

"Living dangerously, ooh! Go on, Shannie, you've eaten enough to soak up a barrel of beer."

She couldn't help smiling. "All right."

"Go on, splash out, eh? Don't need to count the pennies."

She knew Green Bank was a stable that laid heavy bets on its fancied runners. Strictly, as a jockey, Justin ought not to bet, but it was common knowledge that his father put cash his way out of any winnings of his own. This supper was just another of the perks. So she said, "Well, if Charlotte can bring us coffee, I'll have a liqueur with it. What do you think I should try?"

"Now that's more like it!" he said with a flash of his bright eyes that reduced her to jelly.

He ordered Drambuie. She decided she liked it and when he bought her a second she thanked him shyly, which seemed to amuse him.

"I bet you had a rough time when you started with us!"

She thought about it, and said, "I was glad I hadn't got any smart gear to spoil."

He laughed. "Yeah, they buried you in the muck heap. I heard."

"And made me an apple-pie bed — with real apples."

"I noticed Boardman's orchard looked a bit thin..." They both laughed. "So what did you do about it? "

"I hurled them at everybody who came in range and I felt a lot better!"

"Didn't think you had it in you," he grinned and drank to her, still watching her over the glass. "Now when I have a go, I have a real go. Like gentian violet spray for aftershave. Never tried it on a lass, mind," he added, musingly. "The last soft herbert I did it to packed and went back to Mammy next morning. That was when he found the lads had filled his suitcase with shit. I think it was Phil who ended up with his new jodhpurs but I forget. He couldn't ride anyway so he didn't need them. He wasn't as pretty as you, either."

She ducked her head again. "Well... I had nothing worth stealing."

"Darling, you undersell yourself," he said meaningly, and she blushed and looked for a change of subject.

Airily, she said, "Tony let me school today," pleased that the head lad had confidence in her.

"Ash must be getting used to you then," he grinned.

"I'm getting used to him, at any rate." She was not going to admit that the sheer speed and strength of the racehorses had terrified her at first, or that she had been so frightened it had been all she could do not to pack like the "soft herbert" and run home. Only the fact that she had already run away once had stopped her. Green Bank had been her only possible roof and she had to adapt or be defeated. "I wonder what Double Jump will be like?"

"Oh, she'll be all right. She hasn't the strength to put up much fight. I'll soon find out in the morning. The Guv'nor'll put me up to see what she's made of."

Siân felt a twinge of pity for Double Jump, like herself a newcomer and being tested out. But, copying the stable's attitude, she asked, "What's her owner like? Is she quick to 'drop'?"

"Shouldn't think so. There won't be a lot to spare after training fees, but she'll probably like you, so you never know She's schoolmarmish and ever so nice but..." he smiled disarmingly. "For some reason she doesn't react to my charms."

Siân found herself caught by his gaze. *I do,* she thought helplessly, and quickly turned her attention to her Drambuie. *And I'd better not drink too much of that either...*

It was Justin himself who saved her composure. He spotted a group of young men at the bar awaiting their opening pints, and shouted at them to come and join him. Charlotte obligingly cleared the plates and spread clean beermats. The empty table was swamped in drinks, chairs and stools were drawn up, and the conversation became quick and raucous. Siân was eclipsed, so she sat quietly observing the group around her. They were surprisingly non-horsey. One was a bookie's clerk in Burscough, one a racecourse bookie's assistant travelling every day to different courses to work in the Tattersall's Enclosure; the third, Robbie, was the son of a family owning a string of amusement arcades along the coast. She thought the only thing that united them must be a gambling instinct and an urge to take risks. Siân knew that her mother would have condemned them all as being "sharp," but her mother had chosen to leave home, and that in Siân's mind took away any right to judge the company she kept. So she sat quiet and watched, and pretended she was enjoying herself.

Later in the evening, two girls joined the group, tipsy and giggly, wearing fluorescent jewellery and heavy make-up which did not disguise their youth. They looked at Siân as though she were elderly, with pity. But when one of them said slyly, "Jussy only talks to us when Janice isn't around," Justin stared her down, and before long they picked up their black cotton jackets and left.

He stretched an arm along the back of the seat and patted Siân.

"Isn't this nice?" he said expansively, and added to the others, "Don't we get some choice ones at our place, eh?"

They all laughed, and Siân joined in, slightly uncomfortably. When Robbie offered to buy her some nuts she smiled at him, glad he had broken the atmosphere.

She would have liked to go back to the stables but it was too far to walk. She was constrained to wait on Justin driving home, but he ordered another round, expecting Robbie to fetch it. Siân sat on her hands.

The night wore on and customers began to leave. The landlord dropped hints about taxis, but Justin suggested that instead of going home they should all play sardines on the pool table. Siân got up quickly and followed the landlord's directions and found there was indeed a taxi waiting in the car park for fares. She came back and met the lads being shepherded out by the barman.

It was Robbie who gave her her jacket but she overheard Justin's voice: "Little smasher. . . not a bad bit of homework, eh, Danny? I saw you smiling at her!"

Robbie winked and said, "Take no notice," but Siân felt suddenly cold.

Justin came up behind her and tugged her hair. "Us first for the taxi, eh, love? Robbie can come with us. He's going off to Blackpool until flippin' November so he'd best know what he's missing. The rest of you rabble can wait your turn."

The taxi decanted them at the end of the stable drive. Siân watched Justin pocketing his change and knew a fleeting moment of regret that Robbie should be leaving to do the illuminations season.

Then Justin waved the taxi away, and she was back under his spell. He put his arm round her and as they began to walk back up the drive, she could hear his leather jacket squeaking with each step. She found herself giggling.

"What's up, darling?"

"You need oiling," she said. *But if I weren't nervous,* she thought, *I wouldn't have noticed. I wanted to go out with him. Why aren't I enjoying it?*

Near the safety of the hostel door was a beech tree. Old and broad of trunk, it stood in a carpet of crisp newly fallen leaves, and Justin steered her into its shadow.

"Well?" he said.

"Well... what?"

"Do I get invited in for a cup of coffee?"

"If you can stand the noise Frankie will be listening to, yes, I suppose so."

He grinned. "Come on, Shannie, you know what I mean. Frankie was a dab hand at getting her room-mate to move out. She won't take much shifting."

"Hah! You don't know Frankie," she said, before the significance of his words hit her. Her skin fizzed with the shock. "But you do, don't you! You know Frankie all right!"

He laughed. "Yes, of course. But we were finished ages ago. You don't need to worry about her." His hands slipped round her back, caressingly. "Come on, lovey. You're a dream compared to Frankie..."

"And you think I should be grateful!"

"Well, it's a compliment, certainly," he said coolly, his eyes flickering up and down her. His hands pressed closer round her waist. "Don't be cross with me, Shannie darling. You can't blame me for paying you compliments when you look so tasty."

Compliments, thought Siân savagely, are designed to get round people. But she found it hard to keep her anger burning. It was so nice to be held by someone confident and attractive, and he was so unlike the boys she had met at night school when she was still living at home. And she was lonely. It sounded silly, but in the middle of the bustle and crowdedness of the hostel she was alone, and here was Justin, charming and self-confident, wanting her. She couldn't bring herself to turn him away. What if he had been out with Frankie? He said it was over. . .

Doubtfully, she said, "You can come in. But I don't think Frankie will move out. It'll be coffee and good-night."

He chuckled and his arms tightened round her.

"Then I'll wait for a better time, lovey I'll pass up the coffee for once." And, quite gently, he kissed her.

For a moment, Siân stood helplessly. Doubt, astonishment and triumph fought in her mind yet, in a detached corner, a cold little voice said, *If you don't put a stop to this now, you're asking for trouble.* But the voice sounded like her mother, and she closed her ears to it, and only stood under the beech tree, kissing Justin, and hoping everything would be all right.

THREE

Frankie was ruthless at waking time, "Come on, Sleeping Beauty, there's no Prince Charming this morning, so wake up!" Siân groaned and, with half-closed eyes, seized towel and soap and made for the bathroom.

"Not *washing*, are we? Well, well, what a surprise," went on Frankie, sliding back into her limp jodhpurs.

"Why ever not?" said Siân, pausing at the door.

"Wouldn't have thought you'd need it after last night. You won't wash that mark off your neck, will you?" Siân stalked out without answering.

They all hurried over their toast and tea, but Siân sensed an atmosphere of inquiry among both the girls and the lads who had walked over from their house across the fields. Frankie played to it, tossing her head with tight lips, and Siân let her go unchallenged. Penny touched her arm as they went out into the dark morning to collect their mucking-out tools.

"Have a good night?" Siân shrugged, as carelessly as she could. "Not bad."

"Just take it for what it's worth, dear. Pinch of salt, you know? Don't let it get too heavy."

"Personal experience?" asked Siân wryly. She knew Penny now had a regular boyfriend, so her advice was unbiased.

"Fraid so! We've all been where you are. It's no big deal, but it'll be fun while it lasts. Make the most of it. A chap with a car can be useful."

Penny tipped her a wink and set to work. Siân followed more slowly, unexpectedly churned up inside.

She mucked out her first horse, Smokey Ash; then Stickleback and Double Jump. Then she went back to groom Ash, pick out his feet and tack him up.

She had the measure of Ash now; his only trick was to walk round in circles if she tried to vault on to him, but she knew that the head lad would leg her up, and no longer worried. She was put aboard the chestnut and joined the string as it clopped steadily out on to the brightening expanse of the fields. Ash had worked hard the previous day under Justin, so today he would only do a half-speed canter and Siân, with nothing too strenuous to think about, worried instead about Double Jump. What was she going to be like? How much did she know? They were getting on well so far but she had found that the mare was, like her name, quick to react and rather nervous of her new surroundings.

"Daydreaming?" said Frankie's voice in her ear. "I see Prince Charming has been taxied away this morning while the rest of us are working? One over the eight last night was he?"

"He came back by taxi, yes."

"All the little crystals waiting to turn colour for the policeman, were they? Why didn't you drive him home? You weren't half-cut too, were you?"

"Oh, I can't drive," said Siân.

Frankie snorted disbelievingly. "Apply for a provisional, then! You'll get plenty of night driving practice."

Siân steered Smokey Ash away from her, telling herself that Frankie's jealousy was only natural. She coped better with Philip's teasing later at breakfast. When he suggested she wouldn't want to be seen in his elderly Datsun now, she answered firmly that she wasn't Justin's sole property and if she needed a lift she'd demand one from anyone who was mobile at the time. At this point Tony put his head round the door to ask if they'd all gone back to sleep, so off they went again. Stickleback went out for walking exercise on the road and, finally, Siân came back to quarter Double Jump.

The little mare was edgy but she did no more than shiver as Siân put on the saddle and light sheet. Whoever had handled her before had been kind and considerate; Siân hoped she could do as well. She had to adjust the bridle, which was too large for the mare's fine head, but when Tony checked everything over in the yard, he nodded and legged her aboard without comment.

There were only six horses in the last string. Third lot contained the unfit, the mildly lame, yesterday's runners and any new boys Siân rode Double Jump at the rear. paying severe attention to detail, so that any irregularities or odd behaviour could be judged for what they were rather than being blamed on her slackness. But Double Jump was too green to think of evil. Her ears pricked and flickered and listened but she did not know enough to anticipate what might come next and bent kindly to the bit without a hint of argument.

"You're a baby," Siân told her, "but you're a sweet baby with nice manners. You're all right."

"Second sign of madness, talking to yourself," said a voice, and the whip was dragged from her hand.

"Justin!" she said, half-reproachful. "Come on, give it back."

He ranged his big bay horse alongside and handed over the whip. "Here you are, darling."

"Thanks. You've been back for the car, have you?"

"Why? Did you see me go?"

"Frankie did."

"Ah. Well, she would. Don't let her get to you."

"Did I say she tried?"

"She's likely to. Never mind, it's you I'm taking out, not her! Where shall we go tonight? Not a fair question really is it? You haven't been here long enough to know where you want to go. I'll think of somewhere, anyway. Same time suit you?"

"Aren't you riding today?"

"No. Tomorrow. There's a couple of novices going today so Jo Fraser'll be riding. I'm too heavy for them when they start moving into handicaps, you see."

Siân didn't entirely understand the complexities of the handicapping system but she nodded and they rode on together.

"Would you be better off not going out to eat in the evenings?" she said. "I mean I don't mind — you don't have to take me out every night."

He grinned at her. "Managing me already, Shannie? Control yourself. I'm not bothered about putting on weight. I've no intention of dragging round fields every day of the winter for the next twenty years. Another season or two and I'll have shaken the dust of racing off my boots for good. There are easier ways of making money."

"I thought you liked it," said Siân in surprise.

"It's a job," he said and, reluctantly, she had to laugh. "Oh well! Come on, you big slob," he said to the bay, "the Guv'nor's wanting us." And he rode away, Double Jump following neatly behind.

The usual rearrangements ensued. Siân was taken off the mare and put on to Philip's old hurdler; Philip got on to the bay and Justin mounted Double Jump. Siân found herself unaccountably tense. Although she was sitting on another horse, she felt as though she and Double Jump shared the same skin, both closed in and controlled by Justin as he and Philip on the bay horse made for the fibre-sand galloping track. The muscles in her own neck tightened as she watched Justin fighting the mare, trying to get her through the gate on to the unfamiliar surface.

He was enjoying himself; he was naturally athletic and in no danger of falling and Double Jump's efforts to remain on the grass only amused him. When she fought to get her head free and bounded clumsily away from the track, he held her hard, forcing her round until she was parallel to the bay horse and going crookedly forward, and then he shouted to Philip and the pair set off together at last.

Siân let out a long breath of relief. She had to admit Justin's ability but she hated to see Double Jump handled with such offhand, unfeeling force. She was dismayed, too, to see that in spite of that ability he lacked any sympathy for his mount. She wondered for the first time whether his charming manners with people might not conceal a lack of care for them also.

FOUR

Dafydd Owen was studying the Racing Calendar when the phone rang for the fifth time in an hour. It was late September, and his mind was occupied with the pros and cons of two races for one of the improving hurdlers in his care. Habit, however, made him pick up the handset at the first ring.

"Claybrooke: hullo."

"Dava? It's Arthur. Are you busy?"

"Are you joking? You know damn well I am. Aren't we all?" Arthur Whalley was a flat race specialist but his path sometimes crossed Dava's; they were near neighbours and he was well used to Dava's brusque manner.

"This is a bloody awful line. You bought yourself a Boswell phone or something? Put it down and use the real thing."

"I'm on the real thing, as you call it. Do you want something? If you're just panting to discuss your holiday arrangements with a non-combatant, get lost."

"You're only jealous. Anyway it's too early for my holiday yet, as you very well know," retorted Arthur.

"Then what have you rung for?"

"Well, I've an owner wanting to sell a horse."

"And you thought of me straight away! Well, what a compliment. It's a buyer's market for slow racehorses, or hadn't you noticed?"

"Oh all right, skinflint, stoneheart! Look, it's a five-year-old, plenty of scope, but stopped trying. Since the season is tailing off..."

"Yours may be — I'm just getting going and the paper-work must be breeding on this desk. What makes you think I'll want this horse? A five-year-old from you is probably still entire! And you know what I think about stallions going jumping — they don't."

Arthur disagreed, carefully. "It's not unheard of!"

"It's very rare for them to be any real use."

"That could be because it isn't the fashion to race entires over fences."

"Nice try," said Dava. "No thanks."

"You might still be interested," said Arthur slowly, "when you hear how he's bred." He paused significantly on the last word.

Dava controlled a rush of excitement. "Not by Baner? Is this the horse you bought — oh, it must be three years ago! You got him as a two-year-old. A colt by Baner Wen?"

"How in hell do you know?"

Dava said, "Oh, I know where most of Baner's progeny went to... So you can't make anything of him, eh? That sort need an expert's touch, old son!"

"Ah, stop crowing. I bought him for an owner because he was cheap but he's been erratic and I reckon if I keep on with him he'll just turn into a dog. Come on, let's stop beating about the bush. We all know about your love affair with Baner. Wouldn't you like to train one of his sons? There won't be any more, now will there? This one's very like him, too... Dark grey, you know, a hell of a good sort really. His trouble is, he's too bright for the flat. But your job would keep his interest."

Hearing from Dava's non-committal grunt that he had at least secured his attention, Arthur went on to detail the horse's career. Dava scarcely listened. His mind was walking the paths of memory. Baner Wen had been a top stayer, his to train two decades ago when he, too, had handled horses for flat racing; a horse of brilliance and character, winner of the Goodwood and Ascot Gold Cups, gutsy, courageous, never to be forgotten. He was a once-in-a-lifetime horse and Dava had loved him.

In those distant days Dava still sometimes rode exercise on his horses, particularly the older stayers like Baner who could carry his weight — although he hadn't been so heavy then. It had been Baner who had thrown him that windy morning and broken the knee that still caused him to limp; Baner who, as if to atone, had supported the stable's fortunes during his convalescence and kept him from going mad at his limited mobility; Baner whose winning ways brought his lovely owner visiting more and more frequently. This, to Dava, was the ultimate joy. He was captivated by the light in Anna Pritchard's face, and he had dared to express the hope that his world might be brightened by it forever. She refused him. He had been mistaken, she said, quite kindly. That in itself was a cruel blow, but within the month she had moved Baner to

Shropshire in order to have him near her new home, and then she married the Honourable Alistair Selwyn-Hughes, leaving Dava with a lame leg, a deep thirst and a heart like a museum. These days, a burly, grizzle-haired man of fifty, he appeared proof against almost anyone's charms, but it was not surprising that the name of Baner Wen still had power to conjure him.

"Dava! This line's getting very crackly. You still there?"

"Yes!" Dava shook himself. "All right. Whereabouts is this beast? Still with you?"

Arthur told him the name of the stable and got the Owen grunt again. "Armstrong said he found the place in Yellow Pages. He said since the horse hadn't won a race this season, it was the best he deserved."

"Miserable swine."

"It's a recessive trait. That's a joke, by the way. You'll laugh tomorrow. D'you want to see the horse, or not?"

"No harm in it. Not Sunday of course."

"Is that your Chapel upbringing?" chuckled Arthur.

"You are being an old fool today, aren't you? No, bloody owners coming to visit. No rest for the wicked."

34

"Serves you right for being in a leisure industry. How about Monday? Are you racing?"

"No. Lucky for you. Midday then, and a quick one afterwards at the Royal Oak?"

Arthur hesitated. Dava's capacity for drink had become a legend in the years after Anna's defection, and old friends were still inclined to look out for him even though he had long since gone on the wagon. But when Dava got cross and insisted, to the extent of refusing to view the horse if he didn't get a lunch and a chinwag out of it, Arthur capitulated.

"You must be desperate to make a sale," said Dava, pleased.

"For old times' sake," said Arthur obscurely.

Dava chuckled, a slightly wheezy noise. "I must be going mad. Which of my owners is going to take on a failed flat race stallion to go hurdling?"

"Buy him for yourself!"

Dava just grunted. "See you Monday."

* * *

Dava was the first to arrive at the livery stables — not necessarily a sign of enthusiasm, more a manifestation of his character in general. Hands on hips, he barked at Arthur as he emerged from his car: "You're late!"

"Give over, I'm not an apprentice." Arthur grinned, unabashed.

"A good job too." Dava turned away under the yellowing elms and headed for the stable yard. "Do they know we're coming?"

"Vivienne telephoned."

"You didn't bring the owner?" asked Dava, glancing back at their two cars.

"No, I put him off, mean little bugger. He dislikes the horse on the general ground that it costs him more than it wins. But which of them doesn't? You need a real highflyer to look like a business asset."

"You needn't tell me." They were entering the yard by now. "So. Baner is the sire. What about the dam? Gwen Tudor? I couldn't find anything on her."

"You wouldn't. She never raced. She's in the Stud Book all right but I have a feeling that she was a hunter or an eventer and most of her offspring went that road too. The mating with Baner was only an experiment."

"Stamina," said Dava thoughtfully. "She was by Harry Hotspur, wasn't she? Any speed further back?"

"No, only Baner. But I haven't gone into it in detail, Dava. All I can say is, the speed's there if you can find it."

Arthur paused to knock at a half-open door. A young woman, pen in hand, came out.

"Were you wanting a ride? I'm sorry, today is the horses' rest day and they're all out at grass."

"No. We've come to look at a horse. Mr Armstrong's horse, Cymru."

She looked puzzled. "Kumri?"

Arthur obligingly spelt out the name while Dava, a native Welsh speaker, held his tongue.

"Oh yes! Mr Armstrong's horse... He complicates matters a bit... well, here's his headcollar," she said, diving back indoors for it, "and he's in that box over there. Sorry I can't come with you but I'm up to my eyes in paper."

Dava arranged the rope neatly in his hand and together he and Arthur made a diagonal traverse of the yard, Dava taking the lead with his brisk, hitching step.

There was only one closed box. A dark grey horse put out his head on their approach and gave a welcoming whicker. It was obvious he looked on humans as interesting friends.

"He's much darker than I expected," said Dava as he entered the box. "Even as a youngster Baner was never this dark." He haltered the stallion and led him out.

Cooped up though he had been, Cymru's manners were excellent. He pranced a little but did not pull on the confining rope.

"My best lad had the handling of him," said Arthur with regretful pride.

"Hold him for me then," said Dava, disregarding this. He stepped back to get an overall picture, grunted, and came back to begin the routine inspection all horsemen use: are the feet sound, do they match, are they big enough; are the legs straight and have they enough substance to support the weight of the body; have the chest and quarters enough width and depth to do a job of work?

"Why didn't you just geld him?" asked Dava, holding the white-tipped tail out to one side to inspect Cymru's hocks.

"The horse gave us no cause. He wasn't a precocious colt — perfectly kind and amenable. Of course, now it's a bit late."

"Oh yes, it would set him back a long way." Dava shook his head, but Arthur knew Dava. If he talked of gelding, he probably wasn't considering it. This was merely routine, seller praising, buyer disparaging.

Between them the dark horse stood quietly, quite still yet wholly alive. Arthur had always been attracted by his outlook, the way he used eyes and ears to question everything and assess every situation; his intelligence was as much a part of him as his muscular, trim body and thin, boldly veined hide. Dava stood back again, returned, rechecked the smooth legs, then turned to Arthur.

"Well?"

Arthur shrugged. "What do you want know? I never got a consistent response from him. That's all. He's won at Chester and Doncaster and he's been 'also ran, made no show' nearly everywhere."

"In spite of beating some of the Derby entries as a three-year-old?"

"You're slipping, letting on you know that! Oh yes, he won the Chester Vase. It was Armstrong's idea. He wanted something to impress the staff."

"You don't usually give in to an owner's whim."

"At the time it seemed a reasonable thing to do. I only wish we could have repeated the performance. Shall I trot him out for you?"

Dava watched the horse's straight, swinging stride with satisfaction.

"Well," he said to the heavily breathing Arthur, "put him away, and we'll be off. What about that pub lunch?"

FIVE

When Dava got back, he found his nephew Madoc still sitting at the dining table, staring broodily into space.

"I hope to God you haven't bolted all that steak and kidney. I forgot to tell Grace I'd be out."

Madoc roused himself reluctantly. "What? Oh. No need to worry. I never did like it much anyway."

Dava cast an eye over the scarcely touched dishes on the table. "Almost makes me wish I hadn't had that chilli with Arthur. You seem to have restrained yourself for once."

Madoc pulled a wry face. "Am I being given credit for something? How much have you had to drink?"

"Nothing," said Dava abruptly and sat down. "Any coffee?"

"Might be a drop." Madoc pushed the pot across to him and stretched his long frame back to the sideboard for a spare cup.

"God, you are bloody idle," said Dava without heat. "The woman that makes you get up and do things will have my undying gratitude. Pity Grace doesn't have the knack."

"Aunt Grace's talent is temptation. Culinary."

"By that sin fell Adam," riposted Dava over his coffee.

"If Adam had been your stable jockey, we'd all still be living in the Garden of Eden. I mean, how could I go on riding your novices if I got really overweight?"

"You couldn't," said Dava uncompromisingly. They both knew that Madoc took after Dava's tall brother Huw and that before he was thirty he would inevitably be too heavy to race on a regular basis. "But we both know I'll have to find someone else. It's only a matter of time."

The dark blue eyes met his steadily. "What did you suppose I've been thinking about while you were out? The very fact that I'm here and not on a racecourse is a discouraging symptom of my decline." He smiled, nonetheless. "What you need is someone who's light enough and keen enough to enjoy teaching the babies."

Dava grunted. They'd already eliminated the present staff on various counts: of the elders, Bill Houghton was head lad and indispensable to the running of the yards; Jack Brindley travelled with the horses to race and nannied them and their lads with grumpy efficiency; and Ted Gray, the most senior of the lads, simply didn't have what it took to be a jockey — "born middle-aged" was the verdict of Ken Forrester, who was the stable's practising buffoon and was often genuinely too scatty to be trusted with the education of valuable youngstock. That left John Paddy Kinghorn, who was simply too hot-tempered. None of them was light enough or quick enough to be a serious prospect to replace Madoc.

"I did have one thought among the grey clouds," said Madoc. "What about that lass Jo Fraser? She's got a full licence now. She could probably do with the rides."

Dava hitched a shoulder and drank coffee. "I don't fancy putting up a girl."

"And there we have it. Does the Sex Discrimination Act not apply to you? You've never employed a female lad."

"I've never had a girl apply that was good enough. When we need one, which we don't. None of the novices are up into handicaps yet, so there aren't any postage-stamp weights to worry you."

There was a brief pause.

"Well?" said Madoc. "What did Arthur have to offer?"

Dava was silent. Madoc waited calmly, knowing that ideas which merited a slow, considered approach from Dava were usually out of the ordinary.

"Are you still thinking of Afonwen as a stud? The next step?"

Madoc nodded.

"Arthur has an entire horse for sale... a son of Baner."

"Ah." The monosyllable contained a wealth of meaning: understanding, sympathy, agreement, hope. "And?"

"Arthur's had to give up on him. Gone sour, owner fed up, doesn't want to go hurdling, sell now, money back please."

"And Arthur dangled him in front of you."

"Well, a horse of his breeding needs no selling, not to me. He's a stayer, he's sound, big, well made. If he never wins another race, he'll sire superb hunters. On the other hand, he could easily win a hurdle race or two, even a 'chase. It would look good on a stud card."

"Except that I have no capital to spare, with the work Caradoc is doing at Afonwen. Even if jockeys could own horses."

Dava made an irritable gesture. "I know all that. God, I've been in this game long enough."

"Oh, so you don't intend me to give up my licence right away then," said Madoc, straightfaced.

"Ah, you! Look, the first step is for me to buy him. If we then find an owner wants to lease him — lease, mind, not buy — well and good. There's no rush. If you're careful, you won't get much heavier for a while yet. Your improvements at Afonwen can be finished, then you won't have that drain on your income, and by the time you can afford him, we could have something like a racehorse."

Dava pushed his glasses up his nose with a fierce movement and bestowed a wolfish grin on his nephew. "What d'you think?"

Madoc pulled a non-committal face. "I can see a lot of trouble in it. Temperament problems. Difficulty keeping him away from the mares. Retraining. Too much caution over fences... " Dava's face was a picture of mingled disappointment and fury and Madoc broke into delighted laughter. "It has to be a brilliant proposal or you wouldn't be putting your own money on the line."

"I shall want a fair price for him when I do sell," said Dava in retaliation.

"That's only reasonable. And, going back to staff concerns, who's going to do the animal when it arrives?"

"That's no problem. You are!"

"I surrender. Another plot to keep me lean."

Dava sat back in his chair, the action over. "A deal?"

"OK. Provided he passes the vet. And if I like him."

"If you don't, you'll have to think of something else to do with Afonwen. Stallions of quality do not grow on trees at the price you can afford. And you can't farm that small an acreage to make any sort of living. Mind you," Dava went on teasingly, "Huw would turn in his grave to think of his land being used to rear such fancy things as Thoroughbreds, so what would it matter what use you made of it? Turn it into a hotel, anglicise the name, advertise it as a country retreat. A health farm! A wholefood Mecca! Pure country air, non-fattening views and a three-mile hike to the nearest shop. You'd make a bomb."

Madoc played along, became very prim. "Aunt Grace always told us never to let strangers into the house."

"Well, I don't see that taking in other people's mares will be all that different."

"Mares don't pass comments on the view," said Madoc. "And," with a return of his usual grin, "I shan't have to serve them myself."

SIX

Steven Pickering did not encourage owners to come and see their horses.

"If the brute behaves, they wonder what they're bothering to use me for. If it plays up, they think I'm not doing my job. They never believe Thoroughbreds can't race every weekend. I see too much of them on the racecourse and I don't like them on my yards."

He discouraged the lads from being too friendly, which caused resentment because it restricted tipping. Siân had had no practice before Double Jump's owner, Helen Rogers, turned up.

She heard voices outside while she was grooming the mare.

"... settling in reasonably well, considering she's so nervous," said the Guv'nor, as he opened the door and let in a plump, pleasant-faced woman of forty-five or so. "We're keeping her to a steady routine, it's the best way to settle them down. This is Siân," he added, quelling her instinctive greeting with a look.

Mrs Rogers, however, gave her a smile and said, "Well, Steven, you can leave me with her, can't you? I know you've got other visitors and I'm sure they're much more important than I am."

He took only a moment to consider this. Polite disclaimers were not his style and Helen spoke no more than the truth. Besides, Siân was new and anxious to please, and not, so far, mercenary. It would be safe to leave her to answer any questions Helen might put since neither of them knew enough for these to be inconvenient. He went out, bolting the door.

Helen reacted by following him and poking her head out.

"Just checking!" she said. "He's such a fanatic about security he could easily have locked us in." She turned back to Siân. "But perhaps you could have vaulted over, released the kickbolt and rescued me."

Siân responded to the bantering tone with a frank grin. "I'm absolutely useless at vaulting."

Helen grinned back at her. "So am I, which is why I never do it. It's wonderful to have an excuse, you know. People ask me why I don't train Double Jump myself and I just say, 'Oh I'm much too heavy to ride her' and it gets me neatly out of having to admit that I know nothing about getting a licence or entering her for the proper races or even getting to the racecourse on time."

Siân smiled and went back to her brushing, relaxed now. "I don't know very much about that myself."

"But you know enough to look after her. I can see that with half an eye. Does she eat OK?"

"Yes — she's a bit slow because she will look about between mouthfuls but she cleans it all up eventually. Her main trouble is that she box walks. The Guv'nor doesn't think it's a problem, but I know it frets her to be shut up so much. I stay with her as late as I can but of course I have to leave her in the end and you should see the mess she makes of her bed, churning round and round every night."

Helen reached to stroke the mare sympathetically but Double Jump gave a trumpeting snort of alarm and retreated.

"Poor girlie. It must be unsettling for a three-year-old, being on a big yard like this." She persisted with her approach and was rewarded with a cautious sniff.

"There now, you remember me, don't you? How is she when she's working?"

"Oh, she's absolutely sweet. No nastiness in her at all," said Siân, stroking the fine, clipped coat. "Such a baby, but with lovely manners."

"I wonder if Steven would listen to me about the door," said Helen thoughtfully.

"He wouldn't to me," said Siân.

"But I pay him," said Helen, twinkling, and for a moment they were conspirators. Then, with a friendly extension of interest from the mare to her attendant, she asked, "Are you local?"

"No. The Wirral."

"I thought as much. My husband's parents live near Raby. But they just call it 'Wirral' — why do you add 'the'?"

It took Siân a moment to grasp the question and longer to find an answer. "Well... where I lived, 'Wirral' was the grammar school, but 'The Wirral' was the area."

"Ah!" Helen's satisfaction was evident. "What a subtle point! From now on I shall ask everyone who uses the definite article if they went to Wirral Grammar. I suppose you did, then. Did you like it?"

"I disappointed them. I wanted to be a vet, so I gave up the things I was good at and did sciences. They thought it was a mistake and I'm afraid they were right. I just scraped through in everything."

"So what did you do then? Lab assistant?"

"Greengrocer's," said Siân, turning away to brush Double Jump. "My father has a shop and he wanted me at home anyway."

"I gather it didn't keep you very long."

"Longer than I wanted," said Siân, her face as grim as the breezeblock wall. After a pause she said, "Sorry. I'm not supposed to be too chatty. The Guv'nor said."

"I don't see what it has to do with him," responded Helen crisply. "Is there only your father still alive?"

"Oh, no. Only, Mum left home. They're divorcing."

"You'll be glad to be out of it." A statement, not a question.

"When I applied for this job," said Siân in a rather strained voice, "I left my bags in the hedge at the end of the drive so I wouldn't look as desperate as I felt to get away. I was so sick of being a... receptacle.... something they used to pour out all the nastiness they'd been boiling up inside. I was nothing more to them than that," she said, swallowing down the lump in her throat.

Helen gave her time to become composed before she asked, "How messy is it? Are your family taking sides? Are there other people involved?"

Siân shook her head. "No, nothing like that. Thank God, I suppose I should say. But it's bad enough. I never realised until I got out how unhappy they both were. I really thought it was normal for people to be permanently angry, not in a rage, just sort of..."

"Subclinically belligerent?" Helen offered.

Despite herself, Siân had to laugh. "Yes. Grumbling all the time. I'm not complaining, I'm just telling you... Spending all their time apart. Having headaches, not feeling well, never able to agree to anything."

"Typical PMT," said Helen sagely.

"My father?" Siân asked with a slight laugh.

Helen joined in, smacking her forehead. "Oh dear, another facile explanation gone wrong. Well, that shows it's time I went. Problems fascinate me but John tells me I'm a bit like couch grass. I'm not quite sure what he means, but I withdraw on principle. Tell me if I've been too overpowering."

Siân said politely, "Not at all," and then with more feeling, "Really. I needed to get some of that off my chest. I mean, I don't normally moan on about things."

"Of course not," said Helen briskly and for the first time sounded, as Justin put it, schoolmarmish. "Look, I'll give you my address — I must have some of those sticky labels in this bag... and if you want a lift or anything, ring me or come over. News of this lady always welcome," she added, stroking Double Jump.

"Thank you," said Siân, pocketing the little label. "I expect Justin would give me a lift though if I wanted one." She was unable to explain to herself why she felt it necessary to lay claim to him before Helen but the reaction dismayed her.

"I wouldn't count on it, dear. Justin's only sensitive to his own needs. I wouldn't ask him for a hankie if I had a cold, for instance." Helen shook her head and moved towards the door. "Still, that's my son's opinion and he could be wrong, I suppose. Now, I must go and beard Steven in his den. Wish me luck!"

Siân let her go without another word and watched her take her bossiness and kindness across the yard in search of the trainer. She picked the little label out of her pocket and read Helen's address. She had no intention of ever using it but she tucked it back into her coat with the five-pound note Helen had wrapped round it. She knew which was more use.

SEVEN

"Pensioned off are we?" asked Ken, as he passed Madoc on the yard. "No racing yesterday — again — and I see Mr Dava's bought you a nice old hack to potter about on."

Madoc only grinned at Ken's offbeam reading of the situation. "Better be careful or he'll retire you too and you'll end up doing at least four."

"Gah," said Ken, mildly. "Whose is it then?"

"The hack?" Madoc shrugged. "Dava's bought it to sell on. Soon — you lot won't have time to take your turn with it."

"Pity, it looks a useful sort. But then you never know, do you? Handsome is as handsome does. He might not be worth the effort of trailing a barrow all the way up Top Yard."

"Well, I haven't been given a choice. Dava said to put him up there and keep him away from the women."

Ken chuckled. "Poor bugger... I wondered why old Ted was getting in a tizzy but if it's a stallion that would explain it. Expect to hear from him sometime next week." He moved on, grinning.

By this time only the oldest wheelbarrow was left to Madoc. He trundled it over to Cymru's box.

"Bore da," he said. He stepped inside, fending off the horse's greeting. The stable was surprisingly neat, the straw undisturbed and the dung in a fastidious pile in one corner; in a very short time Madoc was crossing the yard with a full barrow.

Ted Gray was in front of him, wheeling a load of dirty straw, slopping along, dark hair wisping from under a greasy cap, sweater tagged with pulled ends of wool yet carefully darned at underarms and elbows. *Somebody loves him,* thought Madoc irreverently as they tipped their loads and tidied the muck heap.

When he presented himself and Cymru to Dava, his orders were brief. "Take Ken and Ted round the fields. And go steady — no larking. Stay in front, then he won't be tempted to be wicked."

So Madoc jumped up into the saddle and Cymru, treading airily, preceded Appomattox and Jackdaw Bay down the drive towards the lodge, then parallel to the busy main road. Madoc's mind, normally switched off during the boredom of slow exercise, today sparked in all directions; working a new horse, with Ken on an excitable mount and Ted easily flustered... He let down his stirrups to what Ken instantly dubbed "amateurs' length," determined to be able to sit out any tantrums the stallion might produce or be goaded into. He saw the long black ears flicker back at him then switch forward, understanding that these adjustments were not instructions.

Appomattox jiggled and bumped Cymru's quarters and Madoc half-turned to choke off Ken's daftness, but Ken only shouted, "Get on! You know we don't like the traffic along here." So he gathered the reins and pressed forward into trot. The stallion stretched smoothly into a gait that left the others well behind, not seeming to mind the others in his interest in exploring; he made no difficulties at all. He was already fit from the summer's racing and his gaiety contrasted sharply with the other horses.

Madoc thought back to their first encounter, only yesterday, when he had gone with Dava to bring the horse home. Cymru had been turned out alone and his greeting had been a flamboyant swing of the head and an immediate spring into full gallop towards them. When he braked clods of earth peeled in front of his hooves and he stood poised at the gate, four-square, with his nostrils widened to catch every nuance of scent.

"Here I am," said his stance. "You sure you want me?"

Despite the obvious challenge there had been, too, a readiness to submit if the approach was right, and when Madoc quietly extended his palm, Cymru stepped forward in perfect trust of him. That moment had begun something: whatever you called it, man and horse were now forging the age-old bond in which the reason of one balances the strength of the other to their mutual advantage.

The roadwork went uneventfully and they came home well pleased with each other.

Madoc expected to put the horse away and unsaddle as the others were doing, but Dava cut in front of him and headed him off.

"Out onto the gallops and walk him round those fences."

"But..."

"Keep him moving. I'll be out when I've had my coffee and seen Grace about the entries."

Ruffled, Madoc turned the stallion to leave the yard by the field gate. Cymru, too, felt unjustly treated. He knew racing routine and he didn't intend to go out into any field by himself when he was expecting, if not coffee, at least a haynet. He jibbed, planting his big feet flatly on the concrete.

"Get on, you," said Madoc, his heels working. Cymru swung his quarters and was promptly swung back to face the gate again. "Get on, I said."

The stallion reared half-heartedly, got a whack on the backside and leapt forward.

"Good," said Madoc. "You do as you're told, boyo, even if you don't understand."

Basic training and good temper prevailed; they went out into the wide field again.

Madoc pushed him on into a trot, taking him under the sycamore trees at the far boundary then circling through the gates between fields, weaving broad sweeps among the black birch fences and the hurdles with their bright orange bars. Cymru snorted and huffed and danced sideways but Madoc kept him moving, now left now right, but always forward. Soon Cymru's flickering attention turned again to his surroundings; he was clearly fascinated by the sheep which scurried off before him and he snatched at the bit, wanting to pursue. But Madoc distracted him by constant changes of direction, inventing patterns for him to trace over the wet grass. So engrossed was he in perfecting a circle around the water jump and the open ditch that he was startled and even disappointed when the arrival of the second string broke into his concentration.

Evidently Dava's orders were for them to keep clear of the stallion, because even Ken did not approach to tease him. Madoc went on working steadily round the fences, keeping an eye on Dava who sent pairs of horses to canter on the figure eight of the gallop but did not call for Cymru. When schooling over the fences began, Cymru tossed his head and sidled, so Madoc took him away, walking, trotting, walking again, revelling in the constant river of energy beneath him, controllable by his own will; it was exhilarating, but by God it was tiring too. He had never come across a horse with such an inexhaustible capacity for work. When Dava at last made his way over to them, Madoc feigned collapse.

"Do you good," cried Dava against the breeze. "I'm going to take the Range Rover up into the top field. The rest are staying down here and you're going schooling."

Madoc nodded, twisting the horse round to get the wind out of his ears for conversation. "What are we doing?"

Dava turned away and Madoc grimaced his frustration. He pulled up his leathers, stood up and let Cymru out into a canter towards the schooling fences.

There were two fences in this top field, both flanked by white rails. One was of regulation height, approved by the Jockey Club inspector, and the other, much knocked about, barely three feet high but nearly as wide. This, nicknamed the Hedgehog, was a novice's first jump at Claybrooke. Madoc walked Cymru up to it and the stallion was still flaring his nostrils when Dava rolled up in the Range Rover.

"Had a good look?" demanded Dava. Madoc turned to him, waiting. "Well then, canter him in. Nice and steady."

"You're not starting by lungeing him?"

"No. Why should I? Remember this isn't a baby. This is an adult, well-coordinated horse. He knows what his legs are for. Get on with it."

The work was familiar enough, if unusually advanced for a horse only just arrived. Madoc walked Cymru down to the start of the short practice track.

Then he leaned forward over his horse's withers, rose in his stirrups and pressed him into a canter.

Cymru spotted the obstacle about ten strides off and swung off the line. Madoc straightened him and insisted he kept going. He wavered, puzzled, but again he was pushed firmly forward and the stick, whose recent sting he well remembered, jutted briefly out into his line of sight. He shortened his stride, was kicked hard and lengthened reluctantly again. Perhaps he could run round the fence? But Madoc whisked the stick over his withers and smacked the shoulder he tried to drop. He bucked angrily, which brought the Hedgehog under his feet. He ducked his head, collected his hind legs for another buck, then changed his mind and made an almighty leap upwards. And everything changed, Madoc laughed, the obstacle was gone and he was being patted and praised. He snorted hugely and kicked his heels, half in pleasure and half in anger still.

Madoc swung him back to Dava at a spanking trot.

"Still there, I see," said Dava drily. "Go on, do it again. Two or three times'll be enough for him to get the idea."

Presented with the same problem once more, Cymru understood well enough what was being asked of him but the emotions it aroused remained. Once again he fought and tried to refuse, but when he found escape was still impossible, he launched himself efficiently upwards with a grunt of suppressed fury. The third time he attacked the little fence with an air of determination, as if transferring his anger from the rider to the jump. By this time, Dava's face wore a satisfied grin.

"All right. Enough for today. Walk down and cool off. Keep clear of the others."

"Right. Dava..."

"Yes?" Impatiently, half into the Range Rover.

"Why the double exercise?"

Dava got back out of the car and laughed. "Why? WHY? Because Arthur, God bless his short sight, has never trained a stayer properly in the whole of his career! This isn't a skinny little yearling. This is Baner's son. With his energy and his stamina and his outlook. You can never get to the bottom of his breed. All you can do is bore them into nothingness if what you give them is repetitive, piddling little tasks they can't be bothered to do. This horse is going to travel the lanes, he's going to go and fetch the papers from the village, he might even go hunting if you have the time; he'll do twice the work of every other horse in the yard and he'll love every minute of it. I don't mean we'll gallop him into the ground, but he's certainly going to spend two hours a day out of his stable with somebody on his back, even if you have to get up an hour earlier or I have to ride him myself!"

The horse was sidling and snorting and Madoc was laughing too. "You can't be serious!"

"Oh but I am, my lad. Believe me. Never more serious in my life."

EIGHT

Green Bank never held back a horse that was fit enough to run. Steven Pickering pushed Double Jump on quickly, particularly once he was satisfied that Siân was competent to school her, since the two got on better than any other combination he had tried. She began to do fast canter work; she learnt, with difficulty, to face the humming strands of the practice start; she was lunged over small logs and then Siân rode her over them before taking her down the schooling lane of hurdles. It was all exciting and new to both of them and Siân enjoyed it so much that it was seldom that she heard the worried little adviser in her ear saying, "But this is only a three-year-old!" The pride of knowing that the filly was fit to run in her first novice hurdle, and by Siân's own efforts, rather deafened her to its voice.

No one else was much bothered about Double Jump's first race. Canterbury, the stable's rising star, was entered for the McAlpine Trophy, a big-money steeplechase intended to become a regular prestige attraction at Haydock. Nobody that afternoon would be paying attention to a raw novice. The whole stable would be getting its cash on Canterbury and hoping not too many bookies realised how well he had come on since his summer's rest.

Siân wished she could be the one to ride Double Jump in her race but she knew there was no way Steven Pickering was going to take out a conditional licence for her even if she had been a strong enough rider. Really competitive riding rather scared her. Although aboard Double Jump she never minded the actual speed and was able to steady her and place her at her fences with an accurate eye, she was well aware that any less generous animal would soon find out her weaknesses and exploit them. In the rough and tumble of a race she might easily lose the sense of oneness that guided her with Double Jump and then she would be lost.

What worried her more than her own inadequacy was the uncertainty about who would actually ride Double Jump in her first races. Novices all carried a reasonable weight, well within Justin's range, so it was entirely up to him whether he chose to ride her or save himself for the McAlpine. Justin was no fool. He knew quite well that Double Jump was talented in spite of her small frame, but he also knew that in her first race she would be startled and out of her depth and likely to be jostled into a misjudgement or a fall. While he didn't mind a fall, he didn't welcome the idea either and he certainly wasn't going to risk missing the ride on Canterbury, with its probability of a good win, a handsome present and a percentage of the prize money. It was only Siân, deep in her insecurity and confused by the conflict of love for Double Jump and infatuation with Justin, who was at all worried.

She was reluctant to face the fact that she had not got Justin's measure. Since taking her out that first night, he had been increasing the pressure on her to sleep with him. He was sharp and confident and he knew what he wanted, and it infuriated him that she blew hot and cold, delighted to be with him in public but fighting him off when, in private, he tried to push his luck a little further. She listened happily — but was there a developing edge of impatience, even boredom? — to his stories, all about racing and gambling successes or the downfall of rivals; she sat in the background when his dubious friends congregated round him; she thought about him with a strangely obsessive constancy which frightened her almost as much as his assumption that, before long, she would sleep with him.

She tried occasionally refusing to go out, as if to prove to herself that she was still free and unpossessed. But when he failed to call for her for several nights running, she lay awake in the small hours listening to Frankie's nasal breathing and wondering if the lads really were running a book on her and whether, as they hinted, there was someone else who regularly took the edge off his demands. Time and time again she assured herself that there wasn't, but she could never quite believe it and the possibility undermined her confidence still further. Yet she had to recognise the strength of his attraction for her. When he looked at her she melted. When he touched her, a current ran through her that shut out rational thought. Away from him, she knew he could be calculating, she even thought he might be dangerous, but it was this unknown quantity that added the spice to her obsession with him. And when she was with him he had only to smile and tease her a little, and maybe stroke her face, and she was lost.

As the days shortened, she began to feel less certain that this was enough. With the rational part of her mind she knew that he was the source of conflict in her life and she ought to make up her mind what she was going to do — sleep with him, or stop going out with him. Either choice was frightening. Sex was outside her experience, a dark country where she knew nothing and had no control and where she certainly did not trust Justin's leadership. Was it enough, on another level, to have status and company only on his terms and not on her own? Was she going to have to sleep with him just to have someone to talk to about other things than earning a daily crust? She tried to keep a grip on herself and her feelings and to resist him in the hope that things would settle down, that she would grow used to walking this tightrope of emotions. She counted herself lucky that he had not realised how great a lever her love for Double Jump might be. But she didn't dare to do without him.

It was two days before the Haydock meeting that her conflicts were resolved. Riding out that morning on Double Jump, she found that when she reached the gallops she was taken off the filly. A wiry girl with a fair ponytail showing under her skullcap was legged into the saddle in her place. Siân had not seen her before but noticed that she was treated with casual respect. Siân watched her walking Double Jump round and talking to Philip on one of the other hurdlers while she waited her turn to school. It was irritating that Justin chose that moment to hop off his horse and lead it round near her, compelling her to walk with him instead.

"Shannie... you're not listening."

"What?" She dragged her attention back to him.

"I said, is it true Frankie's done a runner?"

"Oh. Yes. She must have packed last night when I was out with you."

"Dad's furious. I'm not."

"So long as I don't get all her horses to do, I don't really care," said Siân.

"I'll make sure you don't," he said. "But Shannie, don't you see? You've got a room to yourself now. We'll never have a better chance."

"Mm." She pretended not to get the point, and craned her neck to look for the fair girl and Double Jump — surely they must be ready to go now? "It'll be nice not to have to listen to someone else's choice of music.

"I wasn't talking about music," said Justin. "Not the kind Frankie liked, anyway."

She managed to give him a cool look and turned her head away. Where was Double Jump? Annoyingly, he walked his horse between her and the gallops, but she stopped and went round him.

"Who is that? The girl on Double Jump?"

"That? Oh, well, since she seems to interest you more than I do, that's Jo Fraser. Best nursemaid in the business, if you like that sort of thing."

Siân's attention was on the flying group on the gallops, Jo Fraser bending low over Double Jump's flicking mane, dipping swiftly with her leaps over the hurdles, holding her straight and driving her on with a style and determination Siân knew she could not match. It seemed the Guv'nor had asked to see Double Jump ridden right out, because when she flew across his line of sight, she was eight lengths clear of the two horses working with her.

"Oh, beautiful," said Siân to herself, wistfully, the hairs on the back of her neck rising with excitement. "Oh, I wish I could ride that well."

"I could teach you," said Justin softly but when she met his eyes, she saw again that he was not talking about horses.

"Oh, do stop it," she said, annoyed with herself for blushing. "Look, Jo is so right — she's perfect..."

"You do jump to conclusions, don't you? Why shouldn't it be me that rides?"

"Oh, no, not when Jo can do it so beautifully..." Justin's sudden stillness warned her that her enthusiasm was unwelcome, but she went on, gathering her courage, "I know that's why she's here, isn't it, so she knows Double Jump before she has to race her? And I can see it's right. You're hard on your horses and Double Jump won't take your treatment, she doesn't like it."

"I suppose you don't either," he said sarcastically. "I don't know why you don't just come out and say it. I'm tired of guessing your exit line every night."

She flared up. "What's that supposed to mean?"

"I mean your constant excuses. You can't ask Frankie to move out for the night. It's too cold in the car. You've got the curse. Well, Shannie, you've drawn the short straw this time. Frankie's gone down the road, you'll be on your own in that double room and the door has a lock, so even you couldn't possibly be distracted." He took a deep breath, trying to control his sudden burst of temper. "Shannie dear, I'm only flesh and blood, and I'm dying for you. Couldn't you say yes for once?"

If there had been a touch of tenderness, an ounce of pleading, in the blue eyes fastened so brilliantly upon her, she might have given in. But his own sarcasm had pointed out the truth — she could take no more of him. At long last she realised that he didn't really care about her at all, and with that the spell was broken and those blue eyes didn't affect her any more.

"Justin, *dear*," she said, throwing the word back at him, "get this into your head. I am not going to sleep with you. I'll be in bed in that double room all right, and the door will be locked, but you will be on the outside."

He dragged his horse round to face her. "Oh will I? Well, that won't be any big change, will it? I've been on the outside all this time, haven't I? Long enough to know that the only thing you care about is that puny little mare — don't think I don't know it. I could arrange that Jo didn't get the ride, d'you realise that? I'd only have to tell the Guv'nor I fancied a go and he'd let me. And I wouldn't nurse your little darling, not like Jo! Wouldn't suit you, that, would it? Think about it!"

It was too late now to change her mind, to make Double Jump safe again. She could only hope that Steven Pickering was too good a judge of horse and rider to take Jo off after the performance she had produced this morning. Siân knew that she had burnt her boats.

"It's no good, Justin," she said, walking away towards the mare. "Don't call for me tonight. I've gone as far as I'm prepared to go."

NINE

It was raining when they unloaded the horses at Haydock. Double Jump danced with excitement round Siân as they made their way through the security checks into the racecourse stables, and Siân, newly decked out in smart trousers and waxed jacket, felt equally apprehensive. Jo Fraser was declared as Double Jump's rider but would Justin carry out his threat to replace her? She could not be sure. Did he care so much about his reputation that he could stoop to petty vengeance?

She still had to concentrate hard on getting things right on race days and the discipline helped her nerves. She put protective boots on the mare's forelegs to dampen the rapping of the hurdles; she straightened the rug and put on the bridle. Then they must parade in the preliminary ring. They walked briskly round, waiting for Helen and John Rogers to come with Steve Pickering to saddle their horse. The rain had died down to an ineffectual drizzle and there were few spectators for this first race of the day, so she easily spotted the trainer, unfamiliar though he was in smart suit and trilby.

Helen smiled generally, at the mare and at John, Steven and Siân while the saddle, weightcloth and number cloth were placed and adjusted, but Double Jump was skittish and took some handling, so no one had time to respond. They all hurried to the parade ring, which was already crowded with the other runners walking round for the punters to see. Siân marked where John and Helen stood with the trainer so that, when the order came, she could meet them with the minimum of fuss. She was so relieved when it was Jo Fraser who came out of the weighing room that she rushed Double Jump over far too quickly and unsettled her, and Jo said in her sharp Blackburn accent, "Steady up lass, there's no race till we all get out there, y'know. Let her go, she's just messing about." Then they were gone, round the track and out on to the course, and the travelling head lad was thrusting a sweat rug into Siân's hands and she was alone in the emptying ring. She found a place from which to watch and with rawly cold fingers she clutched the green sheet, the rug and the lead rope as though they could comfort her nervousness.

Double Jump's canter to the start looked very bumpy and uncomfortable. Jo was using all her tact to prevent her from running away. But the pair walked sedately enough while the starter checked off his sixteen runners; then the white flag went up to show they were under starter's orders; the horses faced the tapes and, as these flew up, the commentator said unemotionally, "And they're off."

Jo's riding instructions were based on the trial at Green Bank and she kept Double Jump well back and slightly wide of the main group. Tactics of this sort had to be carefully judged to avoid the stewards requesting jockey and trainer to explain their reasons for "schooling in public," but Jo was handling things well, giving Double Jump a clear view of the obstacles which she then tackled with zest. The fast pace seemed to suit her too; she had stopped fighting for her head and was using an easy, economical stride.

They went out into the country, fading into the drizzle, while the commentary kept the thin crowd informed of the progress of the race. There were groans when two horses fell on the far side of the course and interfered with a third, and Siân quivered, because falling, until now, had not entered her thoughts. She gripped the rugs more tightly.

"Come on, Baby," she muttered. "Just come home safe."

There was a rising murmur from the crowd and she realised that the coloured blot appearing through the murk was, in fact, the race returning.

"Double Jump moving up now," said the commentator, and there the blue colours were, in fifth place, the little mare moving strongly and confidently, gaining rapidly on the four ahead, dancing over a faller at the last hurdle. Her inexperience showed as the field changed direction towards the finish and she faltered, confused, until, accepting Jo's driving, she picked up speed again and galloped strongly for home. Siân was so fascinated by this display of skill and courage that it was a minute or so before she realised Double Jump had come in third.

She hurried down to the gate to meet her horse and Jo, glancing down, gave her a great big grin.

"Damn good little horse. Gave me a great ride. You'd schooled her a treat — it was only the run-in that confused her."

Unused to praise, Siân could only grin back, and hoped it was enough. Steven Pickering would say little, of course, but in the unsaddling enclosure Helen and John brimmed with excitement and pleasure when Jo said, "Give me the ride on this one again, Guv'nor! She'll win next time out."

Helen smiled slyly at her husband and said, "See, I did know what I was doing."

When the loudspeaker said, "Horses away please," Siân was surprised to find that Helen panted along beside her in her smart suit and shiny flat shoes. Double Jump was quiet now but her stride was still long and Helen began to flag.

"Can I — whoof — have a word? Not now – " she waved a hand at the sweating mare and the damp rugs – "but afterwards?"

"It'll be an hour," said Siân, thinking of the need to keep the mare moving while the lactic acid cleared from her muscles, the washing down she must have and the impossibility of taking Helen into the stable block without a pass.

"Fine. No problem. Beside the Tote in an hour."

Siân said, "Isn't that when the McAlpine's being run?"

"I'm sure RTS will have a screen somewhere that we can watch," puffed Helen, gratefully falling back and letting her mare walk on.

* * *

Siân did not skimp on her attentions to Double Jump. She did not leave her until she was sure she was comfortable, then she locked the box door and pocketed the key.

Helen was waiting, as she had promised, by the Tote; the McAlpine was over and queues of successful punters waited to be paid.

"What won?" she asked Helen.

"Canterbury, of course! John is very pleased with Pickering Junior."

"Oh. Well, I'm glad," said Siân without enthusiasm. "I didn't back him."

"I'm surprised at you. I thought you were sweet on the young man."

"Not any more."

"Oh. I hope it isn't too crushing?"

"It's no big deal," said Siân, managing a smile.

"Good, because it may be relevant to what I want to ask you. Let's find somewhere a bit less crowded. I don't want to have to shout this too loudly."

They moved experimentally a few hundred yards and Helen straightened herself as if to face an ordeal.

"Oh dear," she said, "this is going to sound so silly. Tell me if you think it's disloyal. I'd better go roundabout first of all... Are you settled with the Pickerings? Or, now that you say you're not involved with Justin any more, are you contemplating packing your bags and vanishing?"

Siân shrugged. "People do, don't they? Frankie Hewitt did just that last week. Jumped off eighteen thousand pounds of novice chaser and left him trotting along loose beside the string. The Guv'nor got quite lit up about it. He didn't care about losing Frankie, or about the extra work it would make for us. It was the irresponsibility that annoyed him."

Helen allowed herself a small laugh. "I wouldn't expect you to take off quite like that."

"I suppose not, but I might move on. I'm not certain yet. I'm still learning the job and I'm a bad judge of when I should make a move. And I'm fond of my horses, which makes it hard for me to do it."

"Double Jump in particular, I hope?"

Siân said uneasily, "Yes. Is that important?" She didn't want to be blackmailed into staying before she had made up her mind.

"If I decided to take her away, would you consider moving with her?"

There was a pause in which both women became aware of bookies' voices floating across from Tattersall's.

"Yes. Where is she going?" asked Siân, astonishingly calm. The decision seemed to make itself.

"Well, back to your home ground as it happens. We're going to move down to Raby for a time. John's parents are getting frail... We thought at first we'd put Chris that's our son, you know, grown up and dying to have a chance to try out all those ideas from college — we wanted to put him in charge of their holding so they could come to live with us, but they were quite set against that. So we're going to them instead. And, really, I think John would be the better for a rest anyway. So, Double Jump is coming with us, to Dafydd Owen at Claybrooke. He's near Heswall. I wish, in a way, that she hadn't run so well here. I'd have had less compunction about taking her away from Steven."

"When's she going?" asked Siân, unbothered by these scruples.

"Before Christmas." Helen saw her surprise and said, "I'm sorry, it doesn't give you much time to think. What is it today, the sixth? Can you let me know by the tenth?"

"I can tell you now, I want to go, but will it be all right with the other stable? Are you sure there'll be a place?"

"I don't see why not. You'll be wondering about accommodation I suppose. Sorry, I'd forgotten you wouldn't want to live at home. I'd have to ask Dava about it."

"You have asked him whether he'll take me on?" enquired Siân warily.

"Well, yes, in general terms. I said I'd confirm it with him once I had your answer. You see, it would be best for Double Jump to have someone she knows when she moves... and Dava's got a gentler attitude to training, he has a smaller yard and he's more flexible — dare I say more intelligent? I think you'd like it there."

They stood together in the steady drizzle while Siân thought quickly. She could see no reason not to accept. There was only the formality of working a week's notice and, if approached properly, the Guv'nor might let her go sooner. It was a pity she was doing one of Frankie's horses now — it would make him more reluctant to let her go.

"All right," she said, "you're on."

Helen beamed. "I knew you would agree! I'll tell Dava this evening. Now I must fly. John will want to know what you've said, I'm sure. Bye for now!"

Siân watched the plump figure bustle away. *I've done it again,* she thought — *led with my chin. I hope no one's going to punch it for me. And that I can rely on Helen's patronage.*

TEN

Justin came back into the weighing room still wearing the bright grin he had put on for the photographers after the McAlpine.

"Another pair of cufflinks!" he said. "I wonder how many shirts these sponsors think we have?"

His valet glanced at him. "Come on, Pick, get changed. Cunningham's waiting for your saddle already."

"Let him wait," said Justin, still grinning as he stripped off Canterbury's colours. He threw them at the valet. "Take care of them! Father'll likely want them framed."

"If they don't frame him first," said an anonymous voice, to smothered chuckling. Justin's grin slipped a little but he knew better than to show any reaction. He knew that if anyone chose to drop a word in some steward's ear about betting, it could make life difficult for him. He changed swiftly into a fresh set of colours, magenta and yellow, and hurried to the trial scales with his saddle and weightcloth.

"What're you on now, Pick?"

"Just a chance ride. Our two've run already."

"Not that bay thing of Mrs Leverett's?"

"Yeah — called Good Evans." He stood on the scale and pushed lead into the weightcloth pockets until the pointer trembled over the ten stone seven mark.

"These boots are made for walkin'," sang the voice, falsetto.

"All right, smart arse. It won't fall if I can help it."

He took a number from the man by the door and disappeared into the weighing room. When he came back, having relinquished the saddle to Cunningham, he sat down beside Madoc Owen, under a set of crimson colours and a saddle still gleamingly clean.

"You're a late starter today, Madoc. I've won yet another set of cufflinks in our fight for mud or glory and you haven't even got your girths dirty."

"Yes, it's a nice quiet day at the office," said Madoc lazily, ignoring the bait.

"Pick would have had a quiet day too if it hadn't been for Derek getting flu," said five-times champion Jerry Monk, grinning gap-toothed a couple of places away.

Madoc, swivelling to bring him into view, grinned back. "Funny how often Derek gets flu when Good Evans is running."

"You mean it's useless?" demanded Justin. "Aw, just what I need."

"I wouldn't say entirely useless," said Jerry thoughtfully. "But it does fall with depressing regularity – and on a nice wet day like today, as far from home as it can."

"Its one redeeming feature is that Eric hasn't yet dared to send it chasing. You won't have far to fall," comforted Madoc.

"Thanks a lot," said Justin heavily.

"Well," said Kevin Thompson, flicking his whip about, "Look at it this way — a fall would be a good excuse for treatment by that smart nurse of yours. Eh?"

"I don't need an excuse for that," said Justin with a complacent grin.

"I don't know how you keep up with 'em all, it must sap your strength," said Kevin enviously.

Johnny Robson chipped in, "He'll have that many women on the go, he'll have to give up riding altogether. He's already given up one ride today, haven't you Pick? Saving yourself?"

"Something like that. I don't know how busy Janice is tonight."

There were groans at this and a hoot of disbelief from Kevin. "Thought there was a lass at the stables you were chasing, a new one? She run faster than you then?"

"Ah, that one. I've given her up as a bad job. She looks at you as though she was going to write on your school report, 'Could do better.'"

"A woman of taste," said Madoc, fastening his stock.

He ducked Justin's backhander and pushed him lazily towards the door. "Jockeys out, the man said. Is that you?"

Justin pulled on his helmet. "I shall tell Janice it's your fault if she finds the goods damaged tonight."

In a minute more only Jerry and Madoc remained in the changing room. Madoc pinned the neck of his colours and pushed the tails into his breeches.

"You've only got one ride today, I see," commented Jerry.

"Jealous?"

"Don't be daft. I've a wife and kids to keep. What sort of beast is it?"

"A new one, very good. Belongs to Dava."

"What the devil is it called? And how does Dava twist the Jockey Club into letting him have these Welsh jawbreakers?"

"He didn't name it. He only bought it because it's a son of Baner. And Cymru, as you ought to know, means Wales."

"I knew that... You know, I always thought Dava should have had that young one I'm riding for Mrs Selwyn-Hughes. But there's an old feud there, isn't there?"

Madoc shook his head. "Just good friends, that's what I heard."

"Ah well. Musketeer's too good to give away so I'm not complaining."

"That good?"

Jerry cocked his head and appraised Musketeer. "Well... everything worthwhile in the foreseeable future — and certainly the King George and the Gold Cup."

"Can you handle that much responsibility? Are you sure you wouldn't like an understudy?"

"Get stuffed," said Jerry amiably. "My wife adores good horses. They mean I come home in one piece."

"Coward."

"You wait till you get tied down, mate, and watch your priorities change! Hasn't Felicity offered to make an honest man of you yet?"

"We're going up to Afonwen next weekend but I don't think she'll like it." Madoc sighed. "Looks like the end of the road."

"You're a stubborn bastard," said Jerry sadly. "A good woman should be humoured a little, you know."

Madoc shook his head apologetically. "Some things are beyond compromise."

* * *

There was little left of the crowd by the time the last race came round. Only a few hundred hardy souls were dotted across the wet tarmac, with or without umbrellas or waterproofs, and the bookies were not so brisk to keep their blackboard odds legible under the rain. No one thought much of Cymru's chances. The racecard said baldly, "Poor form in last two seasons on Flat. N.H. debut." All the rest of the field, bar the favourite, Sandarac, carried less weight and even a generous lengthening of odds from ten out to twelve to one did not tempt the remaining backers into parting with a pound.

Cymru knew nothing of this low opinion. He jogged round the preliminary ring; he snatched bites out of the air in the saddling stall; he dragged at the rein in Jack Brindley's hand and bucked and kicked his way round the parade ring. The officials took in the battle with critical eyes and, as soon as Madoc had been legged into the saddle, they separated the horse and his angry handler and sent Cymru out to canter to the start alone. He accepted this, surprisingly, as though it were a tribute to his pride, and strode away confidently through the drizzle, his white-tipped tail flicking rhythmically.

When the other seventeen runners, in their turn, came cantering from the stands Madoc kept the stallion clear of them. He checked his girth himself rather than ask the starter's assistant to do it, and when they were called into line he took a station wide of the main bunch — no disadvantage since the first half mile past the stands ran straight. Dava had given him no specific instructions other than "Keep in touch and do as well as you can." It was only a lowly novice hurdle and no one was going to be in a position to dictate tactics other than, perhaps, Sandarac. Madoc was willing to jump a couple of flights at his horse's preferred speed in order to learn how his races should be run.

The tapes crashed up and the line of horses surged forward.

Madoc was unprepared for such enthusiasm. At home Cymru had been gentlemanly about galloping in company, disappointingly so, which had made him suspect that Arthur Whalley had been right to ditch the horse. But today the moderate signals that Cymru used to obey were totally ignored. He charged the first hurdle at reckless speed and threw himself over it a length ahead of the field while Madoc struggled to contain him. *At this rate he'll be burnt out before we've gone a mile,* he thought. *I expected to be buried in the main pack at this point. What the hell do I do now?* But there was little he could do. Cymru was fit and leaping like a tiger, fighting passionately any attempt to regulate his speed and, short of putting him on the deck by continuing to battle with him at every flight, Madoc had no choice but to be his passenger. The other seventeen jockeys followed smugly behind him, delighted to have someone to cut out the work and sure that, before long, he would come back to them, totally spent. But Cymru went on. There was no more than a nose at Madoc's heel now and again, the thunder of hooves cutting into wet turf, the sharp crack and rattle of bouncing hurdles when inexperienced shins rapped against them. As they swung round the left-handed course, Madoc saw the steeplechase fences flick past, those big fences with the Aintree-style drops, and he knew that was the course Cymru should be racing on, which he was designed by God to win on, but, right now, there was the prickle of rain on his face, mist on his goggles, wind in his hat harness, the rhythmic, alternating swing of Cymru's shoulders and the sharp black withers bounding under the gripped reins. There might be no future other than this race if he didn't concentrate.

As they rounded the final bend, Madoc looked back to see what challenge there might be and, sure enough, Sandarac was there, responding cheerfully to Kevin's urging, positioned to drive for the line to the winning post or come round on the outside if Madoc hugged the rail. The moment that Madoc asked Cymru to go he grunted and lengthened his stride, finally displaying the racing spirit which Madoc had feared he lacked. And as Sandarac drew level he swung his head viciously, ears flat, mouth wide, barging him, bullying the other horse out of his stride. Horrified, Madoc struck him hard down the side of the face and he recoiled, then, unbalanced, scrambled clumsily over the final hurdle. Somehow Cymru got his legs together, and somehow Madoc stayed on board instead of falling under the pursuing hooves. Then, with renewed rage, Cymru flung himself after Sandarac.

The favourite won. Kevin's white face and shaky grin and the isolated insults of the crowd underlined Madoc's feeling that Sandarac had been lucky in more ways than one. Neither jockey was surprised to see the E sign go up on the number board, indicating a stewards' enquiry into the running of the race. Dava was called while he was still in the unsaddling enclosure, and Madoc and Kevin as they changed places on the scales in the weighing room.

"Let's hope they want to get home as much as we do," said Kevin calmly, dumping his saddle on his valet's table.

Jack Brindley, left to take the stallion back to the stables, stumped along with an ill grace. "Might have bloody known you'd make a nuisance of yourself," he said. "You awkward sod. Hope they warn you off."

ELEVEN

The atmosphere at Green Bank that night was electric. Penny had won forty pounds on Canterbury and she and Ros were heading for Ormskirk in the company of Penny's student teacher boyfriend and his room-mate. Ros had won an undisclosed amount and was smilingly planning a raid on the Liverpool shops as soon as she got a day off. Siân could hear her pushing things from one end of the wardrobe to another in dissatisfaction as she prepared for the evening: Liverpool was going to have a hard time. Outside the lads' house, Philip, who looked after Canterbury, was washing the front end of the Datsun while Paul washed the rear, and the other lads were piling out in their best gear for a night on the town.

Siân sat on her bed feeling rather left out. Double Jump's third place was nothing compared to the stable coup brought off by Canterbury, and Siân herself had been so absorbed in the prospect of leaving Green Bank that she had almost forgotten that the lads would be wildly celebratory. She sat alone, disconsolately wondering whether it would be tactless to give her notice tonight. It might work: Steven Pickering would be cheerful, whereas tomorrow he would be like a bear with a sore head. Leaving it till the day after would mean she'd have to stay another ten days.

Penny popped her head round the door. "We're off," she said. "Aren't you going out?"

Siân shook her head.

"Ah. You broke up with Prince Charming, didn't you? I suppose you found out about the nurse in Southport."

"No," said Siân. She shrugged. "It wasn't that."

"Why don't you go over and cadge a lift with Phil and Paul? They've got a spare seat in the Passion Wagon. You never know where you might end up. Anyway, I'm off now. See you!"

"Have a good time," said Siân automatically, but her face was empty.

"We will. Tell you all about it when we get back. If we're sober! Tat-ta!"

Siân continued to sit on the bed. So, they had all known how much of a fool she had been making of herself with Justin! How could she have been so stupid? Damn him! She had not fascinated him at all — she was only a bit on the side! The only good thing about the whole sordid episode was that she had not slept with him. Thank God, she had said she would leave with Double Jump! It meant they would both be free of him and she could exult instead of being depressed.

She looked up at the damp, shabby walls of the bedroom. Time she got out of this. She got up and opened the wardrobe and the tatty dressing table with the drawers that stuck — not much in there to pack! She picked her coat off the back of the door and marched downstairs and out across the yards to the trainer's house.

Lights shone from the window of the lounge and loud pop music met her at the gate. Shadows of heads showed on the blinds. So there was a party going on; of course there would be. Should she go back? For a minute she hesitated there among the trim but starkly undecorated lawns. She looked at the smart cars parked beside the house: the Audis and Mercedes, Rovers, Range Rovers, Shoguns and Troopers. Would she have to face all these people — could she, the little outcast, insecure employee, with nothing but her weekly wage behind her, face the moneyed and powerful owners of such cars? They would not know or care whether she continued to work for Steven Pickering or not. She walked up the path and knocked on the door, wondering if anyone would hear over the music.

Her heart missed a beat as a figure approached the brightly lit glass. What if it should be Justin! But the door opened to reveal Mrs Pickering, thin in black trousers and gilt top, a glass of gin in her hand as though to welcome more partygoers. She looked at Siân with disfavour. "What do you want?"

Siân stood her ground, feeling her knees quite rigid with tension. "I — erm — would like a quick word with the Guv'nor, please."

"Who are you anyway? Davies? Oh yes... Mmm. That Rogers woman was on the phone tonight. Steve!" she yelled with no obvious effort. "Message!"

She stood unconcernedly, ignoring Siân while she waited for her husband. The level in the glass dropped steadily.

"Popsy here wants a word with you, darling," she said when he came to the door. "Don't be long."

The trainer took his wife's place with an air of annoyance, looking Siân up and down with the same dissatisfaction he would turn on a lame horse. "Well?"

Siân had spent some time deciding what she wanted to say. "I would like to give my resignation, please," had seemed far too subservient. She clenched her fists and said loudly, "I've come to give my notice."

He just looked at her. "Helen Rogers told me. I half expected you just to go, the way Hewitt did."

"I wanted to do the thing correctly," said Siân, stung.

"It's not exactly *correct* to interrupt a private party. Tony will give you your cards the day the horse goes. I daresay Helen Rogers will tell you before she tells me what day that might be. Goodnight." And he closed the door.

Siân stood on the step for a moment, stunned at how quick it had all been. She had expected much more aggression from the Guv'nor. Perhaps people often gave him unwelcome news and hers was minor. It did not occur to her that she had wrongfooted him in bypassing the usual procedure, which was for her to have spoken to the head lad during working hours. She had simply seen a way to give her notice and had used it. She walked back down the garden path.

She went up to the quiet room in the hostel. It seemed extraordinarily empty without noisy, cassette-playing Frankie. Everyone had gone now. She pulled her suitcase from under the bed, blew off the fluff and put a few of her belongings into it but there wasn't much she could pack in advance. So much of her meagre wardrobe was needed every day. She folded the trousers she had worn at Haydock and the light jacket which still smelled of Justin's aftershave and twisted her stomach with a remnant of his old attraction. She snatched up her heaped washing and went downstairs to crush it into the automatic with unnecessary violence.

As she set the machine off, she thought, *What next? What else is there to do here other than eat, sleep or go to the pub?* She was too restless to sit down and passively watch television after screwing up her courage to face Steven Pickering. Well, she would go down to the yards, in defiance of orders, and talk to Double Jump. The worst that could happen was dismissal and she had just given her notice so that wouldn't matter. Anyway, who would know tonight when everybody was out partying? She put her hands in her pockets and sauntered out into the damp night. Freedom was better than any party.

Double Jump was startled by the opening of the stable doors. Siân slipped in without putting on the light, but she left the top door ajar to admit the glow from the yard lamps.

"Hello, Baby. Are you all right after that big adventure today? Hey? No lumps or bumps? Yes, hello," she said again as the mare blew down her neck and whiskers tickled her ear. She felt compelled to make an inspection while she was there, so she unbuckled the rugs. Everything looked all right. Double Jump had lost some condition but her body and legs were smooth and cool, unscarred by contact with the hurdles. Her manger was empty and licked clean. Siân replaced the rugs.

She was fastening the surcingle when a sound from the yard made her pause. She peered out through the crack of the door.

"That's his car," she whispered to Double Jump, who pressed up beside her and poked her nose out. "Go back, he'll see you. Back... good girl." *Funny,* she thought, *he hasn't gone into the house. I wonder if he's gone to the hostel instead?* She waited a few moments more. "I don't know where he's gone, Baby. I think I'll stay here."

She listened, breathing carefully, hearing her heartbeat accelerate. *This is silly,* she thought. *Cowering here in the dark to avoid somebody I was going out with three days ago!* And then she heard his footsteps. Coming closer.

Justin opened the door and leaned in, smiling in the way she knew meant he had drunk quite a lot. His hair swung over his forehead in a bright wave and he tossed his head carelessly, the smile widening, the blue eyes focusing on her.

"Oh Shannie darling, how lovely to see you."

"Hello Justin," she said quietly. She stood quite still, willing him to go away and not bother her. It was finished, wasn't it? She'd made herself quite clear.

He came into the box and closed the door. "I thought you might be here. Quite a clever deduction, wouldn't you say? I went to the hostel, for a word or two with you, and there was nobody there so I trundled up to your room and there was nobody there either. All I found was a suitcase with your tidy gear packed and a washing machine thundering away in the kitchen, and my razor-sharp brain said, she hasn't gone out on the town in her dirty old working gear so she must be somewhere around. And look, here you are, my lovely. Oh, Shannie, you did me a bad turn the other day. I haven't been able to sleep, did you know that? Lying there, wanting you." He slipped his arms round her. "You didn't mean what you said, did you? Don't tell me this doesn't melt you the way it melts me." And he brushed his lips across her throat, softly.

Siân shut her eyes. He smelt of food, and wine, and that aftershave. She had chased him away and he had come back. She felt helpless. She stood in his arms, not moving.

"Come on, darling. It's a lovely way to say goodbye... I know you're going to do a runner but wouldn't you like to leave me happy? Who knows, you might decide to stay..."

His arms closed warmly around her, his breathing unsteady. Siân felt that current again and a wave of weakness swept over her.

Double Jump pushed her abruptly in the back. Justin swore and regained his balance with such an effort that Siân laughed, but she stopped again when she saw him catch the mare and tie her to the ring by the door.

"What's that for?"

He came back to her, smiling. "To keep her out of the way. She's only got little feet but I don't intend to be trodden on. It puts me off."

"I wouldn't worry about that," said Siân coldly, her weakness gone. "You won't be in a position to be trodden on, not unless you decide to sleep here. I'm going now."

He caught her round the waist, laughing. "You aren't going anywhere, my lovely. You and I are stopping right here."

She pushed him off. "Well, I don't know what you think you're going to do, but it won't be with me. What about the nurse they tell me you go about with? I'm sure she'd be delighted."

He was between her and the door. "Sure she would but she's on duty tonight. That's why I'm home early. I suppose I could take you to the party but I have a feeling they wouldn't make you very welcome. Whereas if you stay with me, you'd be very welcome." He closed in on her. "Very welcome indeed, Shannie darling."

Rage suddenly welled up in her. "Who do you think you are? You think anything is all right so long as you get your own way. A quick hug and a kind word or two and that's supposed to make me forgive you! You're a self-centred creep! I hate you."

He just stood there laughing. She faced him, back to the wall, while he came up to her, still smiling.

"You can't drive me away, Shannie. Don't be too hard on me. You can't expect me to be cool and stand back all the time when you look the way you do. You are a luscious piece, darling, aren't you? I'd have to be Superman to resist you."

He placed a hand on the wall beside her head and leaned forward, kissing her casually. She turned her head away but his free hand caught her, firmly, compellingly, the underlying strength very evident. She knew that he was much stronger than she was. And she also knew that she could never be a match for him, because she was vulnerable and he was not.

"Come on, Shannie, darling."

"No," she said, trying to slip aside. He caught her easily.

"Yes," he said.

TWELVE

Dava turned to Helen Rogers and protested, "You didn't tell me the girl needed accommodation! How in hell am I supposed to fix her up at five days' notice?"

"Give the job to Grace. She'll cope."

"I don't in the least see why she should. I'll get hold of old Fred — he's always at a loose end in winter when the riding schools slow down. At least he has his own bed-sit."

"Old Fred, if he's the same old Fred I'm thinking of, would get blown away by a good puff of wind, and, frankly, I don't want him looking after my horse."

"He's perfectly capable of doing a couple of horses and your filly at the same time. I don't understand why you're so set on this chit."

"And I don't understand why you're so set against her. Move with the times, Dava! Girls have a place in racing, the same as in any other job."

"You know perfectly well," said Dava as patiently as he was able, "that I've never run a hostel for my lads. They all get digs or they come from home. It's easy on the Wirral to get horsey kids living within striking distance. I can take my pick of them. If this girl comes from Bebington, why can't she drive over from home? That would be acceptable, surely?"

Helen, gazing out of the window at the dreary December afternoon, recognised Dava's immovable object attitude and sighed. "She doesn't drive, for one thing."

Dava heard the omission and said, "So what else is there?"

"Oh," said Helen lightly, "broken home, kleptomania, wanted by the police, you know, all the usual things."

Dava laughed suddenly. "All right. Point taken. Come clean, Helen."

Helen cast her mind back to Saturday morning and the picture of Siân Davies, white-faced, bruise-eyed and clearly under the most rigid self-control, telling her that she had given her notice. The interview, brief though it had been, had impressed her with a sense of deep distress. Siân had had no need to come to her; she had accepted the offer of work when it was made. Helen sensed that the unexpected visit was a cry for help and, having not checked about accommodation before she made her offer, she now felt responsible. She could no more back down than she could have drowned a kitten had it been found on her doorstep.

She smiled at Dava and said, "Can't you just humour me for the sake of an old friendship?"

Dava sat back in his chair behind the desk and began to laugh. "Helen, it's just as well you married John because you'd have twisted me round your little finger. Look, I'll toss you for it. Heads, I take on Miss Davies without a quibble. Tails, I ring old Fred. You on?"

Helen crossed her fingers at him and said, "All right! Go on. If gambling is the only way to beat you, I'll gamble. Have you got a coin?"

Dava fished in his trouser pocket. "You've got nerve, Helen Rogers, I'll give you that." He tossed the coin. "Call!"

"Heads," said Helen quietly.

He caught and clapped his hand over the coin, then extended it to Helen and uncovered it. "Well?"

"Tails," she said, lightly. "Well. I'm going to have an unpleasant time telling her she can't come here, aren't I?" She managed a smile but she felt faintly sick.

"Leave it to me then. I'll call old Fred and get his forms from the Registry." Dava was dismissive, clearly expecting her to leave now the matter was settled. But Helen was made of stern stuff.

"Do it now, then. Give him a ring."

"Now?"

"While I'm here, yes."

"Not one of your premonitions, is it?" asked Dava, reaching nevertheless for the phone and punching in the digits. Helen sat waiting. This really was taking things to extremes in support of a principle! She listened to the brief conversation. Evidently Dava had got Fred's landlady. "What? He's got what? Pneumonia? Good God... When's he expected out of hospital? Dear me. Poor old Fred. I'll send him a card. Tell him I rang."

"Well?" said Helen, her hopes rising.

"The poor old bugger got a job sweeping up at a big garage and polishing the cars. I suppose he thought it was a better deal, a bit of indoor work! Now he's gone down with pneumonia and they think he'll probably spend Christmas in Clatterbridge Hospital! Bloody hell. Have you got second sight? You win after all."

Helen thought it wiser not to crow. "I'll tell her she can come, then. Will you organise somewhere for her to stay? There really isn't room at Raby even if John's parents would agree."

"Oh, all right! Debt of honour. I'll do it — or Grace will." He shook a fist at Helen. "You! You'd better buy me a bloody drink when the horse runs, that's all."

"Double orange juice on the rocks," Helen assured him. "Can I give Miss Davies a hint as to the accommodation? Digs? Live-in? Hm?"

Dava stood up and paced about. Each time you thought you'd satisfied Helen, she came right back at you with another request. "Oh God, does it matter? Tell her it's a caravan. There is one. To be accurate, it's Madoc's and it isn't supposed to be here because we haven't got planning permission but I suppose we could rig up a water pipe and some electricity and a gas bottle by next week. Then she could look for digs herself, couldn't she?"

"Sounds... what was your word? Acceptable? Yes, it sounds acceptable," said Helen, just archly enough to raise a smile from Dava. She stood up with difficulty from the shabby old settee. "Is this thing designed to give new owners a sense of their inferiority or of your poverty? Well, I'll be going. You've got stables to see to and it's getting dark so it's high time I went back to Raby. John said we must unpack the books tonight when he'd finished outside."

"All right, Helen." He bowed ironically to her. "Delightful of you to call."

She smiled, making for the door. "Where's Madoc? Hunting for a site for his caravan?"

He followed. "Gone courting. At least, he said he was going to Afonwen, but I know he was taking Felicity, so God knows what time he'll be back."

"Gather ye rosebuds while ye may," said Helen lightly.

"Rheumatism may set in any day — hey?" Dava winked at Helen, who laughed. "I somehow can't see Felicity in that caravan when he takes it up to Afonwen."

"No?"

"He'll have done up the buildings by next year but the house won't be much to shout about. I can't tell how keen she is on him but I think living in a caravan might well scare her off. She likes her comfort. I've known her family for years and nothing has ever been too good for their little girl." He looked owlishly over his spectacles at Helen and she nodded her understanding. "Still! It's none of my business what he does. He might uncivilise his little student teacher after all. Who knows?"

Helen opened the front door. "You take a lot of interest in his future, don't you?"

"He's my brother's boy," said Dava, "and he's a horseman, which the other boy isn't. And he's been damned useful to me. Don't you tell him I said that, mind! I don't care whether he has a woman or not — I've managed without one all these years — but he might as well pick one that will be more use than ornament!"

Helen saluted him with a swift peck on the cheek.

"Dava dear, I think that was a compliment."

THIRTEEN

Siân was given her cards on Thursday morning. The head lad was brusque and she felt again the guilt that had descended on her when she told the others she was leaving. She understood now why more street-wise lads tended just to leave without giving notice at all. Since Frankie had gone the yard's resources were stretched every time a horse and his lad went away racing, and when Penny found that she would have yet another horse to do on Siân's departure, her normally forbearing nature gave way.

"It's a bloody good thing you're taking Double Jump with you," she said crossly. "At least that's one less for somebody else to do."

Siân had swallowed her regret and gone quietly away.

Now, faced with the cold scorn of the head lad, she was equally subdued.

"I didn't expect you to disappear in the middle of the season. You were starting to ride quite well. I suppose you're hoping for better things over at Owen's — conditional licence or something. You won't get it. He doesn't like girls. Surprised he took you at all. That owner of yours must have a pull."

Siân looked stupidly at the papers in her hand. "Don't I get my racecourse pass and my identity card?"

He snorted derisively. "Not bloody likely! How do we know you'll go where you're supposed to? They've gone back to the Registry. When Owen's send in your forms again, the Registry'll re-issue your passes for their use. There's enough villainy goes on without letting people like you loose with racecourse passes."

She was stung by that "people like you," but her spirit was so crushed that she said nothing. What was the use? All her good service had been discounted by the fact that she was leaving when the stable was short-handed. She pocketed her cards and trudged back to the hostel. Her bags were packed, Double Jump bandaged and ready to travel, so there was no point, and too much pain, in staying on the yards to be looked through by the others working. So she went back and sat on the bed. The room was forlorn and the rest of the house depressingly quiet, even Mrs Cox not about yet. Siân thought about stripping the bed but the energy to do it was not there. After a moment she pressed her hands to her face, and tried to rub away the numb inertia which had persisted since Friday night.

What is the matter with me? she thought miserably. *Why am I sitting here like a rag doll? Everyone thinks I'm fit and healthy — they must, or they wouldn't tell me I'm copping out, skiving, sloping off... and inside I'm screaming. Screaming at myself for being so stupid. Screaming because however often I go over the things that happened I can't change them — that suffocating struggle — knowing I couldn't win but not being able to give up trying — and the utter humiliation of losing. And then being treated like an object — just something to be used and thrown away. And somehow feeling that it's all I deserve because if I hadn't been stupid enough to want to go out with him, all this could never have happened! I want to scream and rage and shout what a fool I've been and, in reality, I haven't uttered a word. How can I? Didn't I pretend to Penny and Frankie and Helen that I knew what I was doing? Didn't I leave home to take on the world? Who is there left to talk to but myself inside the brittle glass shell I've built?*

She sat hugging her body, overwhelmed by the urge to bury herself in a dark corner again the way she had that night, and wait for the horror to go away. Justin had gone away — *no, don't even start to think about him, think about Double Jump and her warm, inquisitive breath when you freed her, her gentleness and comforting presence and the hypnotic rhythm of her jaws when she pulled hay from her net. Remember the quiet yards, the empty house, the savage satisfaction of having the shower all to yourself and running off every drop of hot water as you washed and washed and washed...*

It had been in the shower that the great clanging thought finally hit her: *I could have a baby.* She had stood there until the needles of water began to chill, completely stunned as the facts swooped down and fastened their claws in her mind for the first time. She had to see a doctor — tomorrow — and it was impossible. She had not registered here, so the only person who would see her was her old family doctor — her childhood ally Dr Harrison — who was thirty miles away. There was no possible excuse for such a trip except the one, the impossible-to-confess truth.

In the morning she had to wait until third lot had been finished before she could walk down to the phone box. Morning surgery was over at the Bebington Health Centre when she finally got through. The receptionist, no doubt being protective of the doctors, had not been able to give Siân an appointment sooner than today. Siân, by then totally annihilated, had agreed to the appointment. At least it would be with Dr Harrison. She had had to accept that there would be no morning-after medical salvation for her. Leaning on the cold glass wall, she had felt so weary she wished she could sleep for six months. She was even more exhausted now because she had fretted and worried herself to sleep every night, only to wake in the early hours fretting and worrying again, dumb and helpless and alone in a silent room.

The sound of a heavy commercial engine outside roused her from her stupor. She heaved up her bags and struggled downstairs, feeling that once she got started she would find the energy to cope and could keep the awful blankness at bay.

Out on the driveway, shuddering with the vibration of its engine, stood the old blue Bedford which had first delivered Double Jump, and emerging from it, grinning, was the same cheerful young driver.

"By God I nearly went without you," he exclaimed, reaching for her bags. "Mother would have skinned me after all the trouble she's gone to."

Siân smiled faintly at his exaggeration and allowed him to stuff the bags through the living quarters door. At his insistence, she climbed up into the cab.

"The mare's aboard," he said. "You can't hear her because Mother insisted we should put down some of that rubber matting after the last journey. God, she did rattle on that old alloy floor! I was sure she was going to arrive with her legs in a knot." He checked the doors and, with a whirr, slid the wagon into gear. "Here we go! We're full up to the gunwales now. Another consignment of parental belongings to be dumped on Wirral. Wonder it doesn't sink under the load."

Siân barely listened to his amiable chatter. She kept her eyes to the front, trying not to see the too-familiar neighbourhood sliding jerkily by. Chris assumed she suffered from travel sickness and drove with extra care, but she did, in fact, benefit from the noise and vibration. In a peculiar way its physicality, like riding exercise every morning, helped to break the circle of her depression. When Chris shouted, "Aintree!" she was sufficiently aware to nod vigorously and smile as the red-brick entrance appeared on their left and, after filling the windows, slid unremarkably away again.

Going down the Birkenhead Tunnel, he asked whether she wanted to be dropped off anywhere before reaching Claybrooke. "Mother said something about it, so I thought I'd better check."

"Bebington Library," shouted Siân over the engine.

"Want me to wait for you?"

She shook her head. "I'm going home to collect my bike after that. If you take my luggage and deliver it when you unload Double Jump, that'll be fine."

"Could fit the bike in if you like?"

"Too much bother. I don't need to get to Claybrooke until evening stables."

"Ah. Well, it isn't far." He revved the engine to take them up the incline leading from the tunnel bottom.

"I must say thank you to your mother," said Siân, making a conversational effort for the first time in several days.

"She's some organiser."

"My mother? She's the original powerhouse — not very restful. I thought organised people were calm and collected, like you."

"Me! I'm about as organised as a box of liquorice allsorts."

He slapped a fistful of change on to the seat between them. "Practise on that then. I can never remember how much the toll is for wagons, it keeps going up."

He hummed cheerfully as they cleared the tunnel exits and took the dock road. Siân, who was used to the winding route of the buses through the streets of Tranmere, viewed the dual carriageway with regret because it did not pass the landmarks, such as the Oval, which announced that she was nearing Bebington. The old sports ground had been facelifted a good deal since it had been filmed in the Olympic sequences of Chariots of Fire, when some of her junior-school friends and their families had been extras for the crowd scenes. Her own parents had thought it all too extravagant and she had not been allowed to join in. *Story of my life,* she thought bitterly. *How I didn't help win an Oscar.*

She roused herself to direct Chris through the black and white primness of the Port Sunlight estate, and before long she was climbing down from the cab outside the Civic Centre.

"I hope you won't think I'm rude," shouted Chris, "but I won't linger. This is too close to the constabulary for comfort. This old thing hasn't been for her HGV test since last September and I'd rather they didn't come out and investigate how roadworthy she is." So Siân smiled, slammed the door and waved him away.

The Civic Centre was a big complex, designed in the sixties with roughcast concrete walls and tall, narrow, massed windows contrasting pleasantly with enormous circular ones. It encompassed the functions of Town Hall, Health Centre and Library and Siân felt astonishingly homesick when she pushed open the heavy doors and was surrounded by its cathedral-like atmosphere. She had spent hours at her sixth-form studies here, in a carrel in the non-fiction gallery or at a table looking down on to the central checking counter. For a moment she paused, apparently admiring the display of winter foliage plants in the entrance, but, in reality, breathing in the familiar blend of smells, polish, disinfectant and the faint, dusty undertone of books. Then she gathered her courage and turned away from the Library towards the Health Centre.

For the first time in a week, she would have to get a hold on herself and talk. She must tell the truth, yet not the whole truth, for that would involve the law and she was not prepared to face questions. A hundred yards away, across the car park, was the police station, but feeling guilty as she did she could not convince herself that it was Justin who required punishment. She could no more have walked across to demand justice than she could have flown.

She approached the door of the waiting room with a suddenly racing heart. What would Dr Harrison want to know? Would she want every detail of time and place, could she tell Siân whether she was pregnant, would she think her silly and ignorant, would she agree to supply the pill immediately or would she insist that Siân could not take it until she was definitely not pregnant? In those few moments Siân realised how slight her knowledge was. Nervously, she set her hand to the door.

One look inside made her catch her breath. In another moment she had retreated, fumbled for the rear exit and hurried out into the raw air. Round the corner she stopped for a moment, panting. The waiting room had been full, but perched neatly on one of the chairs, shoulder to shoulder with Mrs Bryant and Mrs Johnson, had been Siân's own mother. She had been talking to someone in the opposite corner — not deeply interested, Siân was certain, for even in that brief glimpse she could tell it was just a nervous filling-in of time before her own turn — and she had not even glanced at the opening door. But she was the last person Siân had expected to see and certainly the one she most wanted to avoid.

Her heart hammered as she walked away and her brain darted in all directions. Her mother's appointment might easily be for a later time than her own and there was nowhere else she could wait — if she wanted to see Dr Harrison she must pass through that waiting room. Her watch said it was nearly time.

"I don't believe it," said Siân through clenched teeth. "Why does she have to be here, today of all days? Oh damn damn damn damn damn!"

FOURTEEN

She walked rapidly down the hill to the road, abandoning any idea of seeing a doctor today. She would just have to make another appointment, that was all. If she could collect her bike quickly and cycle across the Heswall, she could easily find a chemist's shop and buy a pregnancy testing kit. It would be no good buying one in Bebington where she was known and the word would go round. *Oh Mother,* she thought, *why do you have to make life so difficult for me?*

She paused from habit in the bus shelter, checking the timetable. Opposite stood the Old Library, raised from its original farmhouse status by the addition of a Victorian clock tower and two cement plaques illustrating proverbs. While she hesitated about catching a bus, these plaques, familiar since childhood, struck her as though she had never seen them before. The classically draped figures of a mother with two children, and a father and son, were too dignified, too full of family authority, to be comfortable in her present mood, and as a child she had confused them with Nativity scenes, which was not helpful either.

Beneath them were boldly chiselled messages: "Take fast hold of Instruction, let her not go; keep her, for she is thy life" and "Wisdom is the principal thing; therefore get wisdom, and with all thy getting, get understanding." It suddenly seemed to Siân that she had lived all her life without applying these two ideas. It was very sobering. *I am an ignorant fool!* she thought angrily. She tried again to read the timetable but it jumped before her eyes and she gave up. Tossing her head at the two proverbs, she set off at a brisk pace. Maybe walking would calm her.

A quarter of an hour brought her to the corner of the street where she had spent most of her life. After the regimented tidiness of Green Bank, its shabby air disheartened her. She was almost ashamed of ever having belonged there, and so nearly allowing it to imprison her. She had to brace herself to walk into the shop.

It had not changed. Old Mrs Fazakerley was buying carrots and instructing a new, male assistant in the niceties of their choice. "I only buy a few, chuck, so they got to be good ones." Siân took advantage of his back being turned, twisted past the counter and slipped into the house.

In the dining room her father had heard her and was on his feet, but he checked, newspaper in hand, when he saw her.

"Oh, it's you, is it? And where the devil d'you think you've been all this time?"

She could not answer. It would need a week's explanation. "I've come to collect some things."

"Aye, all in good time! That's you all over, never say a word to anybody, then expect everybody to fit in with your plans just whenever it suits you."

"I haven't time for all this," said Siân, tired.

"That's no surprise. I take it you aren't back to stay."

"No."

The assistant's round, oily face appeared at the door.

"Are you all right, Mr Davies?"

"Yes, yes, Mark, it's only my daughter. Go and keep Mrs Fazakerley happy."

Mark withdrew. Siân took a deep breath and started again. "I've only come to get my bike and..."

"Now look. You can't just waltz in and start demanding things. Let's have some explanations." He made an effort to be conciliatory. "Cup of tea?" When she shook her head, he went on, "Well then, tell me where you took off to!"

"A stable," she said reluctantly.

"Aye, you look as though you've been dragged through a hedge backwards. I suppose it never occurred to you to tell me where you were going? Vanishing on a Sat'day morning like that. 'Gone to new job, will write.' Doesn't tell you much, a note like that, does it?"

She felt a pang of guilt. She had not written to anyone while she was at Green Bank. The thought of father, mother, grandmother had simply not occurred to her in the immediacy of her life there. The note, which she had forgotten she'd left, had been a hurried defence against being hunted as a missing person. She had not realised it also contained a promise which she had broken.

"Well? I'm waiting for an explanation."

As always, his insistence goaded her. "You never showed much concern for me when I lived here! Why should I tell you anything now?"

"We looked after you, didn't we? Fed you and clothed you? Gave you the chance to educate yourself? You stand in need of a good clip under the ear!"

Siân was suddenly quite calm in the face of his threat. She measured his stooped greyness and knew he could never frighten her again. Quietly she said, "I'm going upstairs to fetch my radio."

"Are you now! Well I've put it in the shop."

She was shocked by the malice in his eyes.

"You took my radio to put in the shop!"

"Mark likes a bit of music."

"Well, well, you never humoured me that way." Bitter contempt came over her that she had allowed the habit to grow up of permitting him to impose his will upon her and because of that, she had behaved the same with Justin. "Does Mark have to clean out the potato bins and carry out the rejects for the pig man?"

"Of course, that's what I pay him for."

"And does he have to remind you for his wage every Friday like I had to?"

"What's that to do with anything? You got your bit of cash, riding and night school and that, you weren't so badly off."

"I wanted independence, Dad, my own life!"

"And what have you been doing with it, these past few months? Tell me that, eh?"

Her mouth opened, and shut. "I want that radio," she said in a stifled voice. He followed her, grimly triumphant, and when Mark protested at the removal of the radio from over the till, he pacified him.

"Let's see how much she intends to take. She's like her mother this one — and she was like *her* mother, the sly Welsh bitch." Siân stepped past him with a closed face and headed upstairs. "God knows what goes on in their minds."

Her bedroom was a shambles, empty boxes and coathangers flung on the bed, the wardrobe swinging open. She picked four paperbacks off the shelf, seizing on them like long-lost friends, before she turned to the clothes: a pair of trousers from the wardrobe, sweaters, blouses, socks. She stripped off her waxed jacket and pulled on two of the sweaters and she was so thin that the jacket slid back on with ease. She hooked a plastic carrier out of a box, sniffed it to check its freedom from vegetable matter, and plunged clothes, books and radio into it.

Downstairs, her father said ironically, "Don't leave too much, will you. I might think you were coming back."

"Where's the bike? Still in the shed?"

"Serve you right if I'd sold it."

She marched through to the kitchen. Boxes of fruit and sacks of nuts for the Christmas trade lined the passageway, something her mother had never tolerated. The kitchen was cluttered and the sink stacked with dirty dishes, the geranium on the windowsill very dead.

"Don't you get Mark to wash up for you?" she sniped as she passed, and thought desperately, *I must not descend to his level.* He watched from the doorway as she lifted the bike from the lean-to and looked at its tyres, strapped the bag on the carrier and wheeled it to the high yard gate. She was reaching for the bolts when he spoke again.

"Pet..."

The name stopped her for a moment. Then, but slowly, she continued to unbolt the gate.

"Pet, I wish you'd write. I do like to know you're all right."

She turned in the open gateway. She knew perfectly well that this brief flash of softness was the way he thought he always was, and she struggled not to make the sharp remark that sprang to her lips. He read her silence, however, and went on, as he always went on, poking at her.

"I suppose you're going to see Her Majesty now you've got what you came for? I daresay you let *her* know where you were, didn't you, eh? You made sure *she* knew you were all right."

Siân drew a deep breath. "You're wrong. You always are wrong, whether you can believe it or not. I haven't written to anybody while I've been away. You can ask her if you don't believe me."

He came out of the kitchen porch, heedless of the cold air. "You tell her I wouldn't lower myself to ask her anything. And it'll be no good her coming round here for anything she's left. I'm getting rid of them. And I've changed the locks, so she needn't think she can sneak in while I'm at the wholesalers." He was out on the pavement now, shouting at her, ignoring people who stared as they passed. She closed her eyes. She couldn't bear any more humiliation. She knew the pattern of his thoughts and the fixed route they followed in detailing all her mother's iniquities and suspected duplicity.

She turned away and mounted the bike. It would be useless to tell him her mother was at the doctor's, because that would drive him to fresh speculation and fury, so she only said, "I'm going to have to go, Dad."

"All right, you tell her, you tell her from me..."

"I'm not going to see her. If you want to tell her something, do it yourself." She would not give him the pleasure of knowing that she had avoided her mother within the last half hour, but what she said was enough. He faltered in midsentence.

"You aren't going to see her?"

"No, Dad, I'm not. I'm moving to a new job. Quite close. If you like, I'll give you the address."

He digested this in silence and then he nodded, tiredly, as though the anger had wasted his strength. "Yes, I'd like to know that."

"It's near Heswall. Dafydd Owen's stable, a racing stable, called Claybrooke."

He nodded, coming closer, trying to think of something helpful to say, pitifully unpractised, and to Siân's eyes suddenly much older than his fifty-four years.

"Used to go walking over there when I was a kid. The far side. There weren't so many houses out there then... but then there weren't so many houses anywhere... People will go on breeding... I'll come out to see you, eh, if I get time?"

Siân was ashamed of herself. She leaned over and kissed his cheek, then, dismayed by her tangled emotions, stabbed by a comment which, for once, had not been intended to wound, she righted the bike and rode away.

She pedalled hard, converting her anger into movement, for nearly two miles. It was almost all uphill and she was panting by the time she reached the main road crowning Storeton Hill, so that she was glad to have to wait for a gap in the traffic.

Facing the woods where, sometimes, as a child she had been taken for picnics, something of the comfort of those days wrapped her. She thought of the peaceful lanes, the bramble-gathering, the barley-yellow footpaths and the road to the stables where she had gone with friends to learn to ride. She ran the bike across the ridge and freewheeled deliciously downhill.

The speed, the flying air and the sense of leaving everything behind cheered her enormously. There were still worries — she must try to get into Heswall and find a chemist's — but she was free of Justin, free of the miseries her parents created, free to make up for the years of ignorance and imagined faults and constant complaint, and the bitterness that tainted everything. She was going to a new future. She must tackle it boldly and not run away any more, which would mean handling relationships more carefully from the start and never being persuaded into doing something she did not want to do.

She found herself singing "O Come All Ye Faithful."

When she reached the line, "Born the King of Angels," her voice faltered a little but she cleared her throat and went on.

FIFTEEN

Claybrooke was redbrick Georgian, older, smaller and shabbier than Green Bank, and indefinably friendlier. Siân investigated the back first, by instinct seeking the heart of the place, the yards where, sure enough, Double Jump was housed in a box with the top door open and looking perfectly at home. Satisfied, Siân wheeled the bike to the kitchen door, parked tidily, and announced her arrival.

Grace Williams was unloading the dishwasher and scarcely paused. "Come on in. Sit down. Are you perished? Or glowing? I'm going to make a cup of tea in a minute, if you'd like one."

Siân perched on a stool while the dishes were packed into cupboards. Grace was tall and gypsy-dark, and the hand she eventually offered to Siân was broad and well kept. Siân shook it, unable to match the grip but smiling at her vigour.

"Dava's gone to Catterick today so it'll be up to me to settle you in," she said, producing a biscuit tin. "Have one? Did you have lunch, by the way?"

Siân, accepting a biscuit gratefully, admitted she hadn't. "I'll make you a sandwich then. You do realise you'll have to cater for yourself here, don't you? No? Well, I'll feed you today and in the morning, but tomorrow you must go shopping. Turn right at the lodge and keep going... Shall I advance you any wages or are you all right?"

Through biscuit crumbs Siân indicated that she had enough cash to buy food. Grace seemed satisfied and, when the kettle began promptly to sing, she moved to the door and yodelled, "Madoc! Cup of tea!"

"Who's that?" asked Siân.

"Dava's nephew — and mine, by marriage. He had a fall earlier on this week — Monday, was it, or Tuesday? Anyway he cracked a collar bone so he hasn't to race. I don't suppose he'll wait until you or I would consider it healed before he cons his way past the racecourse doctor though. These jockeys are all daft."

Her Shropshire accent came through clearly, strong and amused.

"Daft?" said Siân carefully, thinking this heresy.

"Of course! Why else would they go out six times a day to race over big obstacles on silly horses in filthy weather and foul going, hm?" She filled the teapot and brought it to the table with a cluster of mugs. "And Dava's as bad. He's grumbling at the moment that he'll have to find another jockey for the next fortnight. I suppose that's meant for a joke."

She turned back to the fridge and brought out milk and then, as an afterthought, a chunk of roast beef.

Siân watched her assemble a generous sandwich and accepted it gratefully. This arrival contrasted sharply with Green Bank, where she had had nothing until after evening stables and that little enough because Mrs Cox had not known of her arrival until the following morning.

She swallowed a delicious mouthful and asked, "What are they like, the Guv'nor and Madoc?"

"Best of friends. I mean, they must be, they're so rude to each other."

"Who is?" Madoc came in, slightly clumsy with his right arm in a sling. "Did you mention tea?"

"You," said Grace, pouring, and plonking a mug by his hand as he sat down. "And Dava."

He looked gravely at Siân, who smiled uncertainly. "I must be really ill. Not only have I been invited to tea in the kitchen, but I'm seeing double." He blinked and they stared at each other. She would not have taken him for a jockey, for he was surprisingly tall and a thick sweater concealed his leanness, but when she looked at his face she saw that beneath the freckles his skin was washed-out, betraying the rigours of self-denial. Even his hair was pale. But the deep, Celtic-blue eyes were undefeated and they held Siân's attention for an endless minute and then crinkled into a smile.

She looked hurriedly away, seizing her tea and scalding her tongue in an effort to cover the self-consciousness she felt. She heard Grace introduce her as Miss Davies and add, "And no smart cracks, Madoc, she didn't ask to live in your caravan."

"Quite," he said. Siân's scalp prickled at the possible undertones of the word, and she was about to apologise and explain but he went on, "It was Helen's idea."

She looked at him as coolly as she could. "She suggested it, yes."

"Are you always so open to — er — suggestions?"

"No." Siân was beginning to feel embarrassed.

"Just no?"

Exasperated by what she thought she detected in his questioning, she said, "Only from women," and the quiver of his lips as he suppressed laughter told her at once that she had guessed wrongly.

"I see," he said. "Well, I hope you won't find my caravan too much of a comedown from the hostel."

"I hope so too," she said, "but it will at least offer privacy."

She could tell this struck a chord with him, for he nodded and changed the subject at once. "Has Grace told you how many horses you'll be doing yet? No?"

"There's your filly and a nice mare called Aholibah," said Grace promptly. "She belongs to a chap called Lofthouse."

"Knows damn all but he's free with his cash." Madoc looked at Siân. "I did Hollie for a while not so long ago, that's how I know."

"So I'm only doing two? That'll be a pleasant change."

"How many were you doing at Green Bank?" asked Grace.

"My usual lot was three, but someone took off without notice and I worked my last week doing four."

"Oh, innocence," sighed Madoc. "I'd have gone long before that!"

She understood that he was only poking fun at himself but, for some reason, perhaps because of the head lad's comments that morning, she was stung into answering, "Some of us have more pride."

"The starry-eyed rookie," he said, unperturbed.

"You don't stay starry-eyed very long at Green Bank! And as for being a rookie, you can watch Double Jump. I did nearly all her schooling."

"Steven let you! You must be better than his average recruit. Or perhaps you just fell off less than the others?"

"Madoc!" said Grace. He raised an apologetic hand and a faint smile, and Siân realised he had been winding her up beyond his usual level. So she, too, relaxed.

She said, "Oh, no — the Guv'nor liked to see you on the deck at least once a week. I'm afraid I overdid it because with me it was twice or three times."

"Keeping you in your place, eh?" Madoc grinned.

"I'll have to put you on Cymru while I'm grounded, just to keep you in practice."

She blinked at him. "Cymru?"

Grace explained, "A stallion that Dava's bought, and the cause of Madoc being here with his arm in a sling, the fool!" No-one bothered to ask which of the three Grace meant by this epithet, as it clearly covered them all.

"Well, thanks for nothing," said Siân. "I don't fancy tackling a stallion when I'm working with two mares all day! Is he in training? Hurdling?"

"Some daft idea of Dava's," said Grace. "And they say women are sentimental!"

Siân could think of nothing to say to this, so she remarked, "Isn't it odd to train a stallion to go jumping? I thought they got too careful to be any use."

"In that case you certainly must school Cymru," said Madoc, amused. He had refereed the argument between Dava and Arthur on the score of stallions racing over fences and ended up with a curious handful of facts. "Try looking down a stud list in Horse and Hound sometime," and, ticking off fingers, he began, "Broadsword, Cruise Missile, Royal Vulcan. And how about Toirdealbach? He went on running until he was thirteen!" He saw Grace stirring and added hastily, "I suppose it would be fair to say, yes, stallions are unusual in jumping — about as unusual as people who ride four lots of work a day and only fall off twice a week."

Siân was getting used to this split-level conversation and she managed to smile. "Thank you! And I must say it's unusual to chat without coarse comments creeping in, when, after all, we're discussing a stallion."

"Ah, but then we pride ourselves on being a cut above the rest," said Madoc, "and Welsh Methodists into the bargain. Besides, if Justin is anything to go by, the whole stable at Green Bank is a hotbed of lust and incapable of talking of anything else."

Siân went white, then scarlet. She had forgotten that Madoc, sitting calmly in this kitchen, normally worked, rode, changed and showered with the closely knit band of jockeys, and therefore with Justin. The blood thundered in her temples and she had to concentrate hard just to hold her mug upright. She put it on the table hurriedly and heard Madoc say, "But you are obviously a person of taste, since you've left. Which will save you being the toast of the changing rooms in your turn, unless your name happens to be Janice, in which case I've just put my foot right in it!"

Siân, deeply embarrassed, shook her head. "No, no, I know about Janice, but she's a nurse, isn't she? My name's Siân."

"How pretty," said Grace. "Are your parents Welsh?"

"My mother's family came from Clawdd Newydd, but Dad's from Manchester. The surname's only a coincidence," said Siân, grasping the new subject with relief. But she could not help glancing at Madoc and wondering just how, without knowing it, he had managed to shatter the hollow glass. The illusion was gone and she was back in the real world, whole and alive, and grateful.

"I suppose you speak Welsh with a Mancunian accent," said Madoc, over his mug. His English, like many northern Welshmen, sounded slightly Scouse and very familiar to Siân's ear.

She took a large mouthful of her sandwich to avoid having to answer any more questions. Grace looked at Madoc and said, "Well, I suggest you finish your tea and then you can give Siân a look round before evening stables. Starting with the caravan of course."

* * *

The caravan was round the end of the stable block, tucked away from the wind. Madoc turned on the light and, expressionlessly, displayed the small sitting area, the tiny kitchen, bathroom and bedroom. She was still faintly embarrassed by his presence, imagining he disliked showing a stranger into his property, and she made noncommittal replies to his comments about gas bottles, bedding and the electricity meter. He handed her a note which lay on top of her luggage. "Mr Dava says the plumbers will be busy tomorrow after third lot. That's me! Can of water in kitchen cupboard. Luv, Ken."

"He's wacky, but quite harmless," said Madoc. "I expect the plumbing won't leak too much."

"Oh," said Siân, "Good. Madoc — I hope you don't mind me using the van."

"Temporary, isn't it? Anyway, it'll keep it aired."

She gave up. "I'll just unload the bag off the bike, then I'm ready for work."

"Fine," he said.

He agreed the Dutch barn would be perfectly safe for the bicycle and then took her back into the yards. She followed, bemused: rather than a humble employee, she might be a favoured new owner being given a guided tour of the stable in return for bringing her horse. Madoc introduced her to Aholibah and watched, amused, as she made friends with the placid brown mare, then, in his turn, was presented to Double Jump, who approached with interest and, after sniffing, licked his offered palm.

"Well!" said Siân. "You're the first man she's ever done that to."

He shrugged and stifled a wince. "I like horses and they know it." After a quiet word with the filly, he walked on. "We moved a gelding out of that box to make room for her. We couldn't put her on Top Yard next to Cymru, after all — hardly fair!"

The tour of the brick boxes of Bottom Yard completed, he led Siân across to the range of timber stables which stood with their backs to the winter gales. She took in the tidy midden and the row of wheelbarrows upended under a corrugated hovel — what luxury after the mucksacks of Green Bank! But she said nothing because Madoc, with an air of reaching his goal, came to a halt outside the first box and said, "This is Cymru."

At once, the horse thrust his long, handsome head towards her, sniffing deeply, analysing the scent of Double Jump with his top lip curled. Siân patted his neck but his interest in her was clearly not personal. Madoc cuffed him gently and he backed off: then returned to nudge Madoc's sleeve. Siân could not help smiling.

"He knows you all right."

"That's as may be. We have some rare disagreements. If he knows what I want he certainly doesn't show it!"

"Not all the time, surely?"

"Oh no. Just when it's important! Mind, this time I blame Dava as much as the horse. We got beaten last time out and Dava said perhaps I ought to have held him back a bit instead of making all the running. I said, chance would be a fine thing, and he said, damn well try. So off we went to Carlisle and this blighter," he said, stroking the black nose, "just wasn't going to have it. We were still arguing when he went sideways through the second hurdle."

"Ow," said Siân.

"There are some things you can only prove the hard way." His eyes were on the horse, fascinated by the wayward brain inside the handsome head. "Awkward so-and-so — you get off with a scratch or two, and I'm grounded... too damn bright, you are, think you know it all." He punched the stallion's neck, not hard, then stroked him. Siân stood watching. "Cocky devil, aren't you? Hope your Uncle Ken's keeping you respectful for me." Siân was mesmerised by the strong, beautiful hand that caressed the horse with such quick knowledge, and by the soft singsong voice. "I bet he's just going along with your funny little ways until I'm fit enough to take you back, you arrogant nag." Where had she seen that hand before, in what dream had she heard that voice? Why did she recognise them, why did they move her and make her feel that here, in the growing dusk, she was poised on the brink of some great discovery? In this magical twilight, anything could be inevitable and right.

It could not last, of course. In the instant that she grasped the thought, it vanished and the darkening yard glanced with the light of a headlamp and the air was filled with the throaty growl of a motorbike and a jaunty tootle on the horn. Siân shook herself. She was overtired, that was all, reading ghosts into the gloaming.

The bike passenger hopped off and came across with a rollicking stride like a stage sailor, shaking shaggy locks out of his helmet and tackling Madoc:

"'Ello, 'ello, trust you to be the first one in with the new bird! Make the most of it, darlin', 'cos Bill's on his way from the Lodge and the lights'll be on any minute... Didjer get yer gear all right? I'll be along to fiddle with yer taps tomorrer!"

She giggled in spite of herself.

"Shut up, Ken," said Madoc tolerantly. "The other grinning idiot," he added to Siân, "is John Paddy, and

Bill is Bill Houghton, our head man and the only reliable character among us."

Ken and John Paddy raised an indignant chorus and Siân found herself laughing as she had not laughed for months. She caught herself wondering at the change and thought, *it's this place, and these people ... It's nice. It's happy. I'm going to enjoy working here ...* Then she was swept away by the bubbling current of Ken's foolishness and when the lights flicked on they were all chuckling and sparring amicably. The head lad's authority calmed them but Ken remained irrepressible. He sighed stagily as Bill allocated the spare horses whose lad was away with Dava at Catterick.

"Always me, and will I get any thanks from Ted? No... well, come on, darlin', and I'll show you where Carola lives."

He swung the crash helmet as he wandered away, and Bill said to Siân, "Grace says you're to go in for supper when you've finished, and if Mr Dava gets back at a reasonable time he might want your cards this evening. All right?"

"Yes, sir."

He looked at her. "'Sir' sounds funny to a short fat herbert like me. Try Bill, same as everybody else."

But she only smiled, shook her head and trotted off after Ken and John Paddy.

"All right, Madoc?" said Bill Houghton.

"She'll do."

SIXTEEN

On the morning of Christmas Eve, Siân was astonished to find that not only the lads, but also Bill Houghton, Jack Brindley and Madoc all crowded into the tackroom at the morning break. More than that, Madoc was loudly booed for claiming his seat by the door.

"Ratbag, get out, this is for the workers, not the nobs."

"I am a worker."

"No you're not — you just shoved me off Quimby to ride that gallop to show off."

"Had to prove my shoulder's better somehow, didn't I?"

"Go on, get lost, Grace made these for us." Siân recognised then that the unusual fragrance really was mince pies and her nose was not deceiving her. "Anyway that's Siân's place."

"She can sit on my knee," said Madoc cheerfully.

"Go on, Siân, sit on the bugger, and you can intercept his share."

Siân, to her own surprise, took them at their word.

"Well done," said Madoc, in no way abashed. "Now I'm a fixture. You wouldn't deprive a hardworking man, would you?"

"Come on, let's have them pies dished out while they're still hot," said Bill Houghton, cutting through the cries of disbelief. "Mr Dava says he's only allowing Madoc one and he'll have the other spare one."

"Got them counted, has he?" commented Ted dourly.

"Keeping an eye on Madoc's waistline for that novice chase at Kempton more like," said Jack and bit deeply.

"We're goin' to give that Musketeer something to worry about," said Ken.

Madoc, recalling Jerry's confidence, merely said, "Don't bank on it."

"Yah, Quimby'd give 'im weight and still beat 'im."

"Is that filly of yours all right, Siân?" asked Bill Houghton. "John Paddy says she trailed Whisky Tan a long way this morning."

"Wouldn't have got within a mile of us on a racecourse," agreed John Paddy indistinctly, through crumbs.

Siân stood up to take a pie, and said, "Maybe I just have very strong arms." She got a small laugh, but she too was worried about Double Jump's lacklustre gallop, her first since the Haydock race. "I'll keep an eye on her legs," she said to Bill, "Mr Dava said I should."

"Aye, she's like Whisky," said John Paddy. "Very light. It's a wonder his legs have lasted as long as they have, poor old crock."

Siân did not quite dare to sit again on Madoc's knee. Ted stared at her in a disconcerting way, neither friend nor foe, while Ken and John Paddy sat voluptuously munching.

"Keep your strength up," said Madoc, watching her eat.

"What for, what for?" cried Ken hopefully.

"She's schooling over fences with Hollie against Cymru."

"She'll need a parachute! That bloody horse of Dava's is a flyer."

"I thought he was supposed to be selling it," said Ted.

"Not the way it's shaping, he isn't!"

Ted sniffed. "Not a job for a girl, schooling with that."

"I'd better sit down while I can, then," said Siân, feigning collapse between Madoc and Ken. They obligingly moved apart to give her a seat on the bench. "I'm not hurting your arm, am I, Madoc?"

"It's fine," said Madoc, and flung it over Siân's shoulders.

"See?"

"Will you put 'er down," complained Ken. "You've got a woman already."

Madoc maintained his hold. "That's all you know."

"You going home for Christmas, Siân?" asked Bill Houghton.

"No. I've made no arrangements. I can fill in for anybody if they want."

"No arrangements, at Christmas!" John Paddy was outraged. "What's up with your family, then, are they vampires or summat? Don't they celebrate Christmas?"

"Could you fill in for me then?" asked Ted, and was surprised when the others rained blows on his skullcap. "What did I say?"

Siân sat aloof from this horseplay, suddenly feeling rather dizzy. When they calmed down, she said, "I don't mind, Ted. Things are a bit sticky at home at the moment."

"Have to be bloody sticky for me not to get my trotters in the trough," said John Paddy, eyeing Dava's mince pie, now solitary on the tray.

"Yeah, but you're a pig anyway," said Ken. "But I mean, look at this, all this slack 'ere, she's in need of a good feed, i'n't she?" He pulled at the side of her jodhpurs with an air of waiting for the twang.

"We are going to take her to the Two Mills, though," said Ted. Siân, relieved that he had at last made a friendly gesture, was startled by the groans.

"You silly bugger. We were going to keep it quiet, weren't we, a surprise!"

"Oh. Yes. Sorry."

"Prat."

"What is all this?" she asked. The wave of faintness was passing, leaving a familiar ache in her midriff which she was inclined to welcome, guessing, hoping, as to its cause. "Don't tell me there's a party?"

"They have an annual knees-up at the Two Mills," said Madoc. "Bar meals and beer, guaranteed to put weight on." He was still holding her shoulders, almost as though he had forgotten his arm was round her.

"Well, you aren't invited, so stop moaning," said Ken.

"And me a lonely old bachelor."

They jeered, but Madoc shook his head and, with a slight effort, gave Siân a parting squeeze and lifted his arm back to his side. "I am! Felicity finished with me."

"What, no more facilities!" began John Paddy.

Siân took advantage of her freedom to retreat to the toilet and, though she heard Jack reproving John Paddy, she did not wait to hear his reply. Her mind was elsewhere. Perhaps she would finally know she was not pregnant.

She had been worrying for the past five days. Although she had made a shopping list with the words Test Kit in big letters at the top, the assistant who came helpfully to serve her in the chemist's in Heswall turned out to be a gossipy acquaintance from school, whom she had never really liked. She had found it impossible to buy such a thing under Beverley's inquisitive gaze and had ended up with a packet of tampons — and now, thank God, they would be needed. She began to giggle weakly, at first from sheer relief and then from reviewing in memory the comedy of herself trying to shake off Beverley's unwelcome attention. And then, at last, she began to weep.

When she re-emerged, the conversation had taken a different turn.

"So you flamin' well aren't coming with us, cos then you'll be putting up overweight on Boxing Day."

"You miserable lot of Scrooges, all you think about is your money. And I've already told you, we might not get anywhere near Musketeer."

"We've got our money down, so tough. Anyway the other bugger might fall and then you're a certainty," said John Paddy.

"Siân!" pleaded Madoc, "You're going to this party. Invite me."

She looked down on him, her tears forgotten. He spread out his arms.

"Take pity on a poor orphan."

"No, I only take pity on poor orphans if they're single."

"I am, I am," he assured her.

"Then Cinders, you shall go to the ball." She must be careful — her mood was unreliable. But Ken's was more unreliable still.

"As Lord of Misrule," he said, jumping up and clapping his hands, "I decree that your punishment for disobeying my command shall be... to travel to the pub in a miniskirt on the back of Ted Gray's bike."

A shout of laughter acclaimed this. Siân was aware of Ted's normally sallow complexion turning a pinkish olive, and of Madoc's slow, grinning wink.

"All right, your wish, My Lord, is my command."

And, pleased with her ambiguity, she smiled at both Madoc and Ken.

Dava opened the door, stepped in through the laughter, peered over misting spectacles and tenderly took up the last mince pie. "Now, ladies and gentlemen, could I persuade you to exercise a few horses?"

* * *

Madoc had not originally planned to go to the Two Mills party. Normally he disliked social gatherings; it had been a major source of friction between himself and Felicity, although politely not brought into the open in anything so undignified as a row. He had admired her polish and her slightly aggressive air of knowing what was good for him but he was not prepared to let her think that marriage to him would be anything like the life she led now. In childhood he had delighted in the stony solitudes of Afonwen so college socials held few charms. Felicity, dazzled perhaps by the public face of racing and forgetful of the fact that Madoc belonged to the working side, had been appalled to discover that her vision of life with him — consisting of a brisk timetable with lots of socialising and the occasional hunt ball — was entirely discordant with his own plans for the future. Had she been genuinely dedicated to teaching, the thing might have been made to work. Afonwen was not, after all, that far from what Felicity was pleased to refer to as civilisation, and Madoc would not have insisted that she tie herself to the farm. But Felicity had only viewed teaching as an interim step. Marriage to a moderately successful jockey who was soon to become an independent landowner had looked like another forward move. It had appalled her to discover that he clung to his solitude and positively refused to consider exchanging Afonwen for a property in the kinder air of Cheshire.

As her resentment became more obvious, Madoc realised that Felicity had hunted all her life as part of the pack, while he was a fox, a loner. In the pain of the break-up, he wondered how he had ever managed to overlook that fact. Perhaps it was the simple coincidence of two people both thinking of settling down. Perhaps it had been her careful readiness to submit to him that had swayed his judgement. At any rate, he'd made a mistake and, although relieved now it was over, he felt very badly about it all. He couldn't blame Felicity for attacking him and, indeed, he almost welcomed her abuse, for he deserved it; he had disappointed her. It had been a bitter parting and it was only pride that drove him to display his unconcern to the lads by teasing Siân Davies into inviting him to the party.

* * *

The Two Mills was crowded. The lads sat in a congested circle round a small table covered rim to rim with glasses and stacked plates. Ken leaned back and expressed the lads' general satisfaction.

"Good meal that. It's goin' ter be a good night. We'll start by finding a punishment for Ted for openin' his big gob this morning and spoilin' our little surprise. Siân's paid her forfeit."

They all looked at her legs and John Paddy said;

"Tasty, very."

Ken cuffed him perfunctorily. "Manners, serf. Suggestions please!"

Siân raised her hand. "Please, sir?"

"Yes, darlin'?"

"Make him buy the next round. Then, anyone who mentions it again has to buy the one after that."

"Nice one! OK Ted, go on! You heard!"

"If it'll get you lot off my back, I suppose I'd better."

Madoc held out a congratulatory hand to Siân. "Bravo."

She shook hands and blushed, and couldn't think why.

As the evening wore on, hotter and more crowded, the little circle drew tightly together as if to defend itself. Siân sat wedged between Madoc and Ken and felt very happy. Her cramps had been unusually bad but she was drinking whisky and they were easing, so she drank some more. Soon she felt bold enough to cap Ken's jokes, and John Paddy pelted her with peanuts which missed and hit Madoc and bounced into his glass. It was all very silly and harmless, quite devoid of the heavy overtones of her nights out with Justin, and she would not have thought of him had not someone behind her said, in almost the same accent, "Come on, darling!" as a group next to theirs moved out. The sudden jolt of memory made her shudder and Ken whooped as her whisky spilled down his good trousers. Then he laughed and demanded a handkerchief.

John Paddy said, "Use your own, you daft clod."

"Useless, you are," complained Ken. "Here I am, in mortal danger of death by alcoholic poisoning, and my best mate hasn' gorra hankie."

"Well stop pushing her. And anyway, you took that whisky and poured it on your own knee — buy her another!"

Under cover of the exchange that followed, Madoc leaned slightly towards Siân and asked, "Are you all right?"

The gentle enquiry caught her off guard. She wanted to weep but did not dare, knowing she had had more whisky than was good for her self-control.

"I'm all right now," she said.

"Good. Now is all that matters, you know."

She looked at him wonderingly. Why did she feel again that they shared some secret? He tipped her a faint wink and rose to his feet.

"My round," he announced. But Ted refused, saying it was time he went.

"It isn't even ten o'clock!" protested John Paddy.

"I don't like to be too late home," said Ted, getting up and waiting for Siân to follow.

"I'll bet they don't know he's out."

"They don't wait up for you still, do they?"

Dumb under their goading, Ted reached for Siân's coat which lay over the back of her chair, dislodged her weighty shoulder bag, and spilt its contents around everyone's feet.

"You nit, Ted."

"She'll never get home at this rate anyway — you might as well leave her."

Ted's helpless astonishment at the scale of the explosion was much too funny to let Siân be cross with him. She dived recklessly under the table and ferreted between the assorted legs she found there, giggling at the cries of alarm and the jingling glasses above as she clutched handfuls of her belongings. Madoc's face appeared below table level, accompanied by his tie, and she gave way to peals of laughter. "We must stop meeting like this."

"Come on, get up. I'll pick this lot up."

"Why are you wearing odd socks?"

"Get up before you break something."

Ken and John Paddy joined in.

"I bet he has another pair just like 'em at home."

"What are you two doing under there?"

"This is my Wendy house," said Siân, gesturing widely and bumping her head.

"I'm Wendy, can I come in?"

"This is just so silly," came Ted's voice from above.

"Come on out," advised Madoc quietly, collecting up elderly receipts and bus tickets. Siân clutched the bag and struggled back on to her stool, and the men surfaced and drank, while Ted, zipping up his threadbare waxed jacket, waited with exaggerated patience, and watched the others handing items across the table to her.

"You really ought to be careful," said John Paddy, blushing, "throwing these things at us poor fellas."

"Aha!" crowed Ken, "he knows what they are!"

"I have got sisters, fool."

"It looks like your round, Siân. Mine's a pint."

"I'll bring the bike round to the door if you like," said Ted and upturned the two helmets as though worried that female impedimenta might have invaded them. Siân, packing comb and mirror into their rightful places, ignored him.

"She's had too much to be safe let loose with you," said Ken. "You'll keel over from whisky fumes before you reach the traffic lights, and then, with that miniskirt, you'll be at her mercy."

Ted glanced at the clock and shuffled. Then he offered her the spare helmet. "Here."

"No," said Siân suddenly. She was comfortable, owlishly sorting out her muddled possessions and she wished Ted would stop pestering. It was cold and windy on the bike and if he really wanted to talk to her he could stop indoors, couldn't he? "I mean, I don't think I can manage."

"Hooray, she's drunk!" cried John Paddy.

"And it's her round," added Ken.

She fumbled a five-pound note from her purse. "And Madoc's going to get it."

He rose and gave her a pantomime bow.

"Oh all right," said Ted fiercely and, clattering the helmets together, he pushed his way out of the bar.

Madoc brandished the money and vanished snakelike between customers and Ken said with satisfaction, "Well, that's better."

Siân, still sorting with exaggerated care, said nothing. Madoc came back with a whisky and two pints.

"What, are you still here?"

"Yes, if I was going to go, I'd have went."

"Where's yours?" demanded Ken, pointing to the glasses.

"I've got enough fizzy water left to float a battleship," said Madoc. He handed Siân her change, and sat down.

"You're as much of a dishrag as old Ted," grumbled John Paddy.

"Forfeit! Kiss all those present!"

"Him first," added John Paddy, pointing at Ken.

"I never kiss anything that isn't female," said Madoc, carelessly saluting Siân's cheek and balancing his glass of water to defend himself from Ken and John Paddy.

Siân ducked and giggled. *Whatever has come over me, she wondered — I'm feeling quite silly. Perhaps I really am drunk. Drunk and happy. Miracles do happen. I'm not pregnant. I've got away from Justin completely now. I've found men I can be friends with... and a good job... what more can life hold?*

She sat in a sleepy, happy dream for some time. Then she became aware that Madoc was talking to her, stroking the back of her hand to gain her attention.

"Hello," she said, smiling at him.

"Would you like a lift home with a nice sober driver?"

"Are you going my way?"

"Tiddly," he reproached her. "Come on. You'll soon perk up when you get outside."

She found herself gently dragooned into her coat and propelled to the car park where Madoc unlocked an elderly MG and assisted her down into the passenger seat. He quickly took his own place and started the engine.

"Well? Better?"

"I'm somnambulating."

"You're better." He swung the car out of its parking space and took to the road. "How long is it since you had a fling? You looked like a famine victim surrounded by bread."

She smiled again, trying to stay in her sleepy haze, but the chilliness of the little car shook her awake with a shiver. "I'm not drunk," she said suddenly.

"Of course not. Actually you are. But as I'm not in the habit of leaping on intoxicated women you needn't worry about it."

"Oh." Siân was so taken aback by this frankness that she could think of nothing better to say. The MG skipped and burbled along the road with cheerful insouciance, while its heater made ineffectual efforts to dispel the cold. Siân sat up straighter and pulled her coat around her. "I haven't fastened my seat belt," she said, hunting for it.

"No," said Madoc easily.

She half expected him to help her, as an excuse for some advance, as Justin would undoubtedly have done, but he just drove, his eyes on the road.

"There," she said at last. It was ridiculous to feel ruffled and disquieted by this, yet she had grown so used to the obviousness of Justin that she did not know how to interpret Madoc's response. Was it detachment? Calmness? Self-control? Was he actually not interested and was she imagining more attention than she actually deserved? She cleared her throat and said coolly, "Have the lads got much money on Quimby — on Boxing Day? D'you know?"

She saw his smile outlined by the street lamps. "They don't tell me everything."

"Oh, well, nobody does that."

"No."

"Will he win, do you think?"

"If I could tell you that, I'd be a rich man. Not as rich as those who can tell for certain that a given horse won't win, of course." His glance flicked across at her, returned to the road and carefully stayed there.

"I don't know what you mean," she said and gave an uncomfortable little laugh. "I suppose I must still be a bit tiddly, because usually I won't admit that, I just say 'Oh,' or I don't say anything while I wonder what the person meant. But — really — I don't understand. How can anyone know a horse won't win?"

He turned an amused eye on her. "I knew you weren't the type to fit in at Pickering's. I'm surprised you didn't tumble to the fact that it's much easier to make money out of racing illegally than it is to do it legally. It's because it's easier that they make it illegal, of course!"

"And you think..." she began, but before she could say any more, he went on.

"Racing assumes we're all in it to win prestige and prize money. Yes? Placed horses share the loot; owner, trainer and jockey get their cut; lads get a present; end of story, hm?"

"Yes," she said, waiting.

"But the *bookies* don't do it for glory. They work on mathematics. Statistical probabilities. If such and such a horse is the most likely to win, they show the shortest odds against it."

"Yes," said Siân again, rather impatiently, for she knew all this.

"They balance the likelihood of it winning against the greed of the punters backing it. And they always make sure the odds will give them a good return over the race as a whole. A bookie who's bad at maths goes bust!"

"Fair enough," said Siân, wondering where it was leading. "What's this got to do with Pickering's?"

"Well, what I've just described is the legal side. It's tricky and ticklish but it's reasonably fair because it depends on how the horses run and it assumes they run to the best of their ability. But if the bookie gets greedy he can 'make friends' with a trainer. Then he makes some arrangements with him, and when the friend has a good horse going racing he offers slightly longer odds than the punters expect. Longer odds equal more bets, more cash. Then the friend gives the horse a nice, undetectable bucket of water before the race, so that it can't breathe too well. The horse loses, the bookie keeps the bets, and the friendly trainer gets a cut — which might be more than he would have won, even if the horse had been good enough. It's hard to arrange to nobble a horse but it has to be easier than hoping for a winner!"

"And you think Pickering's do that? But if they did it all the time it wouldn't work, would it? Nobody would ever back their horses if they always lost."

He laughed. "You're too literal. Nowhere near devious enough to be a crook! They only do it now and again when the mathematics are right."

"But you'd have to get the lads to join in on a thing like that. And they wouldn't. I mean, I know I wouldn't," she amended, recalling Frankie's lack of concern for her horses.

"It doesn't have to be a lad. Justin, for instance, is a clever enough jockey to lose a race without making it obvious, and greedy enough not to care about what he does to the horse."

Siân fought down her panic at the name. How stupid her body was to react so to words, when Justin wasn't even there! How long would it go on suffering such irrational terror and wanting to react with anger when there was no obvious reason? She struggled to regain control by watching the road ahead.

"You're right," she said, hearing her voice from a thousand miles away. "He doesn't care about the horses he rides."

"There you are, you see. He's on the other side of the fence. Mind you, he's rich and I'm poor so it's hard to say which of us is the more stupid."

Siân managed a smile. "I wouldn't say you're stupid." But she shivered.

"Cold?" he said at once. He placed a warm hand on her leg. "Just testing."

She gave the hand gently back to him. "Better than on that motorbike, thank you."

"Ah well." He smiled apology, and silence fell between them.

So she was not imagining things. But the warm, undemanding gesture, relaxed and friendly as it was, had tied her stomach in a sudden knot and made her heart beat faster in a way that changed all the rules. What was this? Should she be hearing warning bells?

Madoc turned right and the car went bouncing past the Lodge and its two chestnut trees, towards the house and the stables and the spaced security lights. She wished she didn't like him; it made him so hard to fight. She didn't know dearly why she must fight him, only that it was too soon — oh, much too soon — and she wasn't ready to take risks again. She had felt able to flirt with the other lads, could have laughed off a pass from Ken or John Paddy and knew that Ted, for all his thirty years, was a child emotionally; none of them mattered. But Madoc? There was a fire sleeping in that relaxed frame which she knew she could not cope with yet.

The car rolled quietly to a halt outside the garage.

Madoc turned off the engine and released his seatbelt. Then he looked at Siân, at first seriously, then with growing amusement.

"You look like a mouse in one of those humane traps. 'Whatever is going to happen to me now?' Take off your seat belt. You can go if you want."

He sat back into the angle of seat and door, waiting for her response; and because he waited, because she saw that she mattered to him, she released her belt and sat still.

He read her stillness and said, "Are you afraid? Don't be."

She looked away. "Not of you."

"There's no room for anyone else," he said, gently teasing.

"There are people in our minds," she said, half to herself. "I haven't got rid of mine yet and I don't know when I will."

He took a deep breath. "Yes, I see, yes. And I'm the same. As you probably know. I mean, women always seem to know much more about me than I know about them at any given time." He smiled ruefully. "I suppose that means, let's take it as it comes."

She nodded, unable to trust her voice. Neither of them questioned the assumption that something lay between them, because it was as yet too vague to be put into words, merely a feeling, an unexplored connection.

"Well," he said eventually, "I have to put the car away, so perhaps you'd better be off to bed. My bed, you might remember."

There went her heart again. It forced her to pluck up courage and turn towards him, with some idea, perhaps, of a formal handshake and goodnight, but as their fingers touched she knew there had to be more than this tightening clasp and she looked up to see him leaning forward, rather warily. The touch of their lips was gentle.

She was still on guard. The smoky smell of the pub, the feel of car seats, the distant lighting, were all familiar from other encounters and full of hidden menace, so that she was ready at any moment to draw back and flee, but he was different. The scent of his skin and the way he damped down his obvious strength, as though he, in his turn, was afraid to frighten her, were new to her, and sweet. For an endless moment she was drowned and weightless in a warm sea, and then he broke away and pressed his face to her cheek. They sat quite still, not speaking.

Siân found that she was crying. She made no attempt to hide it and Madoc lifted her face with one finger, puzzled by her reaction.

"Did I do something wrong?"

She shook her head. "No. I don't know. I'm afraid of being happy. And that sounds stupid."

"It sounds as though you're out of practice."

"I've got so used to being without it. Thinking perhaps I didn't deserve it — that it won't ever last..."

"Hush. It's all right." His hands held hers comfortingly, for her response had signalled a kind of desperation which he had not suspected. Was she always like this? Or was she rebounding from someone? Perhaps time would give him a clue. "Nothing lasts forever. But if you're happy now, it's enough, isn't it?"

"Too much." She sniffed. "Like you said, I'm out of practice."

He fished out a handkerchief and, dutifully, she dried her face. He was reminded of his small niece being tidied up after a fall, and Siân unknowingly reinforced the image by pecking him on the cheek and saying, "I must go. Thank you for a nice evening," and giving him back the handkerchief.

He pulled a wry face. "We're past saying conventional things like that, aren't we? Go on away to your caravan."

She opened the door. "Goodnight then."

"And practise being happy — it's Christmas."

SEVENTEEN

The short days were lengthening; the year had turned.
Siân remained immersed in the secure solitude of the
caravan and lived a life of steady routine, marked off
with monastic regularity into work and food. Breakfast,
mucking out, exercise; coffee, exercise, lunch; afternoon
off, evening stables, supper; radio, library book, bed.
Despite the constant threat of cold and the hungry
electricity meter, the caravan was a haven in which she
once again began to flourish. Her clothes no longer hung
from her bones and occasionally she lingered at the
mirror as though studying a stranger. She was smiling
more and talking more, but she invited no one in. She
did not go anywhere for Christmas or New Year but
covered for Ken, John Paddy and Ted, shying from their
thanks, knowing that she was using the work as an
anchor. Her father sent a Christmas card with a brief

salutation and a ten-pound note, and she hurriedly sent a card in return. To her mother she wrote not at all.

She was especially wary about Madoc. In the cold light of Christmas Day the aftermath of the party had looked rather different and much too close to the pattern of Green Bank to be comfortable. She had not seen Madoc for a couple of days afterwards. He spent Christmas with his brother's family and went from there to Kempton for the big novice 'chase, in which Musketeer beat Quimby with impressive ease. By the time he came back Siân had almost talked herself into thinking there was nothing in their relationship and was dismissive when Ken and John Paddy tried to tease her about it. But she caught herself on occasion being very careful, very neutral, towards Madoc and, although she could see it puzzled him, she could not help it; she was just as puzzled herself.

She was puzzled, too, by Double Jump who, although much happier in her new home, was not making any progress with training. Dava had seen her schooling, had deduced from her jumping that she had some discomfort and put her at once on to the easy list. Inclined though he was to work his tougher horses strongly, he was contrastingly tender with the less-robust sorts. "No point in pushing her till she's right," he said and, having checked her back and her legs and still not found a cause, left it to the vet to continue investigations. Siân worried a little, but as Double Jump appeared to thrive and was as affectionate as ever, the lack of faster work did not bother her unduly.

By contrast, Aholibah was bouncing out of her skin. Eleven years old, experienced and tough as the proverbial boot, she was just the sort Dava liked, a specialist over three miles, a superb fencer and a regular runner. On her, Siân had learnt to sit on over the big schooling fences and pretend that she was teaching the mare, when everyone, including Hollie, knew very well it was the other way round. As January drew on, it was routine for Aholibah to be included in the list of entries for Wetherby. With its stiff fences and easy turns, it was a course Madoc enjoyed and on which Dava's horses tended to do well. Quimby had won there in November and Hollie was fancied. Cymru, still an unknown quantity, was entered too.

"It's a sharp hurdle course," said Dava to Madoc, "but you never know, a good gallop might just settle him and stop him fighting early on. There's a decent field today he'll have a job to get away from this lot."

They were driving up the A1, Dava at the wheel of the Range Rover, peering round the wagon in front. "That is, assuming you're still in one piece after your encounter with this novice of Cunningham's in the first.

Why you agree to nurse his dodgy jumpers at all beats me."

"I always think, maybe this one will be better."

"And it never is."

"If you'd let me school over there more often it might be."

"I'd rather you schooled mine."

"All right. I still get a fee to ride them. You pay me sixty-five quid to sit in the changing room and I'll pass up his money and his dodgy jumpers and welcome. No? Afonwen Building Fund will be taking Cunningham's cash, then."

When the dodgy novice duly fell at the fourth hurdle, Madoc trudged back through the wind and rain cursing Dava's accurate forecast of its chances and Cunningham's inaccurate optimism. The only bright spot was the early return to the changing room with no damage done. Everyone else was getting at him: trainer ("Should've stuck on that, lad, he only pecked!"); valet ("Clean breeches already?"); doctor ("First today, try not to come in again!"); and, of course, Dava, to whom he gave his saddle after weighing out for Aholibah's race.

"Got passed fit all right?"

Madoc only looked at him and sighed.

"Make sure you damn well are then. Not overweight, hm?"

"Of course not."

"All right." And he was gone.

"Blast and bloody hell," said Madoc at his retreating back, and felt better. At his elbow Kevin and Justin waited for their trainers to collect weighed gear. Justin was complaining of tiredness.

"I'm even having to ride work, just ordinary work, not gallops."

"You don't know when you're well off," said Kevin, whose mornings were occupied with travelling to various trainers to school their horses. "All yours are on the doorstep. Too many late nights, that's your trouble."

Madoc went back into the changing room and spent the remaining time fidgeting with the silk on his skullcap.

His mood lightened when he went out into the wet paddock. There was Aholibah, with Siân bustling to keep up with her long, calm stride. Cheerful Mr and Mrs Lofthouse stood under a huge umbrella and chaffed him and Dava about racing in such weather. He assured them their four-legged darling had been schooling well and silenced Siân with a wink before she could reveal the realities of the exercise; with unhorsey owners, tact could be a very funny thing. Dava gave Madoc a leg up and the old mare kicked out the way she always did, so that he laughed in spite of the weather and Siân looked up at him, startled. As she led him away, she said, "I take it you're all right?"

"The doctor said nothing was about to drop off so I could go on riding until it did."

"After what Grace has told me, I'm inclined to believe you."

Madoc shook his head, waiting impatiently for her to slip the lead rein from the bit, but he smiled. "You don't need to worry about me on this old lady."

The "old lady" was feeling well and the heavy ground suited her. She set off happily in the field of six, holding her ears out stiffly against the rain but lobbing along with a carefree air as if humming her way through an undemanding task. She was an old love, thought Madoc as he crouched over her short, lapping mane. *God bless you, you big Irish dear, you love these big fences and you could potter round here with your eyes shut. We'll just take it easy, nobody's in any hurry, not with three miles to go on this ground... well, maybe*

Justin, but who knows what his riding orders are?
Don't rush things, old dear, I'll tell you when to put the
pressure on him. . . Four fences from home, he told her.
She forged steadily ahead, dropping Justin's mount in
her wake, taking her fences with deadly accuracy. Her
only challenger came up with a rush, misjudged the
second last and turned over, and Aholibah cantered
home to win by a length and a half.

"That," said Madoc to an excited Siân, as the mare
walked steaming into the winner's enclosure, "was what
is known as an armchair ride."

* * *

Jack Brindley turned Cymru in to be mounted.
Cymru didn't behave well for him — the gusty wind
made him sidle and kick and Jack's growls and chucks at
the rein only aggravated him the more.

"Stupid great sod," grumbled Jack to Dava who was
stripping the rug off the horse. "Why don't you geld the
bugger and have done with it?"

Dava didn't answer. He legged Madoc up and Jack
held tightly to the stallion's bit while Madoc got his feet
into the irons. Cymru tossed his head and fretted. Jack
struggled and swore.

"Let him go, Jack, you're just making him worse."

Only because Dava had given him a direct order would Jack acknowledge defeat by letting go. Cymru's progress to the two mile start was bouncy in the extreme.

The stallion stalked about irritably, while Madoc checked the girths and considered the nineteen runners circling around him: inexperienced, excited, all heading out for two miles of sodden turf in the dim hour before winter's dark, hoping to clear the clattering hurdles and not be bowled over by someone else's mistake. *Damn you, Dava, telling me not to race from the front. On this horse, in a field like this, it's got to be the safest place...*

The rain stopped. They lined up, jostling, and Cymru jibbed and swung away. Madoc brought him back and someone else was facing the wrong way. The stallion bounced and sidled and was sworn at, and then, "Come ON!" and the tapes went up.

Cymru plunged forward, fighting control as the other horses surged around him.

"Bloody hell," said Madoc. He was swept into the lead and over the first hurdle.

Dava and Jack Brindley stood together, watching.

183

Dava put binoculars up to his rain-smeared glasses as the field raced towards the stands.

"What does he think he's doing? He'll have him on the deck." He lowered the binoculars impatiently. "Can't see much." Jack offered him a handkerchief but was waved aside. "Bloody hell, what a pace. I wish he'd listen when I tell him... "

They swept past in a thundering bunch and the wet earth trembled.

"Madoc's having a terrible fight," said Jack.

"Don't sound so bloody pleased about it. It's still too fast."

They watched the bobbing figures go out round the bend left-handed and into misty distance. Siân, too, was watching, tucked into an inconspicuous corner, finding it easy for once to read the race — the near-black horse out in front in the red colours was impossible to miss. Siân could not help gasping every time he met a hurdle, for his leaps were so huge that each time they looked like a mistake, but there was no crumpling fall and no avalanche of horse and rider to be galloped over by the blur of following hooves. As the field came round the far turn, it was clear Cymru still intended to lead at all costs, and Siân, observing the evilly flattened ears, wondered whether he meant to be first home or simply to dominate the rest of the horses. She could see that Madoc was not fighting him any more but sitting close as though waiting. Did he feel the horse tiring? Was he waiting to beat off a challenge? Siân looked at the strung-out field, assessing them, and realised with a jolt that one of them seemed familiar. She recognised her old friend Stickleback, with Justin crouched, tight and efficient, in the green and blue colours, crowding him up against Cymru's quarters. By listening to the commentary she learnt that the black horse with the orange colours in third place was called Tandem Leader. There was a growing gap between these three and the rest of the field as they came to the final hurdle.

Cymru still led, Stickleback clinging to his right side, and Tandem Leader surging suddenly forward so that all three rose like a wave together. Cymru leapt high and clear. Stickleback touched down first and nipped into the lead. Siân saw a sudden flurry; Stickleback swerved into Tandem Leader whose jockey swore at Justin. They both pulled their whips through to their left hands and Siân winced to see the great slashing arc Justin made between Stickleback and Cymru. Tandem Leader recovered and for a moment she thought he was going to win, but then the wickedly lowered head of Cymru thrust forward again, Madoc's whip flicking alongside his eye, and she could see he was gaining ground once more, his long aggressive stride seizing the trembling turf and flinging it in flying clods behind him. Then there was the post. And Cymru had won.

As the field pounded past, Siân leaned into her corner, drained. He had won. Madoc had won. She thought of the confusion at the last hurdle and the speed with which the jockeys had reacted compared with her own bewilderment; she could never hope to ride like that, let alone win a race. She set off towards the winner's enclosure, full of admiration for the everyday skill needed to win a little old novice hurdle.

There were very few people about and she saw Dava and Jack Brindley ahead of her, arguing as they went. Dava clutched his hat against a gust of wind and she heard him say, "That bloody enquiry signal again! What the devil is it about that horse?" And Siân woke up: it was one thing to want to hail Madoc's victory and quite another to stand foolishly within range of argument when Justin was involved. She carefully drifted away before the placed horses arrived, unaware that she had been spotted far earlier in the day.

* * *

Madoc changed back into street clothes and claimed a cup of tea. He was tired, more by the discipline of the low weights than by the riding. Although this had been a full day, it had been a good one: two winners, a second, an also-ran, and only one fall. He sat on the bench and drank thirstily while the jockeys talked around him and packed up and left. Kevin and Johnny Robson said goodnight. Madoc watched the ever-busy valets bagging colours to return to trainers, heaping dirty breeches, stocks and gloves to be washed, wiping wet mud from saddles and boots. He ought to meet Dava now but he was curious about the outcome of the enquiry and it made a good excuse for sitting there drinking tea instead of listening to the usual precise instructions Dava would be giving Jack about caring for Cymru and Aholibah and driving them home.

Eventually Justin and Derek came trailing back, mildly grumbling, to finish changing. Justin cast an eye over Madoc's sprawled form and poked a toe into his leg.

"Knackered, are we? Serves you right."

Madoc ignored this. "What did they have to say?"

"Oh, the usual pronouncements about proper use of the whip. You're lucky they didn't call you. They're a different set from the stewards at Haydock and they didn't realise you had anything to do with it. That bastard of yours always looks so evil, the cameras didn't show much."

"We were that close you couldn't see anyway," said Derek. "And you were the one who rode me off my line, Pick."

"Sure, and I'll do it again if I get squeezed between you and him. You saw the bugger go for me!"

"I didn't, which is why I didn't mention it to the stewards."

"Yeah, well, it made no difference as it happens, he beat me all right." Justin pulled on a heavy sweatshirt and added, "And you needn't thank me, Madoc, I just wanted to get home at a reasonable time. Last race, miserable day, we can all do without a tale-telling session. But I'll be the first in with the objections if that bastard of yours goes for me when I'm in with a real chance any time. So watch out."

"Fair enough," said Madoc, finishing his tea.

He stood up wearily and went over to arrange with his valet that his gear was to go to Carlisle for the next day. When he came back with Aholibah's and Cymru's colours, Justin was carefully combing his hair.

"That isn't your job. Next thing you know, you'll be valeting yourself. You've got to draw the line somewhere."

"Give it a rest, Pick. The world would be a far easier place to live in without your demarcation lines." Madoc swung the bag over his shoulder, ready to go, but Justin went on talking as though settled for a cosy chat.

"You want to ask that new girl about demarcation lines."

"Which new girl?" asked Madoc, blankly but alert.

"Oh come on. You know: came to you with that black filly."

"What about her?" Madoc knew he ought to have ignored Justin. There was a gleam of devilment in the bright eyes which he might have thwarted by leaving twenty seconds ago, but he found himself waiting while Justin slipped on his jacket and straightened his collar.

"Just a friendly warning. Can't swear it's gospel of course."

"Friendly?" said Madoc sceptically.

"Well, I could have dropped you in it with the stewards, couldn't I? Course, if you don't fancy her it wouldn't matter, but it's always safer to know, isn't it?"

"Know what?" asked Madoc, furious with himself for asking but unable to resist.

"Well... it's just something I heard. She'd be better put to the test, you know? Fools rush in and all that? You never know what you might catch."

"Caught it off you, I suppose," said Madoc automatically. "No wonder you're going about with a nurse these days."

"Me! Pure as the driven snow, I am. Would I cheat on Janice now, would I?" His smile was dazzling. "Shall I ask her about it for you? She'll soon tell you how you can find out."

"Get stuffed, Pick." Madoc turned away contemptuously.

"You'd know where to draw the line then all right!"

The door shut without emphasis and Justin let him go, still smiling. He'd seen the looks that passed between Shannie and Madoc before the handicap chase — something there, definitely! More than she'd had for him, too, whatever Madoc might pretend. The chance to twist his tail had been irresistible, especially after the incident in the last race, though he'd have done it anyway just for the sake of tormenting him — a serious character, old Madoc, not given to frivolity, and in danger of becoming a bore. Justin turned up his collar, shook out his hair and did a dance step with triumphant style.

EIGHTEEN

Claybrooke had a carnival air in the first days of March. In those wild and blustery precursors of spring, the horses were fresh and leapt willingly up the gallops. John Paddy whooped as old Whisky Tan schooled beside Double Jump. Cymru bucked and fly-kicked as he waited to tackle the fences.

"What is this?" Siân asked Ted Gray. "This — euphoria?"

"You what?"

"Why is everything... jumping?"

"We're getting ready to go to Bangor." He shrugged. "Happens every year."

* * *

There were six horses going to Bangor-on-Dee and Siân rode in the second horsebox, hired for the day. Everyone was going because the course was so near there was no nonsense about leaving lads behind to see to the non-runners. Ken and John Paddy were ahead in the Claybrooke horsebox with Jack; Siân and Ted sat in the hired wagon's cab with the driver; Madoc and Dava, as usual, shared the Range Rover, leaving Bill Houghton and Grace to hold the fort at home. Siân began to understand the festive air surrounding the stable's day out. Even the mundane presence of Ted Gray could not dampen her enthusiasm, nor spoil the cheerful sunshine on the brassy yellow daffodils in gardens and roadsides, or the mist of green through the trees where the winter buds were breaking. Double Jump travelled quietly alongside Iron Duke and Siân, knowing that Helen Rogers had gently pressured Dava to engage Jo Fraser for her, was happy and confident and beginning to be excited. Under the masking note of the engine, she began to hum. The driver winked and joined in with a cheerful whistle, although Ted pulled his cap over his eyes and began rubbing dust off the sleeve of his 'best' jacket with a sour expression as though he considered *Mae hen wlad fy nhadau yn annwyl i mi* in bad taste when they hadn't even crossed into Clwyd. Siân surprised herself by risking a wink back at the driver, and went on humming.

The last month at Claybrooke had been very quiet for her. She was wholly involved with the stable, at ease with her horses and the other lads and enjoying the security of routine, while the minor excursions that always cropped up prevented life being boring. She banked her wages, shopped, mended harness for Bill, lingered endlessly in the warmth of the nearest library and occasionally treated herself to new clothes. And just now and then she began to lift her head and wonder briefly — rather carefully — whether she might do something else in an evening other than read in the caravan. She hadn't yet dared, but she knew her courage was returning. A great deal of her confidence stemmed from the fact that John Paddy and Ken, though they teased her, never pursued her, being busy dealing with Ken's optimistic sprinkling of Valentines across Heswall. And if she sometimes found herself sweating when Ted Gray walked past the doorway of Double Jump's box, at least he never came in, and everywhere else she knew she could cope with him.

She saw very little of Madoc. He was determined to keep his weight down and complete the season as profitably as possible, so when he wasn't riding, schooling or racing for Claybrooke, he was doing those things for Eric Cunningham or any other trainer who would employ him, and when he had spare time he would be jogging or wasting less energetically in the sauna in Chester. Even on Sundays he was busy and would disappear in the MG immediately after morning stables. It was a long time before Siân dared to ask Ken where he went and the offhand answer that he'd probably gone to the building site was not very informative. Not wanting to attract Ken's attention, she hadn't asked any more and had tried very hard not to let her eyes follow Madoc when he did happen to be home and on the yards. She was determined not to throw herself at him, partly from a sense of her own dignity but also because there were still times when she was confused or self-conscious, or sometimes frightened, and in spite of the friendliness of Claybrooke she did not want to make a public spectacle of herself. She coped by keeping busy. She applied herself to learning saddle-stitching and, under Bill's tuition, stitched new bits into the racing bridles and helped him to maintain leathers and girths. In the evenings she read voraciously or listened to the radio. So she found a measure of security. But as far as Madoc was concerned, anything might happen.

* * *

Regular punters at Bangor knew that Dafydd Owen made a speciality of raiding in force at the March meeting and, accordingly, the Claybrooke horses attracted a lot of money. Madoc worked his way happily through them, from Iron Duke in the opening hurdle, to Carola, Whisky Tan who ran bravely second, and Quimby who galloped contemptuously away with the main handicap chase. And then, his last ride of the day since it was Jo Fraser who would ride Double Jump, there was Cymru. He was to be a steeplechaser from now on, to Madoc's satisfaction. Although his debut in that role at Carlisle turned out to be argumentative, Dava had sent him 'chasing as soon as he felt the horse had mastered the schooling fences at home.

"I get the feeling," he had confided to Madoc, "that we're working against time with this horse. We've caught his attention for the moment but how long will it last? Let's try him at the job he's really made for, before he gets it into his head that hurdling is easy."

So they had gone north. Cumbria had had snow and with the thaw the ground at Blackwell was desperately heavy but Dava said that the stallion's long-striding gallop and bottomless inherited stamina should cope. "Always assuming that you don't let him gallop himself into the ground in the first mile!"

Madoc found this habitual caution frustrating. He felt that Dava was wrong to consider Cymru young and green. Being a stallion, he was physically very strong, and growing wilful. The Carlisle turf came up to meet Madoc yet again as Cymru, jealous of other horses alongside him, totally misjudged the first open ditch. Madoc had been sufficiently infuriated to tell Dava that unless he was allowed to ride Cymru fast and out in front from start to finish, the horse would have to be gelded. There was no room for Afonwen in his thoughts just then.

Now, nine runners gleamed under the sun at the quiet end of the course. The novice 'chase, described with typical Bangor approximation as 'about' two and a half miles, started way out in the country, and its contestants usually hacked from the paddock bend in a quiet little group. Not so Cymru. After fighting Jack in the paddock, he had discovered good ground beneath his feet and he wanted nothing more than to run freely, so Madoc let him. There was a small flurry of cloths on the bookies' boards, lengthening the odds as word came that he was running away. Then, having taken a few extra bets, the odds shortened again when it became clear Madoc was perfectly in control.

Cymru stood at the start like an onyx statue. He liked the sun on his back and the nearness of the River

Dee had attracted his attention. Madoc quietly tightened girth and surcingle and he did not move.

"Fancy a swim?" asked Kevin, drawing up alongside.

Cymru turned one ear at his chestnut horse and concentrated again on the river.

"Hope not," said Madoc. "What's that you're on?"

"This is Diaghilev."

"Pickering's? Where's Cock o' the North then?"

Kevin's good-natured, ugly face split into a grin. "You mean you haven't heard?"

The assistant starter, having checked all the other horses, called to Madoc, who indicated that his girth was tight, and then the starter himself asked them to form a line. As they turned towards the tapes, Kevin said, "Tell you later — it's too good to waste!" And they set off side by side.

Madoc let Cymru go on as fast as he dared and he was surprised to find Kevin driving Diaghilev along to join him. As the two horses jumped the first fence together, Cymru began to pull. Momentarily Madoc resisted him and then relaxed, letting the horse go on. Diaghilev slid out of view. He came forward again as they approached the second fence.

"What's this then?" shouted Madoc to Kevin.

Kevin glanced across with a scowl of concentration but didn't answer. Again, they jumped the packed birch together and then Kevin, using his advantage of being on the inside, began to push Diaghilev gradually into the lead. It was crazy — nobody jockeyed for position so soon in a two and a half mile 'chase, and the strangeness of it alerted Madoc. He knew the next was an open ditch. Had Kevin had orders to half-length him, hoping for a repeat of the Carlisle fall? Diaghilev was well fancied and there wasn't much else in the race that would beat him if Cymru fell. Madoc let out the rein and drove Cymru on at the black fence and its staring guard rail.

"Go on, get on!"

Cymru stood off from the fence, leaping high and strong and clear, and Madoc exulted, knowing the danger past even before they landed. Diaghilev was still there but Cymru would not let him past, not now, with Madoc conspiring with him to keep the lead. The energy he would normally have used up fighting the rein was there at his disposal. Madoc raked a hand down his crest and the black ears flickered, back then forward, comprehending, then dismissing the praise in his eagerness to run. Madoc let him go, guessing that Diaghilev could not stay with him for long after using energy to sprint to the front so soon. Cymru measured the next fence, flew it and swung into the left-hand bend a clear length ahead of the chestnut.

After that, the race was an easy one. Madoc allowed the stallion just enough rein to keep ahead of the field, neither checking nor urging him, sitting as steadily over his withers as he would in a schooling canter. And Cymru, moving with oiled precision now that his instinct was not being frustrated, negotiated the sharp paddock bend in three tidy strides and, changing on Madoc's orders to the opposite lead, went flicking away towards the far end of the course once more, over the water and another open ditch and, with another switch to the left lead, round yet another sharp bend. One circuit, and a mile and a half completed. Madoc glanced back at the strung-out field. Diaghilev, visible across the curve, was a long way back in seventh place and only Black Letter, who had won the Carlisle race, followed Cymru with any appearance of a threat.

"Come on, my son," said Madoc with the nearest thing to a smile that he could manage. "Spit in his eye."

Fence after fence, the open ditch again. His lead began to lengthen. Four lengths became five, then six. They were less than half a mile from home. Seven lengths, eight, nine, the crowd roaring like distant surf, ten, the last fence. Was that John Paddy and Ken jumping up and down outside the wings and yelling like

Irishmen? Madoc shut them out, concentrating on the wind, the stallion's grunt of effort as he took off, the hush of flight, the thump of landing and the intoxicating pulse of the gallop as he rode for home. Cymru had found his style, and the small country meeting, its heart captured by a good horse, cheered him from its grassy grandstand in full-throated celebration.

Siân heard all the excitement but was not a part of it.

When Cymru was passing the post, she was bringing Double Jump across the road from the stables and, during his unsaddling, she was in the preliminary ring. She could make the right noises about the win (the commentary had been good) but her attention was focused on Double Jump, making sure the cheeky breeze did not flip the blue rug off her quarters, that her plaits were still neat and the bit comfortably level on the lead rein. The little teacup hooves made faint clicking noises as the light racing plates hit the tarmac, the black, slender legs strode out confidently, making the silky tail swing. Double Jump was enjoying herself.

So was Helen and, very evidently, so was Dava when Siân took the mare into the parade ring.

"Shall we see whether we can make it three wins, eh, Helen?" he said, as he legged Jo Fraser into the saddle.

"I'll give it a go, anyway, Guv'nor," said Jo.

Helen gave a wide smile and said, "Good luck!" as Siân led Double Jump out towards the course among the other horses. Infected by their cheerfulness, Siân almost forgot to cross her fingers when she let the mare go and watched her canter down to the two mile start. She found herself a place near the top of the bank, pleased that, for once, Jack Brindley had kept the rug after he had saddled Double Jump. Spring really must be on its way.

A hand touched her hair, stroked it, settled on her shoulder.

"Madoc!" she said, startled to find him among the crowd, and so near, so suddenly near. He wore a jacket loosely over Cymru's crimson jersey; he was still in racing boots and breeches. He was clearly still as high as a kite after his win.

"*Aha, yr eneth dlos!*"

"What?"

"*Fy eneth dlos,*" he said, hugging her, "*yr eneth dlos iawn!*"

"*Yr ydych chwi'n ddrwg,*" she said, blushing and disengaging herself politely.

"*Dwyf i ddim!*" He went on speaking, too swiftly for her to follow and, seeing her incomprehension, translated, "I didn't know you spoke Welsh!"

"I don't. Not much, anyway. And certainly not here where everyone can tell how badly."

He laughed. In the afterglow of Cymru's win, it had seemed important that he should find her and watch beside her as Double Jump ran her race, so he didn't mind this confusion.

"I shouldn't think anyone's listening."

"Mm. Hope not." She was watching the start, trying to concentrate in the hope that it would quiet her leaping emotions; and he, still bubbling, remained good-humouredly silent. He had intended to watch Siân herself, but the race started and, from force of habit, he found he was watching the horses. It was Siân who, glancing at him, forgot Double Jump and saw only Madoc, drawn away into the action, still, vital and dangerous. How thin he had become: he was almost gaunt, his fair skin transparent and tired bruises under those extraordinary eyes. How long could he go on doing this to himself? Surely it was too much of a strain for someone so tall to go on starving himself and wearing himself almost literally to skin and bone, just to ride horses?

He looked down at her and, with a shock, she realised the race had gone more than half a mile, had passed them and she had seen nothing for looking at Madoc. Her face crimsoned.

"Beautiful," he said. And before she could speak, he added, "That girl can really ride. That turn is difficult for a novice."

Siân opened her mouth and shut it again, bewildered, and decided she had better concentrate on the race.

The runners bobbed away towards the river, a mingled, coloured blot; you could never see much of what was happening in a race going away from you.

"Do you think she's got a chance?" asked Siân.

"Well..." Like Dava, he was not a great admirer of lightly built horses and he had not been paying attention at Haydock when Double Jump had first run. "What do you think? You've done all the work with her. Is she fit?"

"I think so. She would have been able to work more easily if Dava had an all-weather gallop. Our ground's awfully heavy. But I think she's fit enough."

"She's got as much chance as anything else then. The ground's beautiful today."

"Is it?"

"Lovely. I haven't hit it once." He grinned at her, and she blushed again and turned her attention to the race.

Double Jump now lay in the centre of the main group as it came round the home turn, but it was clear to Madoc, and eventually to Siân, that Jo was getting to work and finding nothing there. She was shaking the rein and niggling with her heels. Among the other horses, between the slapping whips, punching heels, straining flanks, the order changed every moment. The second last hurdle was ahead and Jo was telling the mare that now she must go, now or never.

"Oof," said Madoc in sympathy, "that was a bit crooked."

An ugly screwing movement of Double Jump's quarters over the hurdle had nearly thrown Jo off, and she only saved herself by flinging out an arm to regain her balance. Two strides on, she was still gathering the reins, and the mare had visibly lost ground. Now she was fourth from last and Jo gave her a slap down the shoulder, then another.

"Going backwards," said Madoc resignedly.

Siân held her breath. There was one more hurdle to Jump.

Jo suddenly gave up the fight. She dropped her hands and sat up, allowing the mare to slacken pace and the other three horses to pass her. Now Double Jump was only cantering, bumpily, unlike her usual fluent self, then trotting, very unevenly. Jo turned her carefully aside from the last hurdle. Then she was walking. Jo jumped down to lead her and her head nodded sharply, painfully, with every other stride.

The race was coming up the straight and all around the crowd was shouting encouragement and only Madoc was near enough to hear the moan that came from Siân. He put out a hand towards her, but she dodged and began to run down the bank, between the people, towards the course where Double Jump was limping home.

NINETEEN

When Helen Rogers came visiting the following day, she came in the Land Rover, towing a trailer. In her box, the mare stood quietly pulling at a haynet, while Siân crouched in the straw, removing a bandage from the injured leg. Helen watched without comment as Siân applied a plastic bag of crushed ice and bandaged it into place. Double Jump turned her head briefly towards the door and touched Siân's hair with her muzzle but otherwise did not stir. Helen waited while Siân checked the bandage supporting the other leg and collected a wet, empty plastic bag and a discarded bandage.

"Morning," said Helen brightly. "Morning," responded Siân, automatically. "Ice cubes?"

"Cheaper than fancy packs from the saddlers."

"That sounds like Dava," said Helen with a wry smile.

"Yes." Siân squashed the bandage together and said abruptly, "Have you come to take her away?"

Helen blinked. "Yes. Yes, I have. There seems no point in her being here when I'm only two miles away and she could equally well be resting in my own stable at next to no cost."

"I suppose so," said Siân, crushing the bandage hard.

She kept her head down.

"She'll have a good long rest," said Helen practically.

"Yes, of course," said Siân. In the silence that fell between them the noise of Double Jump munching hay sounded suddenly loud. Helen cleared her throat.

"Is Dava about? Or Bill? I ought to ask whether it's convenient to bring the trailer into the yard."

"They're out with the second string. Should be back any time now. Then you'll be able to come in and load up. And take her away," she finished harshly. She stepped back into the box, into the gloomiest corner, so that Helen should not see her face. Double Jump nudged her. Tactfully, Helen turned away from the door and walked down the yard towards the field gate.

Siân began slowly to unfasten the roller and stable rug that Double Jump wore. She talked softly, stroking the velvet coat, caressing the fine nap on the mare's muzzle. Double Jump nibbled her fingers gently in a mute appeal for reassurance, a gesture she had used a lot in the past eighteen hours, and Siân's eyes filled with tears. "Don't, Baby," she said. "There isn't enough time for that stuff." There never is enough time to say goodbye, she thought. Double Jump touched her nose to Siân's shoulder and wiggled her top lip, begging as she would to another horse for grooming and attention. Out of habit, Siân obliged by scratching her withers. "Oh, Baby," she said softly, "what am I going to do without you?" And the tears trickled slowly down her cheeks.

Outside, the clatter of the string coming in marked the shortening time she had left; voices, chatter, boots on concrete, doors shutting, bolts clicking home. Ken stomped past, looping up a trailing girth over his saddle. *I must not cry,* thought Siân, *I must not cry. I am a professional and this is part of my job.* But when she heard the engine of the Land Rover start up, she choked. Outside, there was the chink of clips being released and the squeak of springs as a ramp was lowered. Siân swept the rug into a warm curtain over her arm and drew her hand over Double Jump's smooth coat. "Goodbye, Baby," she said. The stable door opened. From now on there would be no moments to share with the mare alone.

Helen came in first, carrying her own rug, and Bill followed.

"Oh, good girl," she said briskly and flung the new covering over Double Jump's shoulders. Siân, wordless, helped her to fasten it. Bill replaced the stable headcollar with Helen's blue webbing one.

Double Jump stood like a rock during these ministrations, and Siân's heart was full of bitter pride at the quiet trustfulness she displayed. *Claybrooke was the answer to your nervousness,* she thought. *But racing has asked too much of you.*

They led the mare slowly out of the box and up the ramp into the big trailer. Her progress was pathetically uneven. Helen found it necessary to chatter, covering her feelings by remarking on the borrowed trailer, saying that the wagon was still in Lancashire and, anyway, this was better, not such a strain to get into, and she wouldn't be tempted to drive too fast going home. She had put down a specially deep bed for Double Jump and Siân must be sure to come and visit as often as she could. But Siân could not speak. They closed the gates and put up the ramp.

Rather hesitantly, with a glance at Bill, Helen brought an envelope out of her pocket and held it out to Siân. "I — er — put some money in this for you. I'm afraid it isn't very much really, but I wanted to say thank you. I know how much effort you've put into looking after her for me."

Siân could not meet her eyes. She muttered thanks and pushed the envelope into her pocket.

"Keep that box free," said Helen brightly to Bill. "We could be back next season!"

Madoc was grooming Cymru in his box on Top Yard but his ears were on the stretch for Helen's Land Rover pulling away. He had been unable to do anything to alleviate Siân's distress yesterday, for she had devoted herself to Double Jump, travelling with her in the horse ambulance and the wagon and hanging on every word uttered by the vet once they arrived back on the yard. But now she was separated from the mare and, he guessed, quite lost without her. It would take a heart of stone to ignore Siân this morning but, for the sake of her pride, he must find her alone. He knew very well that it would embarrass her to break down in front of any of the other staff.

When the Land Rover moved off, he put down his brush, removed the tack tray from Cymru's investigative reach and walked down to Bottom Yard.

Double Jump's box door was open. Inside, Siân stood with her head against the wall, the rug clutched in her arms, bowed over the empty cloth in a storm of grief. She made no sound but until he stepped close to her, she did not even know he was there. He reached out, wanting to comfort her sorrow.

"Oh Siân, love, I'm so sorry."

She turned her face away to hide the tears, afraid to reveal the depth of her need for Double Jump, that confidante and dumb comforter, solace of humiliation and loneliness.

"Don't. Go away. I'm only being silly." She retreated, avoiding his touch.

"I know how you loved her," he said.

Her face twisted. "I did try not to."

He wanted to hold her, to soothe her, but somehow she held him at bay with her rigid clasp on the thick material.

"Stop it," he said. "Nobody can be that strong. What good would it do anyway? You were in here nearly all night, weren't you? And before Bill came this morning?

You could hardly have done more for her. What's wrong with calling that love?"

"A rose by any other name would smell as sweet," she quoted bitterly. "Please don't be kind, I can't bear it."

He didn't understand why she should want to hide her emotion behind someone else's words but he went along with it in an effort to sympathise. "Oh well, if you don't think you deserve kindness, OK you don't, but there's no law about it, you know, it just happens — or if you insist on the Bard, it droppeth as the gentle rain from heaven — "

She made an angry sound and whisked past him, out of her corner, beyond his reach. "Damn you, Madoc, why do you have to go one better all the time?" And, clutching the rug, she hurried blindly out, leaving him wondering.

He had all afternoon to ponder this strange behaviour.

Claybrooke had no runners and he was not engaged to ride anywhere. Wearily, he muffled up in his running gear and set out round the Thornton Hough circuit, so familiar from start-of-season roadwork that it needed no thought. As he pounded along he turned over things she had said and done and, more oddly, the things she had not. Why couldn't she just cry on his shoulder like any other female? What lay behind her resistance? She seemed prepared to stifle any emotion that might make her vulnerable. He had been observing her long enough to be sure there was no other man in her life. Since Justin had sowed the seed of doubt, he had watched her, and he saw she was the most single, solitary girl he had ever come across. He doubted whether anyone had even set foot in the caravan since she arrived. Why? What was wrong with her? Was she hiding something? What was she afraid of? He could not find an answer.

Evening stables provided him with an unexpected clue. He was in Cymru's box, ostensibly talking over the stallion's performance at Bangor but, as usual, the discussion had veered towards theories and Dava was expounding on his favourite subject.

"The trouble with 'chasing these days is that there are so many flat horses doing it. I mean, look at Quimby! Real, strong 'chasing types like him stand no chance against these little whippets, not until the ground gets soft. Then they daren't run them — or, if they do, look at the wastage! Like that filly Helen took home this morning. Plenty of speed on fast ground but so delicate! If she ever comes back into training she'll be like old Whisky Tan — legs that need cotton wool treatment all the time. I know we've got the odd race over the years with the old crock but it's all wrong. If we've got to race in winter we should be breeding animals that can cope with the conditions, not spindly things that go wrong after every third gallop."

"That sort can go on the all-weather courses," argued Madoc, fending off Cymru with a practised hand.

"You needn't play devil's advocate because you know as well as I do they aren't a forward step. Before you know it, we'll be copying the Americans, with standardised tracks, and little fiddling fences and nothing being bred to cope with varying conditions..."

"All right!" Madoc surrendered. "Haven't you dinned it into me for the last fifteen years? All I want to know is, what do we do now with this fellow? You know my feelings on the subject. But I suppose all the 'chases at Aintree have already closed."

"Unless you want to wait for the ones in November, I'd say, yes, they have."

"I suppose you've got Quimby entered for that new McTay Trophy. I haven't seen the latest Racing Calendar — have you been hiding it or something?"

Dava's eyes gleamed. "You'll find he's entered for the Sun Alliance at Cheltenham." He watched with satisfaction as Madoc's face creased into a slow grin. The Sun Alliance 'chase was, effectively, the novices' championship, run at the National Hunt Festival meeting. "I thought that would amuse you."

"I wish you'd stop confusing me. I thought we were just running a couple in the smaller races? I thought you decided Quimby wouldn't run against Musketeer?"

"He won't. Peter Walbrook has taken Musketeer out of the Sun Alliance and left him in the Gold Cup. Jerry Monk did say something like that to you, after all, so I thought the entry was worth the risk. We could always have ducked it at the acceptances stage."

Madoc laughed. "There's one thing about working for you, Dava, life is full of surprises. So are you going to run Quimby at Aintree too?"

"When Musketeer's entered? I don't think so, do you?"

"Did you enter him? Or is there something else you haven't told me about?"

"I entered Cymru," said Dava, turning to study the horse.

"Now I know you really are crazy! You must have put that entry through when all he'd ever done was jump a couple of fences and hurl me into the open ditch at Carlisle. You're either crazy or clairvoyant and I know which my money's on."

"You don't want to ride him round Liverpool, then?"

"Haven't I just said I do? What I want to know is, why do you want it? Why the secrecy?"

Dava said irritably, "I don't have to give my reasons for everything! The horse is mine, he fulfils the conditions of the race and I think he can win it. Do you want to ride him or not!"

"Of course I damn well do! But, Dava, Musketeer may well have won the Gold Cup by the time the McTay comes round."

"So? They were both horses who hadn't won a 'chase at the start of the season. If you want to chicken out, I'll put someone else up."

"This isn't anything to do with Anna Selwyn-Hughes, is it?" asked Madoc. "Suddenly, with one of Baner's breeding, you've got a chance to rub her nose in it? Like I said, you're crazy."

"It's got nothing to do with Anna," said Dava stubbornly. "The fact that she owns Musketeer is only a minor consideration."

"And the fact that I'm crazy too is a major one. I'd argue black was white if it gave me the chance to ride Cymru round Aintree but I'd rather be sure it was on his merits."

Beside them the stallion swung his head towards the door, ears pricking to the darkness outside.

"Who's that?" said Dava, welcoming the interruption. "Siân, is it? What d'you want?"

She hovered just outside the lamplight. "It's nothing important. I wondered if Madoc was there. I wanted a word."

"Yes, he's here." Dava bestowed a brief pat on the subject of the argument and moved briskly out of the box. "Nice timing! We've finished. Is Bill on Home Yard?"

"Er, yes. At least, he was in the tackroom."

"I'll find him. Goodnight."

"Goodnight, sir."

And off he went. Madoc came out of the box and closed the door with care. He switched off the light.

"Hello there," he said slowly.

"Hello," said Siân nervously. He seemed very guarded and she added, "I hope I wasn't butting in."

"What? Oh, no. At least, I don't think it would have made any difference. Dava is not the man to admit that there's no fool like an old fool."

"No," she said with a little laugh, "he is not. Though I don't know what that's got to do with anything."

"The woman who owned this horse's sire is now a widow," said Madoc thoughtfully, "and as Dava was once very smitten in that direction I begin to wonder whether two and two are four, or rather more than that."

"Oh," said Siân.

He laughed. "Meaning that you don't understand. Well, never mind." He looked at her kindly enough. "You wanted me? At your service."

Siân trembled. She had nerved herself to apologise for this morning and now she could not bring herself to say anything for fear of sounding clumsy. Instead she asked, "Is he well? Cymru? After yesterday?"

"Oh yes." Madoc turned away and looked back into the box, where the horse had transferred his attention to his haynet. "You'd hardly know he'd had a race."

"I missed it but according to Ken, 'e ran a blinder?"

She caught Ken's accent so accurately that Madoc could not help laughing and suddenly Siân found it easy to talk. "I'm glad he's justified your faith in him. He's been so difficult, hasn't he?"

"Correction: Dava's been difficult. I've been telling him since Christmas that this is a front runner, not just a strong-headed runaway."

She looked straight at him and said, "Unlike me this morning."

His expression sharpened but he said with some amusement, "That was your privilege — you didn't ask me to come poking my nose into your feelings."

She could have shouted with relief. "I'd forgotten where I was. At Pickering's I had to be so careful not to show that I was fond of Double Jump. So when you came in..." She paused, then finished, "I ran. I'm sorry."

"No harm done," he said easily. There was silence for a moment and they both looked in at the stallion. In the darkness he turned momentarily from his hay and ceased to chew as he listened for some sound. He gave a deep chuckle, chewed, paused to listen again, then blew his nose disgustedly as though the promised response had failed to come.

"I wonder," said Madoc, "how long we can go on... keeping the balance between work, boredom and mares? Spring is on its way!"

There was only a slight catch in her voice as she said, "At least the Baby won't be here to add to his temptations."

He nodded. "No, it's a shame. But these things happen."

"Yes." She accepted the great platitude, recognising that he had not queried or ridiculed the nickname. A liberating sense of shared intelligence and sympathy swept over her and she said, "I know Helen will look after her — why shouldn't she? But — oh, I will miss her!"

"Of course you will. I would miss this devil here if Dava decided to part with him! There are some horses you never do more than look after, and others you get involved with, just like people."

"Yes," she said. Trying for a lighter note, she added, "I expect Dava will make sure Bill keeps me busy."

"Yes, we'll have the best kept tack in England. And you'll have more time for your books too."

"What do you know about my books?" she demanded.

He grinned at the sharpness of her tone. "Grace is of the opinion that you spend a lot of time in the library."

"I don't see how she can know that but it's quite true.

It's cheaper than heating the caravan. That meter positively eats money."

"Well," he said reasonably, "you are supposed to be looking for somewhere else," and was surprised at how stricken she suddenly seemed.

"Maybe." The caravan suited her so exactly that she had not troubled to hunt, and the thought of trudging round looking at bed-sits and flat-shares filled her with horror. "Still," she said as brightly as she could, "now the weather's getting warmer I shall be able to read in the caravan without needing either electricity or gas."

"Oh, feel free," he agreed ironically, yet meaning it.

"I'm sorry," she said in a small voice. "I forget sometimes that it's yours."

Her bowed head, silhouetted by the yard lamp, seemed to him full of a sad beauty and, moved by a sudden generous impulse, he said, "I shouldn't tease you. I don't need the caravan yet and I don't want you to move out." And when she looked up at him he added, "I really do need a neighbour who can quote Shakespeare."

She gave him a reluctant smile. "I was so angry with you for that! I didn't know I was quoting and I thought you were laughing at me. Oh I was angry!"

And frightened, too, he thought, but said nothing.

"Well," she said, squaring up to him and taking a deep breath so that, for a startled moment, he actually thought she was going to hit him, "I came over to extend the olive branch, so I'd better do it. Will you come and have coffee this evening?"

"In my caravan?" he asked, with no hint of a smile.

"In your caravan," she agreed, stiffly.

"Yes, thank you, I will. About eight? All right." And as she turned away, too abruptly, as though escaping, he called after her, "And I'll bring you some books, shall I?"

TWENTY

Siân was very nervous.

She had tidied the caravan and swept the carpet, had a bath, set out mugs and a kettle of water in the kitchen, dressed carefully and then realised that she had left her dirty boots behind the front door. Her mood swung wildly from patience to a fierce resentment of all the fuss she was making. She turned the radio on and off, unable to bear the silence yet equally unable to bend her mind to the programme being broadcast. By the time Madoc tapped at the door, she could have done nothing and taken all night to do it.

He took in her state with one look as she opened the door.

"Parcel for yer, Missis, will yer sign for it?"

The play-acting over a carrier bag was sufficiently unexpected to dispel her sense of unreality and, with a strong feeling of being roughly woken up, she said, "Don't be so daft — standing there in the rain! Come on in."

He came in cautiously, giving her time to retreat.

"I'll put the kettle on," she said, with a nervous cough, and abandoned him in order to light the gas.

Madoc surveyed the sitting room, where the settee was drawn comfortably close to the electric fire. There was no other chair, so no interpretation could be placed upon this arrangement. He sat firmly in the middle seat, opposite the glowing bars, feeling the atmosphere lurking coldly as though heat had only recently been switched on.

"Gas bottle all right? You don't need a fresh one bringing?"

"No," she called, glad to have a neutral subject.

"Grace checked on Monday. She's very organised."

"Even sorted out which day you can use the washing machine, I gather."

There was no response from the kitchen, so he waited patiently until the kettle boiled. *First time doing the honours in her own — my own — kitchen,* he thought. She held her ground beyond the partition.

She came in at last with the coffee, handing him a brimming mug without meeting his gaze. "Black with no sugar," she said.

"Quite right."

She hovered, sipping at the too hot liquid, and he said, "It's quite a thing, this settee, isn't it? They must have put it in here before the windows were glazed — they'd never have got it through the door, would they? What's it like to sleep on?"

She sat down quickly, tucked into the corner of the settee. "I don't sleep on it."

"No? I rather thought you spent your first night here on it. Covered in a quilt, with the fire on?"

That caught her, he thought, as coffee slopped down the outside of her mug. She looked at him accusingly, saw the twinkle, and decided she was overdoing the prickles. "Yes. God, I was tired! I imagined all sorts of things when I woke up and I couldn't think who'd been in."

He laughed. "Dava sent me to find out whether you would fill in your forms, and there you were, spark out.

I covered you up and put a few shekels in the meter, and that was it. I'd forgotten about it until now."

"I never had the courage to ask who it was."

"No, I suppose it looks bad to make your debut by asking who put you to bed last night!"

"Actually, I thought it might have been Grace. It looked the most — comfortable answer."

An interesting choice of word. He said, "Oh?"

"It was thoughtful. And the lack of fuss looked like tact."

"How disappointing to find it was me. Or I? English is so confusing."

"*A ydyw'r Gymraeg yn hawdd?*"

"*Ydyw,*" he said, laughing. "You've been practising. How do you come to speak Welsh?"

"My grandmother taught me some when I was small. I'm very rusty, I know. Gran used it for a while as a way to get back at Granddad for leaving Wales after the war." She smiled a little. "I don't know whether she felt it did him any good; I was only seven when he died."

"Whereas, to me, it's my mother tongue. Dava and my father came from Conwy and you can't get much more insular than that without going into Môn." He raised an eyebrow, testing her.

"Anglesey," she translated without hesitation. "It never occurred to me that any of you spoke Welsh until yesterday. Owen is such a common name round here."

"Thanks for nothing! Mind, Grace doesn't speak it. She married my mother's brother Gwylim — she comes from Oswestry. She thinks Dava's being rude when he speaks Welsh because he knows she can't understand him." He did not go on to tell her how Felicity, when taken to Afonwen, had provoked the local ladies into taking refuge in their own language and had indignantly dubbed them "deliberately ignorant." "I suppose that's how we get our reputation for being secretive. It's only self-defence really."

Siân understood only too well and just nodded. They sat for a few moments without talking. Siân finished her coffee, but since Madoc's was too hot to drink yet, he looked round the walls, curiously. There was a stack of plastic-jacketed library books in one corner and a pile of newspapers and magazines, but no pictures, no photographs other than one of Double Jump propped in the middle of the mantelpiece, no clues to her life before she came to Claybrooke.

He waited for her to choose the next topic of conversation. It was clearly an effort for her but eventually she said, "Well? I assume the parcel contains the books?"

"Take your pick," he said, nodding. His choices had been swift but not random and he was curious to see how she would react.

She handled the complete Shakespeare with a kind of hunger which she tried hard to disguise. "It is yours to lend? You're sure?" She checked the endpapers. "From Aunt Grace. Ah. She wanted to make sure you were well grounded in English literature as well as Welsh?"

"Don't be sarky. She was very good for Gwylim and me — that's my brother Gwylim, not my uncle Gwylim. She always bought us books for our birthdays when we were at school."

Siân pulled a face and said, "Damned with faint praise."

Poor Aunt Grace, she thought. *Good for them rather than to them.* He'd only read two plays, to judge by the thumbed pages: *Romeo and Juliet* and *Merchant of Venice.*

Before she could trace in her memory the phrase she had used that morning, he broke in, "All right, Sherlock. She was robust, English and commonsensical, and you can't introduce a woman with those qualities into an all-male Welsh household without striking a few sparks."

Siân paused in her examination of the other books.

"All-male? What happened to your mother?"

"She died. Not long after Gwylim's first birthday. It was very sudden and I don't remember much about it except that I walked as far away from the house as I could get, right up through the top fields, up towards Tal-y-fan. Grace said she'd gone to Heaven, you see."

He ducked his head quickly to his coffee, and Siân said inadequately, "I'm sorry."

He shook his head. "Don't worry, it happened a long time ago."

"Did Grace bring you up then?"

"Oh no!" He laughed. "Heaven forbid. She stayed with us for a few weeks until Dad got organised and then she went back to her own house. She was expecting a baby of her own so she couldn't really take us on as well."

"You've got a cousin as well as a brother, then."

"Cousins. Both married. There's an awful lot of us about."

"Whereas I'm the only one, and my mother and father were only children too." She turned over the books in her hands and seemed to dismiss the subject of family. "Josephine Tey, H.E. Bates, Dorothy Sayers. You seem to like the same authors as the television companies."

"I'm making no suggestions about chickens and eggs."

"I'll give you credit for having read them before they were reprocessed. Is Aunt Grace responsible?"

"She always signed her presents," he said seriously, and laughed as he saw her suppress a twitch of the fingers on the covers. "Got you! If you don't want to borrow them, I'll allow you to peek. I can't actually remember which ones she bought."

"I'd like to borrow them all," she said, "though *Strong Poison* is the only one I haven't read before and the title gives me the creeps a bit. Did you know Ken got Ted to put a rat in here the other day? They found one that was half-dead after Bill put the poison down. Ted left it in my sink and it was too far gone to climb out."

"What did you do about it?" he asked, a faint smile on his face.

"I yelled blue murder at Ken and he came and shifted it on a shovel."

"You were sure it was Ken's idea, then!"

"Well, I should think so. I'm lucky Ted didn't put it in my bed! He admitted that's where it was supposed to go."

"Be thankful for small mercies," grinned Madoc.

"I wonder why nobody told you about it." There was a pause. "What surprised me was that Ted was willing to do the dirty work. He's usually so timid."

"They probably offered him a drink. Did you see him yesterday?" Siân shook her head. "They pushed him into the other wagon in a little snoring heap once you and your filly were loaded. Didn't you notice he rode with his eyes shut most of this morning? He only drinks when he goes racing but it's definitely his biggest weakness."

Siân reflected that she had been too busy with Double Jump to care what Ted Gray's hangover had looked like. "Why does Dava put up with it?"

"Well, most of the time he's a sober citizen and he doesn't go on a bender until his horse has been looked after. It was just bad luck that, yesterday, that left him most of the afternoon to get drunk in."

Siân shivered slightly. Drunkenness frightened her these days, like any sign that someone was not in control. To cover her feelings, she stood up and put the books with the library copies in a little stack. "I thought he was a non-drinker after the do at the Two Mills."

"He's careful of his licence, that's all." Madoc got up and strolled across to study the books Siân had already borrowed.

"*St Mawr?*" he said, "that's a strange name. D.H. Lawrence. What's it about?"

She gave him a faint smile. "It's about a wayward, brilliant stallion. That's his name, St Mawr. You ought to read it."

"Is it as good as *Lady Chatterley?*"

She stared at him for a moment, unable to answer.

Under the naked light bulb his hair gleamed golden and his kind eyes were shadowed, and just for that moment he was not Madoc, her friend, but...

"I've no idea. I haven't read *Lady Chatterley*," she said shortly, and turned away, hurrying back to her place in front of the fire. "And I don't know why you think I should have done. What do you think I am? I don't read books like that, what makes you think I do?" She sat down, trembling.

"Well," he said easily, "if you read one book by an author you very often read another. And millions of people read Dick Francis without wanting to be champion jockey themselves. I didn't mean what you appear to think and, if you did, then I apologise." He rubbed the back of his neck, deeply puzzled, before deciding to return to the fire and the settee. And he thought carefully before he sat down, in the centre once more.

There was a very long pause this time. Madoc sat perfectly still, a trick of relaxation that had persuaded many a frightened, newly broken horse that he was not a predator although he sat on its back. All the same, he had to wait much longer than he expected before Siân's eyes cleared and her clenched fists slackened.

"Sorry," she said, rubbing a hand across her face. She relaxed the fingers and asked with a forced laugh, "Did you think I was going to hit you?"

"You nearly did."

"Yes. I was afraid I was going to. How did you know?"

"I've ridden horses professionally for so long it's second nature. The smallest movement is enough sometimes to tell a very long story."

"You must be able to read me," she said bitterly, "like the proverbial book."

233

"No. Obviously you want to stay hidden here in the caravan for some reason, but I don't mind what it is. A desire for privacy isn't a crime, after all."

She looked at him then, and the kind eyes were visible once more. Justin would not have understood her need for solitude, but Madoc did. She sighed. "I'm sorry. I'm not being very rational, am I? I invited you here and I seem to be driving you away. It's stupid."

"You're worn out," he said practically, "and you've had a rough twenty-four hours. It doesn't make for intelligent reactions. Sit back and relax. I don't need entertaining — I'm a very undemanding soul, you know."

She was still inclined to resist, but he was right; she had reached the hamster-in-a-cage sequences of thought that tiredness produced and she knew, from experience, that they would do no good. So she gave a defeated little smile and wriggled herself into the cushions.

"That looks more like it. You can shut your eyes if you like. I won't leap on you if you fall asleep, I'll just quietly leave."

She did shut her eyes then, to control the vivid images, but she opened them again after a moment, and turned her head towards him. She gave him her hand. "I seem to remember kissing you once," she said. "I don't know why I'm fighting you like this."

He gripped her fingers lightly. "Nor do I. Except that you told me you were afraid of being too happy. And, of course," he went on, "you were slightly tiddly and reasonably warm. If you had a drop of alcohol inside and a warmer jumper outside, you might feel a lot braver."

The laughter in his voice made her laugh too and she made no remark as he reached an arm behind her shoulders.

"Come on, move up and let's be comfortable. You're like a perishing ice floe. Here!" He pulled the open flap of his jacket around her and she was comforted by the heat of it. He covered her cold hand with his warm one. "There. Get the other one burrowed in somewhere warm too. Go on, I can stand it. Ouch! Haven't you got any thicker clothes?"

She risked a chuckle. "I had to put on something clean in your honour."

"And were all the warm things dirty? Don't answer that! I know Grace's washing sequence."

"I'm afraid that's it in a nutshell."

He chafed her fingers, absently. "And the meter swallows money." He felt her nod and held her carefully, staying relaxed and letting her lean into him gradually as his warmth slackened the tight, cold control she held over herself. He was thinking deeply. Here he was, holding his emotions on a tight rein to see how she reacted, and for the wrong reason he seemed to have done the right thing. She really was shy. She really was afraid. It was not the front that Justin had implied and, because he had sat and waited to see what she would do, she had trusted him.

"Well, when I move this heap up to Afonwen I can't spend my life putting coins in a meter. I wonder if I can get the box unlocked? Then you could re-use the coins you've already put in... Dava won't ever think of collecting them, anyway." He shifted subtly nearer to her. "That would be a better arrangement, wouldn't it?"

He looked down at her bent head. Her hair really was beautiful. The scent, which he had been trying to remember, filled his nostrils — apricots, or was it peaches? "Listen to me. I'm trying to buy you with my extraordinary generosity."

She had not been listening to him with the upper part of her mind, and the rambling sentences had flowed over her like sleep. The warmth and security of being held so quiet and close, the steady beat of his heart and the musically Welsh intonation of his voice all lapped around her like a tropical sea. Her intellect slept somewhere in this wonderful simplicity of physical comfort and she could not begin to disturb the tranquillity by looking for it.

"That was a joke," he said, moving very slightly.

"Mm," she murmured. She looked up, faintly bemused. "What?"

The soft sleepiness of her face so close was too much for his self-control. He leaned forward and kissed her.

She felt no surprise, only a subtle shock of recognition, and a flame of desire that grew even as she discovered it. She spread out her fingers upon him, and the mouth that was gentle and exploratory on hers became silently more demanding, moving down her cheek and throat, while his hand settled with assurance on her thigh. There was a long moment when neither of them breathed.

"I have not mistaken your knee for the gear lever," he said, with the faintest tremor of a chuckle.

She pushed her face into his neck to smother a laugh, and he hugged her swiftly, glad she remembered that Christmas encounter. She gasped then: here was that sleeping fire ready to wake to a full blaze. Her fears and inhibitions had already been scorched once by it. Now they seemed meaningless, only there were no words to say so. She had the feeling she must move, she must do something to fill the hollowness of her own yearning. And as she asked herself, *do I dare?* the light touch of his hand made the pulse of her blood sing, *Yes!* With breathless care she unfastened one button on his shirt, then another. He was quite still in astonishment: did she mean it? He moved to look into her face and her answer was unmistakable. She leaned towards him and kissed him, at first timidly, then with a growing power. Slowly, in disbelief and wonder, they began to explore each other.

* * *

She woke quite suddenly. The light was still on, because he had replenished the meter. He lay warm beside her in the three-quarter bed, vulnerable in sleep, very beautiful in his stillness. How strange to wake beside another human being after so long lying alone; strange and wonderful to find that the fiery collapse of her defences meant no longer fear, but safety. She lay considering him, thinking how swiftly the evening had moved from conversation to passion, as though they both had known from the beginning, from long ago, that this was bound to happen, and they were only waiting for the right moment to arrive. She had no doubt that it was right. Had it been wrong, she would now be sitting fully dressed in the main room, willing him with every muscle to wake and go, not lying here drowsily snuggled into his side, listening to the rain on the roof... he turned over and reached sleepily for her, pulling her closer, and she relaxed into him, feeling the recurring ripples of pleasure washing over her at the touch of his hand and smiling at the biblical phrase it brought to mind — *At thy right hand are pleasures for evermore.* She had never been religious, possibly because her grandmother had been a strict churchgoer and had been known to express the opinion that "the Song of Solomon wasn't the sort of book you ought to find in the Bible." Siân had immediately gone to read it and been captured by its lyrical beauty. Now she understood it:

His left hand is under my head, And his right hand doth embrace me.

I charge you, o ye daughters of Jerusalem, By the roes, and by the hinds of the field, That ye stir not up, nor awake my love,

Till he please.

Oh yes, she understood it now. It was with a kind of awe that she realised how spiritual pleasure could be. Although she had never before cared whether the soul might be immortal, or whether the fleeting joys of life reflected eternal values, for a moment, she thought, *I know why God is important...*

She dozed a little and roused again. Madoc still slept, the rounded muscle of his arm lying smooth and elastic across her ribs. She recalled him coming to find her that morning after Double Jump had gone — knowing she needed comfort and not ashamed to offer it. She was sorry she had turned from him then. Some day she would explain it all, but not yet. It was too soon. Let contentment become a habit before she recalled unhappiness.

Her eyes lit on the packet of condoms on the bedside cabinet. She had been surprised at his caution, startled, but touched rather than repelled, which was perhaps why she had not explained about the pill... or was it simply that words had failed her? That words had become unimportant as she let him take and give pleasure and learnt to her own astonishment that she could do the same? Never mind why. It was such a small knot to undo. The memory of pleasure still warmed her and she pressed herself to him so that he stirred in his sleep and murmured, and she answered, feeling again the hollow yearning for him, which deepened as he woke and turned to her once more.

TWENTY-ONE

The rain was still falling in the morning, a curiously quiet, vertical rain that set Siân tingling to do things, go walking, dance under the sycamores. She mucked out Hollie with vigour, hearing with a small, private smile the sweet whistling from Cymru's box as she passed with her loaded barrow. Exercise went by in a dream. Though her hands were raw and rain dribbled down neck and crotch, she didn't care, the work was easy and she felt wonderful. She schooled Hollie upsides with Madoc on a five-year-old just learning to adapt from hurdling to, chasing, and neither put a foot wrong. It was as though a magical bubble protected them, thought Siân hazily, as she rode back to the yard. Even the rain seemed warm.

She trotted through the puddles back to the tackroom, carrying Hollie's soaked gear. She was glowing with the rubbing-down she had given the mare and happily returned Ken's damp grin.

"How do you manage to be first in every day?" she asked, as she dumped the wet saddle on its rack and reached for a cloth to wipe it.

"I cheat," said Ken, dropping a teabag into his mug.

He still wore his chaps and waterproof; he had still another lot to ride and couldn't be bothered to strip off only to replace wet clothing. Wisps of hair stuck to his neck below the rim of his helmet and water dribbled from the woolly hat pulled over it. He looked completely bedraggled. Siân was no better off, but she had finished riding for the day. She wiped Hollie's bridle and hung it up, and soon her own wet coat was dripping on a hook.

"Kettle's nearly boiling," said Ken, and pushed the coffee jar towards her with a reddened hand.

"Ta. You'll make somebody a wonderful wife."

She spooned coffee into her mug, unaware of the speculative look on Ken's face. Smart cracks were normally his province. He unplugged the boiling kettle and filled up both mugs while Siân took biscuits from the cupboard. Steam billowed between them.

"Not many of these left," she said. "I'll go shopping later and get some. Pass me the kitty."

He gave her the battered mustard tin. "In this rain? It's supposed to get worse this afternoon, windy, and you're soaked."

She only smiled. A funny, secret smile, but, being a cheerful soul, he didn't resent it. He liked people to be happy. It sometimes backfired — witness his current efforts to sort out the results of his Valentine cards — but life was never dull.

"Oh well, if you're set on it, I like them ginger ones."

He noticed her gaze constantly returning to the open door and the yard. "If you're lookin' for Madoc, soon's he got off Zama he went off to Cunningham's to school. Then he's going on to Wolv'r'ampton. He won't be back till tonight."

"Oh." Her disappointment was so obvious that Ken felt sorry for her.

"Aw. Didn't he tell you last night he'd be away today?"

A spot of colour glowed on her cheeks. "I didn't realise everyone watched me so closely."

"They don't. Just me, eavesdroppin'. Dava was complainin' he hadn't been able to find Madoc yesterday evening. An' seein' you smilin' away there, I jus' put two and two together." He sat down beside her in his usual matey fashion. "I won't say anythin' if you don't want 'em to know."

"Yes, fine," she said absently from inside the bubble.

He leaned confidentially against her shoulder. "So you were too busy to talk about where he'd be today! Who's naughty gerl then?" She began to giggle, and Ken gave her a quick, wet hug. "You'll be all right. He's a good feller is Madoc."

Ted's appearance in the doorway prevented any further confidences. He came in with a darkening face, dripping ostentatiously round his tack. "Oh, excuse me."

Ken, with his arm round Siân, said jauntily, "She promised to buy me my favourite biccies when she goes shopping, so I thought she deserved a cuddle. I like to keep me women happy."

Ted snorted and dumped his gear. Ken grinned at his back and began to whistle "Pretty Woman," stopping only because Ted turned ferociously on the kettle and he couldn't whistle and laugh at the same time. Siân sat in her careless daze as before, while John Paddy came clumping in, grumbling that his elbows were leaking, and Ted snapped at him for brushing the saddle against him as he passed. She scarcely heard them. So Madoc was away for the day. She must get used to that. It hadn't bothered her before but, of course, things were different now...

Bill Houghton came to the door. His round face was serious beneath the rain-darkened cap. "A word, Siân."

She got up, startled by the quietness of his voice. Her heart beat queerly. "Is something the matter?"

"Well..." He glanced into the tackroom, where everyone was drinking and pretending not to listen. "I'm sorry, but with Double Jump going, I'm afraid we haven't got work enough to justify keeping you on."

"What?" she said, stupidly.

He spread his arms a little, excusing himself. "John Paddy'll tell you... Mr Lofthouse says it's time to retire old Whisky. The old lad's the same age as Hollie and that's ancient for a hurdler."

John Paddy agreed, morosely. "His legs fill up every time he runs. It isn't fair to ask him to go on struggling against three-and four-year-olds."

"But what's that got to do with me?" asked Siân. "There won't be plenty of horses to go round."

"So I've got to go?" Was she going to have to find a new job and new accommodation just when she thought she was settled?

"Last in, first out," said Bill apologetically. "Mr Dava said he'd give you a good reference. We can put you on to a stable or two that always need staff."

"But —" said Siân, and stopped, aware of the listening ears. Bill, poor soul, looked uncomfortable enough. "All right," she said. "How long have I got?"

"Oh, till next Friday — and I suppose Madoc might let you stay in the caravan till the Monday. Better ask him." He gave her a nod and went away, relieved to have got the job over.

Siân stood motionless at the doorway for perhaps ten seconds before sheer rage overwhelmed her. It was monstrously unfair that she should have all this upheaval yet again! And did Madoc know? Was that why he had gone this morning without comment? She balled her fists and gritted her teeth and growled in frustration and nobody behind her dared to speak. Perhaps they had all guessed, too, that this was about to happen! She strode back into the tackroom and flung on her wet coat and disappeared out into the rain.

She walked for over an hour, disregarding the wet trickling through her hair and down her scalp and spine, and from coat hem down her knees and into her boots. Once you were wet, you couldn't get any wetter and, anyway, what did being wet matter when the world which you thought you had got glued together from the last disaster suddenly fell apart again? She noticed angrily that the cosy bubble she had felt around her had vanished completely now. She would know better than to mistake tiredness for safety in future.

She found herself out on the coast, by the golf course, facing out over the bleak marshes and the Dee estuary and the rain-obscured shapes of the hills on the other side, in Wales. The wind was getting up, blowing prickles of rain into her eyes. Damn it, why hadn't she seen that the stable was going to be over-staffed yesterday when Double Jump went home? Answer on a postcard: *because I was thinking about Madoc. And he came neatly on cue to take Double Jump's place. He probably knew Dava would have to sack me, and decided there'd never be another chance to get me into bed.* Staring into the gusting curtains of rain, she saw that Wales had vanished, and she began to shiver.

* * *

Madoc and Dava sat after the evening meal, reviewing the progress of the horses during the week. In general, Dava felt things were going well. Quimby and Cymru had won and the stallion's prize money was a pleasant bonus; Zama was learning quickly; Aholibah was fit to run next week. On the down side, Double Jump had gone but, never having considered her particularly promising, Dava did not mind.

"When does old Whisky go?" asked Madoc, sipping his coffee.

"Some time next week. And he's another — poor rickety old thing. I don't know what they'll do with him. What job can you give an eleven-year-old with dicky legs whose entire life has been dedicated to going flat out over obstacles? Lofthouse can't ride, and Whisky is no elderly hack for his daughter to potter about on. I know they've got a lot of grassland but none of it's fenced. I give the poor old bugger about three months of trampling on Mrs Lofthouse's rose garden before the great dogmeat can swallows him."

They grimaced briefly at each other, too familiar with the realities of the game to want to comment. Dava went on, "Of course, we can make some savings when he goes. That girl will have to find another place. We haven't got an excuse to keep her now."

Madoc put down his cup. "I thought the Lofthouses were going to buy that Irish gelding?"

"Oh, we'll manage, we've done it before. They haven't bought it yet and they might not when they hear the price." Dava shuffled papers into a neat stack. "I've given her her notice, anyway."

"You did what?"

"Well, Bill did. You'd gone off to Cunningham's, though what good you think it does..."

"You did what?" repeated Madoc, with a fixity of stare that eventually captured Dava's attention.

"Sacked her. She will have to go, Madoc. Sorry if it gets in the way of your hunting, but she'll soon find another job. I'll recommend her, after all."

Madoc shut his eyes. "What have you done," he muttered under his breath. Last night sprang vividly into his mind and he stood up. "Don't lock up. I'll be late." He went out through the kitchen, grabbing the first coat that came to hand, thrusting his feet into Wellingtons. Dava followed him as far as the kitchen door.

"What have I done? You've gone mad. I haven't done anything."

Grace stood arrested in her loading of the dishwasher.

Madoc opened the back door, strode out, slammed it. She looked at Dava without humour.

"I told you, didn't I? You are a callous old bastard sometimes."

* * *

Bang. Bang bang bang. Bang bang. Madoc's fist shuddered the caravan door.

"Siân! For heaven's sake open up!" The gusty wind hurled rain at him as he stood on the duckboard in the black tunnel between the caravan and the back of the stable block. What was she doing? Why wouldn't she answer? He imagined her in tears. "Siân! Let me in!"

The door slowly opened. She stood outlined in light, one hand in her jeans pocket, and looked him up and down, expressionlessly. "Yes?"

"Thank God! Let me in. There's something I've got to explain."

"Is there now?" She stepped back coolly. "Then I suppose you'd better come in so that I can keep the place warm while you do it. You won't mind if I go on working. You see, I'm sorting out what I need to throw away. What I needn't take with me. It isn't a big job. I think I can concentrate on your *explanation.*" She gave the word a sarcastic twist and he damped down his temper. As he kicked off the Wellingtons she said, "I see you haven't made such an effort tonight. Last night was a one-off, was it?"

How she had grown bolder in twenty-four hours! This was no grief-stricken girl, ready to droop in his arms. She'd had all day to hone the edge of her anger and he was going to have to stand up to it. He felt absurdly at a loss standing there in his socks beneath her scornful eyes.

"Well?" she said, putting her hands on her hips.

"I don't know where to start, really..."

"You seemed to know well enough last night."

"That has nothing to do with it."

"Hasn't it? I must have made a mistake then, I thought it had everything to do with it."

"And it has, but not in the way you mean," he said impatiently.

She turned away and knelt on the floor, sorting newspapers, magazines, horsey catalogues of the kind that came inside the magazines.

"Well? Go on, tell me what I mean. How do I know what to think?" She picked up his few paperback books and slammed them down again. "Did you know I was going to be sacked? Last night?" She looked up at him, her eyes blazing. "Did you?"

He stared down at her, equally angrily. "Of course not! What kind of creep do you think I am?"

"You're telling me you never thought, here's an opportunity I've nearly missed, get in quick before it goes?" She flung two magazines into a corner with a solid thud.

He ignored them. There was the echo of another mind in what she said — nothing loud enough to be worth a comment, but memorable. "Is that what you thought of me?"

"I'm only a girl, and pretty stupid. I can be kept in the dark and then I won't know what to think." She squared up two piles into one and then banged them down so that the floor shook. *To hell with thinking*, he decided, and he knelt swiftly beside her and took hold of her furious hands.

"Siân, on my mother's grave, last night was not a farewell fling."

For a long moment she remained stiffly resistant, her eyes blind with anger and pain. Then she blinked and looked at him for the first time with indecision. "Well," she said, "it fitted the facts. It's a pattern. I'm used to treachery, you see."

Quietly he said, "But I play fair. Siân, if all I wanted was to get you into bed, I could have tried any time since Christmas. Don't judge me by the standards of your past lovers." Her hands jerked in his but he gripped them tightly, stilling her protest. "There's more to it than that. I swear to you, my intentions are honourable."

A gust of wind shook the caravan and the floor quivered.

This time her fingers gripped his for reassurance and, feeling the change, the slackening of her anger, he said gently, "Siân, I love you."

"Very convenient," she said automatically.

"It isn't convenient, it's hell. All right, if you hadn't come here I couldn't have met you but don't hit me over the head with your 'very convenient' like that. I can't stop loving you because you're being pushed to go. It can't be turned on and off like that and if you think it can, what you've had before wasn't love."

He stared at her and she lowered her head. In the silence, the wind tore past the walls of the caravan and rain began to hit the windows in a jagged assault. Madoc shifted his grip on her hands and sat on the pile of magazines to look her full in the face. He had to speak more loudly over the clatter of the storm. "If it means anything to you, I don't want you to leave. If I can manage it, you needn't move out. Dava says he'll recommend you when you start looking for another job."

"But I don't want another job," she said.

"Well, that's encouraging, but if Dava can't employ you, you'll need to start looking. It needn't be permanent."

She sniffed and tried to laugh. "Why? Is this a proposal?"

He laughed too. "I don't know. Let's take it one step at a time, shall we? If you have to move away, I'll come and see you. Never think you'll lose me that way."

She shook her head, thinking how gladly she had shed Justin by exactly that method. "I can't face going into a hostel. Sharing a room. Dossing on someone's floor when your room-mate brings a boyfriend for the night. Everybody knowing what your underwear looks like. Cheap cracks and jealousy."

He sighed. "If you want to work in racing, you haven't much choice. Still, if I get some names off Dava we can soon work through it. Did Bill say how long he'd given you?"

"A week."

"All right. You can relax for tonight at least." He released her fingers. "Trust me. I'll help you all I can."

In the pause, the wind racked the caravan again and rain sputtered from the far corner in an audible stream against the stable wall. Madoc looked around the room, at the furiously scattered possessions. "You haven't much to move with, have you? Rolling stones and all that. Not if that corner contains the sum total of what you're throwing away."

"I put the smaller stuff in a box." She suddenly clapped a hand over her mouth. "Oh dear! There was something of yours. I thought you wouldn't want it again."

He blinked. "Of mine?"

"Yes. I'll get it." She jumped up, fetched a box from the kitchen and rifled in it. "You left these last night, and this evening I was so mad at you I threw them in here. Sorry. Perhaps you'd better have them back." She dropped the small packet into his outstretched hand with a funny little smile.

He was taken aback. She put the box down and knelt in front of him, while outside the storm screamed on, disregarded.

"Hussy," said Madoc, stroking her face. "You're supposed to be angry with me."

"A token of reconciliation," she said.

TWENTY-TWO

Saturday followed and was confusing. Siân finished work at lunchtime and not being on the duty rota for the weekend, ostensibly had a free afternoon. However, armed with the list which Grace had provided, she spent that time, and a good deal of money, in a phone box.

She came out looking blank. Not one trainer had a vacancy. Not one, in all of Cheshire. It appeared that the combined attractions of Cheltenham in ten days' time, and Aintree three weeks away, held the local staff in a loyal grip. No one was going to pass up the chance of attending winners there. One secretary had even gone so far as to suggest that Siân waited until after the Whitbread meeting at Sandown: "The season's a lot less classy then. You might pick up a job almost anywhere." Siân thanked her despondently, calculating that her thin bank balance would just about feed and roof her until Aintree.

She placed these problems before Madoc in the evening when he came to find out where she planned to go job prospecting. He was sympathetic, but he had fresh problems of his own.

"Doesn't trouble always come when you can least do with it? Just as well you haven't got to go for interviews tomorrow, because I couldn't have taken you. I've got to go to Afonwen. Grace tells me Gwylim rang here this morning with a message from Pant Coch ‑ that's the farm below. They'd noticed some damage after the gale, so they called Gwylim to have a look at Afonwen. And half the roof's gone. I've got to meet Caradoc and discuss what's to be done." He sighed. "Still if you've nothing on tomorrow, you could come with me."

She agreed, but her mind was still on the job problem.

"I suppose I should go to the Job Centre on Monday. Sign on. I don't know the proper procedures."

He put his arms round her. "Neither do I, but I do know you can't do a thing about it until the place opens. Worry about me for a change."

She slid her arms round him in return, grateful for his presence. "I'm getting paranoid."

"Look, don't fret. So long as nobody goes and tells the planning people you're no longer an employee, you can live here indefinitely as far as I'm concerned."

"Only I must earn some money."

He kissed her, swaying her a little. "You won't go short, I promise. Stop worrying."

* * *

Sunday looked uncertain weatherwise, but Madoc predicted it would be fine on the coast and drove the MG rapidly towards Queensferry. Siân enjoyed the route, remembering coach trips with her grandmother.

"She was a bit of a tartar, but she must have spoiled me when we went out because I remember these roads with pleasure."

He nodded. "They're easier in winter time when there's no tourist traffic."

"Is this where you go every Sunday?"

"Mostly. I didn't go so often when Dad was alive, though I should have done. You never realise until it's too late." He fell silent, so she did not press the subject but, after a while, he went on, as though thinking aloud. "Being tied to the land isn't all it's cracked up to be. He was always busy, always tired, hard to please. I think he was disappointed too. Gwylim decided figures were easier to push around than sheep, and I clung to the horses, which meant Dava."

"Has he been dead long?"

"Just over a year. They found him up on the mountain, after someone realised the sheep hadn't been fed for a day or two... He'd turned the four-wheeler motorbike clean over. Broke his neck. Ironic, really. He'd always predicted horses would do that for me." The little car bounded on, fiercely driven towards the sunshine and the sea.

At Llandudno Junction the expanse of steel rails shone blindingly and from the long bridge over the sparkling Conwy estuary Siân could see the moored boats swinging to the pull of the returning tide. As Madoc steered carefully through narrow streets, seeking the back roads to his destination, he recalled a softer moment.

"It used to be a treat, when we'd come in to do the shopping, to walk along the path by the river back there and have our lunch watching the boats. We usually had chocolate biscuits, Penguins. And for some reason we always met at least one nun along there — black robe, white head-dress. For years afterwards, it was a family joke to refer to a nun as a *pen gwyn*. Nobody English ever understood."

She was still smiling as Madoc swung the car into a narrow lane and began to climb rapidly. Before long the lanes gave way to farm tracks where she had frequently to open and shut gates. After the third farm, she was moved to ask how much further there was to go.

"That was Pant Coch," said Madoc. "Next stop Afonwen."

It had been mild at sea level but the air had sharpened each time she got out of the car and now the March wind blew again, fresh and chill across stunted sloe and hawthorn. She could feel the intractability of the land, rocky bones poking through the thin earth, heavy rain rusting away the gates that she lifted and swung. Water trickled down both sides of the track and sometimes across it. But the steep fields were grazed tightly by sheep and the earliest lambs lay tucked into sunny banks like obedient toys, while under the walls and hedges celandines glittered and dog violets and anemones drew up their first buds, life fighting persistently against difficulties.

The car breasted a final rise, sweeping sharply into the eye of the sun so that Siân had to shade her face with her hand, then across a noisy little river to draw up in the triangular yard of a low, solid, white house. When Madoc switched off the engine it was like waking in another world; just the sound of running water and, high above the farm, the faint mew of a buzzard. Madoc got out.

"If Caradoc is here, he'll have parked round the back. We didn't have to open the gate, so I imagine he's about somewhere. You stretch your legs while I go and find him."

He was gone almost at once, striding away, lean and relaxed, with his jacket flapping in the wind. She sat in the MG for a minute, getting her bearings. The house, between her and the sun, presented her with a shadowed face, rising straight out of the bedrock of the yard, its walls prim and reserved in their coat of whitewash and in sharp contrast to the adjoining barn of random stone and the angular new building at its corner. Behind the house, a small garden, rough with winter grass, dropped away in a sunny slope towards the stream. Siân climbed out of the car to investigate. Afon Wen, already strong and well filled by yesterday's rain, flung itself briskly against the spur of ground on which the house and buildings stood, only to be pushed aside to flow noisily away under the bridge. She recognised now that they had crossed it several times on the way up from the coast but when she looked back across the yard and the bridge, windswept hedges obscured the track and the fields dropped away, curving, secretive and unhelpful, back towards the unseen Conwy valley. Behind the buildings the ground rose determinedly, slanting away upwards, sheep-cropped to the skyline. Siân guessed that Afonwen had been built to withstand whatever hard weather blew over the mountain. The recent damage seemed an affront to its pride.

From the yard, its roof and deep windows seemed untouched by the storm. It was only when she walked round, through the garden gate, that she saw the piled broken slates, a mound of swept-up fragments and a pathetically small stack of re-usable pieces. Because of the slope of the bank, it was hard to get a clear view of the roof but it appeared that the storm had found out a weakness in the slating between the barn and the house She wondered how much of it lay open to the fickle smiling sky. Earth, air and water, she thought, the basics And the fourth element, fire, at the moment subdued, the hearth unkindled.

Below, the Afon Wen rollicked down its stony course filling her ears with the never-ending shout of falling water. She stood absently in the sunshine and its clamour washed through her head until she felt she knew it in all its moods, thickening after rain, coloured by gravel and peat and flecked with churning white water, high and boisterous, then shrinking to a murmur in summer chuckling under its sparkling surface as though tickled by the wavering tails of the small trout and minnows.

Into this near trance came voices. Madoc was arguing — laughing, but definitely arguing — with a short, dark man perhaps ten years older than himself. In a cap, tweed jacket and collar and tie, he was the image of Sunday primness and Siân wondered how Madoc had persuaded him to come out and do business today.

"Caradoc is trying to tell me this is a blessing in disguise."

"*Bore da*," said Caradoc politely to Siân, ignoring this provocation. They shook hands vigorously.

"Everybody knows builders like making work for themselves," Madoc went on.

"*Digon o waith i'w wneud*," protested Caradoc to Siân, gesturing at the house.

"I know," she said, hoping the conversation would not continue entirely in Welsh; her childish vocabulary did not include building terms.

Madoc, perhaps seeing her difficulty, pursued his subject in English. "The rafters are sound, but he wants to felt the roof before he re-slates."

"Cheaper now than later, isn't it?" Caradoc's English had a far stronger lilt than Madoc's. "And you'll feel no pain if you aren't living under the roof while I'm working on it."

"That depends on the size of the bill," said Madoc wryly.

They walked together into the house, ushering Siân first through the shadowed door. Two rooms opened to either side of a small hallway, with stairs beyond flanked by two more. A blaze of sun, striped with the pattern of slate laths, declared that the stair well at least had been stripped by the storm, but Caradoc waved the problem aside and crunched upstairs over the fallen plaster. Madoc followed but Siân, unexpectedly, felt shy, an intruder. She listened to them, arguing again in Welsh as they moved chunks of ceiling from a doorway and padded across sodden carpets. She was surprised by the old-fashioned air of the house. Perhaps Madoc's father had never felt the urge to update anything. The kitchen would be much sunnier if that tiny window was only larger. The pot sink beneath it had a wooden draining board, grimy now instead of regularly bleached and scrubbed. She felt a sudden rush of pity for the widower, working alone in the kitchen he had once shared with wife and children, and stoking the tiny range to cook his solitary suppers. Why had he not moved down into Conwy? He must have valued the little house and its memories more than the world's companionship.

There was no furniture left downstairs and from the way Madoc's and Caradoc's voices bounced off the walls, none upstairs either. What were they discussing? Something about changing this into a bathroom ... Siân caught some joke about horses too, and on an impulse she went out into the yard and looked again at the new building which, at first, she had ignored. Horses ... She ventured inside and recognised what Caradoc had been working on. Loose boxes, big and comfortable, snug enough for mares and foals. Of course ... Cymru.

She didn't know the terms, but the future was plain. The two men found her sitting in the sun on the garden wall.

"I'm just going to get my cheque book," said Madoc, "so I don't suppose Caradoc will be going anywhere, but chat to him all the same. Give him a few ideas."

"For building," said Siân.

"Of course." He grinned. "What else?"

"Drat," said Caradoc. As Madoc walked away he watched how Siân's eyes followed him, fitting the man into his real surroundings and adjusting to the new slant on his life. "*A wyt ti'n ei garu ef?*" he asked with a chuckle.

Without looking at him she answered, "*Ydwyf*, oh yes." And she felt, rather than saw, him smile at her instant response.

When the business had been transacted, Caradoc thanked Madoc and, with a courteous farewell to Siân, took himself off. The battered blue pickup bounced out from the rear of the building and disappeared down the track and Madoc said, "Walk up the fields with me? There'll be a good view today."

She jumped off the wall and landed lightly, smiling at him.

"Let's go," she said.

He caught her hand. *She belongs here*, he thought gladly. *She conquered Caradoc in half a minute, just sitting there on the wall in the place I always used to sit. Could she take the loneliness? If so, there is only one problem left to solve ...*

Caradoc's mark was evident in the new, tidily hung gate between the barn and the new building. It swung at a touch and closed smoothly behind them as they climbed up past the sheep pens. There were stacks of long posts, rolls of sheep netting and coils of high tensile wire.

"The Pant Coch sheep are crossed with antelopes. If I want grass, I've got to defend it!"

"Even from those little lambs?" she asked.

"Especially from them. By September they're as big as their mothers and twice as active."

"But you've got sheep on this grass now," she said, surprised. "Are they yours?"

"No, they're ewe lambs from Snowdonia. They use the grass till after lambing then they go back to their home range."

"Who looks after them?"

"John Williams, from Pant Coch. They're no trouble once they've settled where the walls are supposed to be. They aren't in lamb, so they're no work."

"And this field is yours?"

"This, and the little fields lower down. I'll show you in a minute, you can see better from the top. I had a hell of a job persuading Gwylim to let me have all the sheltered bits," he said, opening a gate at the top boundary. "This is the highest part but we can go right up on to the mountain from here."

She followed, interested.

At the summit the wind seized them, brisk and free, and they gasped and laughed and staggered together. Madoc held Siân up to face the view.

"Well?" he said.

Before them the wide semicircle of the earth's curve shimmered with light. The sea was a wintry grey-green to the horizon with the land fawn and sage against it: Great Orme in rocky layers beyond the shoulder of the mountain; Anglesey flat and fading into distance; Puffin Island cloud-shadowed for the moment but with brightness returning even as they watched, while the mountain was soft-shaded green, taupe, brown and grey. Siân said nothing. She put her cold hands in her pockets and gazed and gazed. Her face wore a small smile.

Madoc stood back and waited, watching her absorb the vastness of the scene. It had been here that Felicity had made up her mind on that cold autumn day and she had not stayed to argue about it.

Siân seemed fascinated.

"If the house had been built up here!" she said.

He shook his head, knowing how the weather would crucify a building so exposed. She had passed all his tests now bar one, and he felt suddenly mean, being unable to offer her all he wanted to offer because of that one, final condition to be fulfilled. He was tempted to ignore it. He wasn't even sure any more that it was important. But the fact that it nagged away in the back of his mind must mean something and so he didn't speak after all. If Siân noticed, or minded, she said nothing and so, after a while, he began walking again, taking a more oblique route back down to the farm and pointing out the extent of its land.

"Gwylim and I had to divide it, of course. I would have liked all of it but I couldn't buy his share as well as the house and I needed cash to make alterations."

"For Cymru."

"Clever girl. Not many people know about Cymru."

"Dava still owns him."

"Of course. I can't. I'm not ready yet to hand in my licence."

"Better be certain Dava doesn't accept another bid before then."

"He might not part with him at all," said Madoc with a half laugh. "He trained the sire once and lost him. Who knows what price he'll put on Cymru now?"

Siân took his hand, comfortingly. "I know I've got nothing to offer that would help, but I'm sure it'll work out."

He wrapped his arms round her to stop himself making the answer he longed to give. *Not yet,* he thought. *Soon, but not yet.*

"Is he worth such a lot?"

"After the style of that win on Wednesday ... fifty, sixty thousand? Until you put him on the market, you can't be sure, and it isn't a thing I want brought into the open yet."

"A secret," she teased.

"Private, anyway."

"Comes to the same thing."

He moved impatiently and she let him go. They started walking again.

"It's going to cost you a lot to buy him," she said, "whatever the method."

"I might raise a loan on his stud potential but whether my bank manager will look kindly on a steeplechaser still running over fences is another matter."

"He'll go on running then?"

"He might as well. At the rate things are going, shan't be ready for him here this season anyway."

"You're planning a long way ahead," she said soberly "Taking a lot of risks to secure your future."

"Yes," he said, knowing them all, knowing too that there were still some he could not discuss. "Still, I think I can be sure of Dava. Blood's thicker than water."

She was silent. She liked Dava, even though he had just given her notice. But could he be trusted not to profit from a gold mine? She had good reason, hadn't she, to believe in the smallness of his margins at Claybrooke. If somebody came along and offered the huge sum that Madoc said Cymru was worth ... She was not sure how far her trust in Dava went.

They walked back down to Afonwen, each hiding the reservations in their hearts.

TWENTY-THREE

By Wednesday Siân had cleaned every bridle in the tackroom and had started on the saddles. In her semi-idle state, small details which normally had not bothered her began to be annoying, and when her wheelbarrow developed a squeak she went about looking unsuccessfully for an oilcan.

She prodded Ted into joining her in the search and, after a scuffle under the tackroom sink, he produced a dusty, greasy, long-nosed object but, instead of giving it to her, he trailed along with her to the barrow and squatted down to look at the wheel. He turned the victim over and rocked the wheel on its spindle.

"A spanner wouldn't hurt either. Got a couple in my bike kit — adjustable. I'll get them." Siân, surprised by

273

this generosity, stood up and let him go. Ken trundled past with a loaded barrow.

"Curing the squealbarrow are we? I think I'll nick off with it when you go. It'll be better than this one."

She was resigned by now to leaving but she still found Ken's insouciance hard to take. "I'm not doing it for your benefit."

"You and Ted make a lovely pair when you're grumpy. If old Jack's feeling in a mood when he gets here you could..." Bill Houghton came out of the house, and Ken ducked Siân's backhander and moved on hastily.

Ted appeared with a spanner in each hand. "Maintenance," he said, as Bill fell into step beside him. Sheepishly, he crouched over the wheelbarrow, setting his pair of spanners to the nuts and puffing slightly as, with a creak and a groan, the rust gave way and the fittings tightened.

Bill nodded and straightened up and said to Siân, "Well, that could be worthwhile. It looks as though you're reprieved."

A smile grew on her face as his meaning dawned.

"Reprieved? Oh, Bill, really?"

He had to smile himself at her evident joy, although his eyes were worried. "As soon as our grease monkey's finished, you'd better muck out Carola and Did Ya See Me. Jack's missis has phoned to say his back's gone funny again and she's driving him to the doctor's."

Ted groaned. "Does that mean I'll have to drive the wagon?"

"I might have to, and so might you, but let's hope we don't go racing before he comes back."

"Who are you trying to kid?" muttered Ted, touching the oilcan to the spindle. "His last spell off work lasted months."

Bill said to Siân, "Even if he comes back fairly quickly, he'll probably only be allowed to drive, not to lift things. So Dava says you've to take over both mares indefinitely. Push along now, both of you." He nodded and moved on. Siân watched his stout back bustling across the yard and felt so many emotions she thought she would burst.

"More blooming work," said Ted, standing up and slapping the spanners together into one hand.

"Oh, shut up," she howled, not knowing whether to laugh or cry. She hugged him. "It's the best news I've had in months." And seizing the barrow handles, she whooped across the yard, crying "Geronimo!"

Ted touched his sleeve where Siân's hand had squeezed him. "Loopy," he said.

* * *

She was very happy for nearly a week. Madoc had never seen anybody bloom so suddenly. Although her high spirits rubbed off on him, he was troubled, too, because he wanted to find a moment to discuss their future together and her purring contentment held that need at arm's length. How could he disturb her hard-won calm with questions? They spent all their free time together, rejoicing over Cymru's easy win at Uttoxeter and sharing their pride in the horse who would found Afonwen, wrapped up in each other physically but not talking of the remaining secrets that lay between them.

However, the Monday before Cheltenham saw a change in Siân. Though they sat in front of the fire, both staring into the red bars, she was restless and Madoc felt he must hold her by his own stillness. He knew she was upset that he would be away for three days at the National Hunt Festival but there was nothing he could do to change it. In old-fashioned style, Dava ran horses on all three days and spent the intervening nights in a hotel. Madoc had rides on outside horses as well as on Jackdaw Bay, Quimby,

Appomattox and Zama, so the meeting would be a reasonably busy one and there was no way he and Siân could meet until he returned late on Thursday night. They both knew this perfectly well, and also that Siân would have her hands full coping with the horses left at home, for Jack was still semi-crippled and off work, and Ken and Ted would be needed at Cheltenham, leaving only John Paddy, herself and Bill Houghton to run the yard. Madoc knew his part in the proceedings was a comparatively easy one, although responsible, and he felt faintly guilty in the face of Siân's attempts to come to terms with the first challenge to her security.

"You'll give me the phone number of the hotel, won't you?" she said and, even as he agreed, he could see she tried to lighten the question and hide her uncertainty with a smile: "I'll want to check they're looking after you properly — you know, one concubine per room and two spares?"

He had to laugh. "Trust you to think of that! Look, three days away from you are necessary to charge up my batteries," he kissed her ear, "for when I come home."

She sighed. "I'd rather you didn't have to go."

"I know. But you'll be so tired, you'll just fall into bed in the evenings and die till morning. Believe me! You won't even have time to read."

"Well, I suppose you could be right. But I'm glad old Ted is going with you and not staying here."

"Why?" he was surprised.

"He's got his eye on me — I can feel it. It's a bit creepy."

"You're imagining things. Ted! You'd get more fun out of the motorbike."

"I'm not. He's all right when you're around but I see him looking at me sometimes and I know."

"Just as well he's going to Cheltenham, then. He'll be drunk for two days. . . "

"Or nights."

"More than likely — and you'll be tucked up in your virtuous bed reading Nevil Shute or whoever the library had in this week."

"Actually I went mad and bought a copy of *Lady Chatterley*," she said archly.

"What! bought it! You rash creature." He grinned. "You'll still fall asleep, I bet you."

"I thought it was all inflaming passions and things?"

"Sorry to disappoint you. It's a lot less inflaming than some women's magazines."

"Oh." Then, with a half twist in order to look at him, "And where have you been tempted to read women's magazines? Don't tell me Aunt Grace is a secret devourer of Cosmopolitan!"

Trapped, he said, "Felicity used sometimes to put out articles she thought I ought to read — she'd leave the magazine open where I'd be, well, bound to find it."

"Funny woman," said Siân, wondering. "How bossy! And did you read them?" She refused to ask where Felicity had thought to leave them.

"Sometimes they were quite interesting," he began, but she was not to be sidetracked.

"I'm surprised you put up with it. Being manipulated like that."

"Well," he said slowly, "there are times when you can put up with all sorts of things... if you have to. Reading the odd copy of Cosmopolitan is quite a mild sort of duty compared with some other duties that I've heard of."

She went very quiet at that. Feeling the muscles tense under his hand, he simply went on holding her. He had not forgotten the trick of relaxing and letting time pass, and if there was to be any confrontation he was not going to be the one who drew back. But she did not say anything. After a while she reached up and kissed him, pleadingly, and although he knew the distraction was deliberate, he was unable to resist. She needed sometimes to test how gentle he could be, to reassure herself of his control by driving his responses ahead of hers. He understood that. He had seen her astonishment at learning to accept love, to dare to offer it, and he'd watched with pride as her confidence grew. What worried him was the unseen, unspoken catalogue of past disaster. There was something there, still, that she could not cope with. He heard an echo of it in her desperate whisper. Despite the brave, almost jaunty smile, with which she led him into the bedroom, he was haunted by a sense of unhappiness.

TWENTY-FOUR

Ted Gray sat happily in one of the Cheltenham bars, smiling into his brandy glass. What a horse, that Jackie boy, eh? Nobody had really expected him to win, had they, not even Mr Madoc bloody Owen, perched up there so proud? He put his hand into his pocket, to make sure the winnings were still there. You could never be too sure in a big crowd like this. He drank another mouthful. He wasn't needed again today and he could always outface Dava at evening stables. Who was he to preach temperance when he'd damn near gone bust all those years ago through drink? He sipped again, chuckling.

Somebody joined him at the table but he paid no attention. He had nothing in common with smart young men whose clothes and manners indicated that racecourse bars were beneath them. Gradually, however, he absorbed the fact that this particular young man was watching him. Sipping at a pint, lounging in his seat, but with blue, bright eyes steadily fixed on him under a fringe of yellow hair. Ted looked back at him with a frown which eased as recognition dawned.

"I know you," he said. "You're that jockey, what's his name, you won that hurdle race, didn't you? Bloody good odds, wish I'd been on it. Cheers. Well done. Congrats." He lifted the nearly empty glass in a hazy salute.

The other acknowledged it with a twisted sort of smile. "I wish I'd been on it, too. Quite the reverse, unfortunately, but we won't go into that."

Ted grappled with the thought for a minute but its meaning eluded him. The bloke had ridden it, hadn't he? Surely he'd do well out of a win like that? But that was his own business. He gave it up. "Drown your sorrows, then," he said, and drained his brandy.

"Want another?"

"Flush, are you?" Ted focused on him. "Can't be that bad, then, can it? Go to hell."

The newcomer put two fifty-pound notes on the table neatly, side by side. "Those say I'll buy you a drink and you'll listen to me for ten minutes."

After a moment, Ted put the empty glass in front of him. "Buy it then. Time's cheap." And the young man took it up steadily, sniffed it and went away smiling.

The customers were noisy, restless brutes. They took no notice of the television screen which was showing the last race of the day. They were all celebrating ⁃ or drinking to tomorrow ... The stranger came back, lowering the little glass tantalisingly in front of Ted's face.

"There you are then. A double. Mr Owen doesn't mind you drinking?"

"Let him try and stop me," said Ted. "Cheers!"

His companion sat down and took another token sip of his pint. "I see you've taken over old Jack's responsibilities. Travelling Man. Has his back gone again? Shame. He was a crusty old character, but a good man."

"I'm a good man myself," said Ted. "Sober's a judge tomorrow, you'll see. Big race. Favourite. Can't let the stable down." He raised his glass. "To Quimby!" He began to giggle. "Thass the name of a man who makes cartoons, y'know. Silly name."

The young man picked up one of the fifty-pound notes, consideringly. Ted snatched at it. "Ah, ah. You gave them to me."

"I put them down for you to look at. They're still mine. Still, maybe I'll give you this one." He pushed it towards Ted. "You can have the other one when you've done a favour for me. Mm?"

Ted raised the glass to his lips while he thought. Fifty quid for listening wouldn't compromise anybody. He tucked away the money and the young man's attention sharpened.

"Right. Start listening. First off, I'll need your address. I'll post this," he tapped the second fifty, "afterwards. Get me into trouble, if they saw you taking it from me then. See?"

Ted drank and tried to look as though he was thinking.

Then he gave him the address. The other wrote it down, neatly, on a piece of paper from his wallet.

"Brimstage Close, Gayton..."

"Not got an address book?" Ted waved his glass at the paper. "Fifties everywhere and can't afford an address book?"

"This is enough. It's more easily — lost — when I've finished with it. Are you on the phone?"

Ted shook his head. "Thought about it for the old folks. Haven't got round to it yet."

"You could afford it now — and a lot more if you're clever. You've got fifty smackers tucked away there to start with, six races tomorrow ... of course you'd need the right bookie. And a bit of inside information."

"Now," said Ted, with an effort to fight off the haziness, "that is the problem. Quimby. Short odds, no guarantee."

"You've hit it. A guarantee, that's what we want. A guarantee that a horse won't win. You're in the right position to see to that."

"Here," said Ted with sudden alarm, "not tomorrow! Not Quimby!"

The other laughed. "No, not Quimby. It's too soon; got to sow the seed before you can harvest it, see? But Aintree's only a couple of weeks away."

"Get on," said Ted, "you're cracked if you think I can get at a National runner."

"Oh, no, I wouldn't push you that far. But what about the Friday? Seen the Racing Calendar? There's a very interesting list of runners for the McTay Trophy. Have you seen it?" He pulled out the stiff paper and laid it in front of Ted's frowning face. "Lovely race, that. Limited handicap, lots of publicity. Look at the top weight, there."

"Musketeer," said Ted, focusing with increasing difficulty. "Can't do it. Not him. Not get anywhere near."

"Wrong again. He's the draw, the spice in the cake. His odds'll be so short, everyone'll be backing the others. And look who's down among the others. Go on. Number five. Walked away with his last two races. Jumps for fun. The sort of horse old ladies love to bet on because he's always out in front and they can see him."

"Cymru?" said Ted puzzled.

"Got it in one. You're going to help us clean up. Cymru is not going to win, although the odds are going to be very tempting."

Ted was getting out of his depth. He prevaricated.

"Oh, I dunno. Find someone else. Walbrook's lads maybe. I can't do it. Stop Musketeer, 'seasier."

"Oh, we'll try. If he wins on Thursday we'll try. A Gold Cup winner coming to Aintree? What do you think? But that's not a certainty, is it? There's no guarantee a novice can beat all those seasoned chasers. If he goes down, your boy's going to be fancied for the McTay. And then we'll want the word that he isn't going to win."

They sat for a moment, looking at each other over the Racing Calendar, poised on the seesaw. Ted had no great love for Cymru or for Madoc, but he'd never been approached like this before and the sense of power it generated made him inclined to push his luck. He drained the brandy and pointed a finger at his opponent.

"You got to be desperate. Hm? Thass worth much ⸤ much more'n fifty now, 'n fifty after." He swallowed a hiccup. "I want to know what y're up to."

"If you can't work it out, I'm not explaining for you."

"I wan' a better offer," persisted Ted.

The young man gave a cold smile. "How about family security," he said, "at Brimstage Close?" And he folded Ted's address and put it into his wallet. "If Musketeer gets beat in the Gold Cup, I'll be in touch. Wherever you are."

Faced with those wintry eyes, Ted knew that "why" no longer mattered.

TWENTY-FIVE

Madoc reappeared in the middle of Friday morning, bounding out of Dava's Range Rover into preparations for third lot. He burst into Carola's box, picked Siân up, and waltzed her round the stable.

"I'm home, woman, say something!"

She squealed as he bumped into Carola. "Shut the door before she gets out."

"A fine welcome for the conquering hero." He let her slide to the ground and shut the door. Then he made another dive at her and although she shrieked, she did not flinch. He hoisted her aloft.

"Tell me I'm good," he demanded, bouncing her.

"You're terrific."

"And Quimby was good. And Jackie."

"They're amazing," she said to the roof.

"And that you love me."

She looked down, and he stood still, waiting.

"You know I do."

He let her slip to the floor, then squeezed her tightly. "Grrr... Have I missed you!"

"I missed you too," she said through his jacket. "I thought you'd be home last night."

"Didn't Grace come and tell you? We were invited to the party."

"What party? Grace never came near me."

"Oh. Maybe she disapproves of parties."

"Or of me!"

"Don't get mad. There was a bit of a bash at the hotel and we sort of got swept along. Dava's been mates with the Lambourn lot for years and they insisted he came on the strength of Quimby's win."

"That's the stable that trains Bartholomew Boy?"

"Mm. It was all rather spur-of-the-moment. Gold Cup fever. I did think of you... I'm sorry Grace didn't pass the message on."

"Oh, well. No real harm done, I suppose." She smiled, reluctantly. "No wonder Ken was cross last night, having to come home and miss the fun."

He laughed. "We'd had a few on Wednesday night. He didn't do too badly."

She wriggled out of his arms to catch up a trailing rein from Carola's feet.

He said, "Look, there's something important I must do in Chester this afternoon. Can you come with me as soon as you've finished for lunch?"

"You're not riding anywhere?"

"I turned it down. This is more important."

"I'd better say yes, then."

He stood back to let her out with the mare and gave her a leg-up. As he watched her out into the fields, he thought, *This afternoon I'm going to stake everything on one throw. Luck had better be on my side.*

* * *

"Any chance," asked Siân, "of going first to Helen Rogers's to see how Double Jump is getting on?"

Madoc turned the MG on to the drive and consulted his watch. "Do you mind if we don't? Helen is a lovely lady but I have things to do today which I don't want delayed."

"Oh," she said. "It does sound important."

"Well, fairly."

Siân wound down the window and the slipstream blew her hair about. "I must get it cut," she said, pulling the flying locks away from her mouth.

"Don't. At the moment you remind me of that girl who was always flitting about in a helicopter. All you need are the earphones."

"Thanks very much," she said, laughing.

"I always thought the pursuing cameraman had a nice job."

She went along thankfully with the banter but, as the journey unwound, she realised he was covering an inner tension, and more and more she heard the beating of her apprehensive heart. She was not entirely surprised when, at the college traffic lights on the outskirts of Chester, Madoc drew a deep breath and, looking at the chapel, remarked, "It's a wonder this car doesn't have its indicator on."

"Oh?" she said guardedly.

"Felicity is in her third, doing physical education. Up to Christmas I was a large part of her syllabus. Then she realised... well, she couldn't cope with me. So we split." He grimaced. Siân, warily, offered no information in return. The lights changed. They both preserved a careful silence until he had parked, just outside the bounds of the city proper, and locked up the car.

"What is this important thing you have to do?" she asked, as he pocketed the keys. "The thing you've passed up a riding fee to do?"

"Bottom weight in a selling handicap at Nottingham," he said wryly. "Not that big a sacrifice."

"Madoc!" she said angrily but he had started walking. "Let's walk, shall we?" he suggested. "I find I can talk more easily if I'm doing something. Let's be tourists for the afternoon. Do you know Chester?"

She gave a rather sour smile. "Not as well as you do, I'm sure. What with Felicity and everything."

"Let's see, shall we? You be the guide. Let's go up on to the Walls and take it from there."

"All right," she said, and lifted her chin.

From Northgate they walked for some time without speaking, both inhibited by the knowledge that Madoc had walked this stretch a hundred times with Felicity. Every now and again they met a self-sufficient knot of students, briskly discussing college business, or sometimes a solitary, be-scarfed female lugging the weekend provisions back to digs.

"Are we likely to meet her?" asked Siân, hardily.

"She has lectures all afternoon on a Friday," he said, frowning, matter-of-fact, but more disturbed than he would admit.

Siân stayed on the Wall, still going south. Her instinct was to skirt the city, even though, so early in the year, it was not heavily visited by tourists. She wanted to take the long, quiet route down to the river, staying open to the sky, where eavesdroppers could be seen coming. The constant reminders of history, Roman wall, Georgian houses, ancient racecourse, were reinforced by little plaques and inscriptions. Siân, aware of the continuity, was nevertheless nagged by a vague sense of trying to recall something important among all these items. The settled, self contained cosiness of the medieval city was at odds with this, so that she almost wanted to attack it. She wished Madoc would say something.

"Did you ever ride on the flat?" she asked, as they walked past the pretty, toylike Roodee spread out below and to their right.

"No, I was always too heavy. And anyway Dava gave up after he lost Baner Wen. Or rather, after he lost Anna. Do you know about her? Mrs Selwyn-Hughes?"

"The woman who owns Musketeer? Only vaguely."

Madoc explained, briefly. "Dava was hit very hard when she married the Hon. Alistair. He used to get drunk a lot, couldn't pay his staff, had to mortgage the stables and the farm. It was a long haul back when he finally got a grip of himself."

"He's more sensitive than he looks, then. Dava."

"Everything's relative," said Madoc wryly.

"Ha, ha."

"Baner was Cymru's sire. Dava isn't quite rational on the subject, in spite of being a hard-headed businessman."

"You're an unusual family," said Siân thoughtfully. "After working at Pickering's I thought I was really odd, being fond of a horse. But you and Dava get just as involved as I do."

"It's an occupational hazard. The flat boys don't have the time. Two seasons, and their horses are over the hill. We have them so much longer."

"That isn't the whole answer," she said.

They negotiated the traffic heading into Wales over the Grosvenor Bridge and Siân continued to follow the line of the Wall, ignoring the castle and the county buildings which backed on to it in municipal stolidity. Madoc, perhaps associating the dreariness of this stretch with the break-up of his link with Felicity, said hesitantly, "I came out intending to discuss — well, you and me. But that isn't fair without talking about other things as well."

Siân said warily, "I had a feeling you were thinking a lot more than you would say."

He said, almost angrily, "I'm not the one keeping secrets, Siân." And when she did not answer, he said, "Look, I can't pretend it wasn't fun being with Felicity. For a while it was ideal. We were both busy during the winter and had the summer free, so when I was riding she wasn't demanding because she had her own work. But she started to drop hints about settling down, giving up the teaching, branching out socially. I didn't mind — Dad died and I could see prospects at Afonwen — but I had doubts. For me, there's nothing worse than having to guess what someone else is thinking and feeling in order to do the right thing all the time, so I took her to Afonwen to see how she'd react."

"Like you did with me, I seem to remember," said Siân, rather sharply.

"Yes." He admitted it reluctantly.

"It felt like a test, but at the time I didn't mind." She tossed her hair. "I suppose that means I do now. I don't like the idea that I'm one of several who've been offered the sights of Afonwen to see if I can take it."

"Not several. Just you and, like I said, Felicity."

"Well. And how did she take it? Didn't she pass?"

"It was a miserable wet day," he said apologetically. "She was appalled at the isolation and that long track with all the gates on it. She said it was like a prison."

"Maybe she had a point." Siân set her face and marched onward, deeply unsettled.

At the old Dee bridge, she hesitated. She could go straight on, towards the Groves; or she could turn right, across the river. On other visits she had usually chosen the wide walk of the Groves where, in summer, the visitors crowded aboard steamers or sat on benches and ate their sandwiches amid a mob of greedy swans, pigeons and sparrows. That way led on to the park, and the gardens round the ruins beside St John's church; but today she veered away. Legend said an errant nun had been walled up alive there, and with Felicity's comment on Afonwen in her mind Siân knew she could not face that. She set off across the bridge.

It was so narrow, the traffic filled its single carriageway, leaving room for only one pavement and an abbreviated kerb, and it was along the kerb that Siân danced, darting from one haven to the next, where the triangular starlings split the grey, incoming tide. She did not look back to see whether Madoc followed. She knew that, today, she could not escape him.

She waited for him at the Handbridge end of the crossing.

"Up here there's a bread shop. We'll buy lunch and have a history lesson."

She still would not meet his eye, so he agreed neutrally.

She bought sandwiches and a sticky bun and marched with her carrier-bag into a grassy patch that seemed to have no other purpose than to set off a children's play area.

"You can have my bread," offered Madoc, picking out the beef from his sandwich. Perched astride a swing, he reminded her of a gawky heron, all legs and over-large wings.

"You look positively gaunt," she said bluntly. "Will one sandwich really put you out of work?"

"Until I give up riding, yes, I really do have to be careful."

"Stubborn," she said, munching defiantly.

She couldn't finish the sticky bun. Madoc was watching her with a terrible air of patience and as she tidied up the sandwich wrappings and pushed them and the fragment of bun into the flimsy carrier, her fingers trembled. Still he waited.

"Well," she said eventually. "I suppose it's my turn."

"A history lesson, you said."

"You elected me guide for the day."

"There's nothing here."

"You wait," she said. "I came here last summer as part of a night-school trip. There was a chap called Tom O'Neill whose big thing was Roman history — the biggest thing about him actually, he was only about five foot four. He spent most of his time arguing with the lecturer and the rest of the time trying to persuade me to go out with him. You'll get some idea of what he was like if I say the other night-school women called him Toenail." She could not help a giggle at the nickname, but went on seriously enough. "When we visited the

Roman sites, it was this one that really got me. This is the soldiers' shrine to Minerva." She swung gently round, inviting him to look. Beyond the play area he saw a blackened sandstone bluff, quite unremarkable except for the set of railings which had been let into the rock as though to shut off a small cave or cell, and a lumpy carving in the stone, framed by a sort of doorway.

"Nobody on the course thought much of it. They preferred labels on things in museums, and mysterious shoelaces being brought out of muddy trenches. This was too common. Too accessible. You just walk up to it, no tickets, no turnstile. The kids play round it and nobody takes any notice, it's just there. Poor Minerva. It probably never was a very good carving anyway."

"The goddess of Wisdom," said Madoc. "Wisdom or knowledge? Or learning? Which? Did they say?"

She shook her head, not looking at him. "My mother once said, when she was angry, that wisdom was not what you knew, but what you did with what you knew. I thought she was exaggerating at the time but maybe she was right."

"Wisdom is the principal thing, therefore get wisdom."

She turned on him. "How did you know I was thinking that?"

"I didn't. It's in the Bible, Proverbs I think. A reasonable association with the lady over there."

Siân's mind had been jerked away from the shrine to the grey cement pictures on the Old Library which had so struck her on that day in December — the incised lettering, her childish confusions, the grinding awfulness of that week when she left Green Bank. She got up abruptly and walked to the shrine, leaving the swing oscillating. The breeze blew her hair out behind her and the plastic bag rattled in her clenched fist. He followed.

"Siân, you didn't come here just to tell me about Roman history or even your friend Toenail, whatever he was called, now did you?"

She said in a thin voice, "Isn't it horrible the way people leave litter all over the place. Even here — cider bottles — Coke cans — crisp packets..." She began to pick up the debris and poke it angrily into the bag and he wondered at the passion she put into it, the power this unimpressive place had over her. The little columns let into the stone were no more than five feet high, and the flat lintel over them an obvious replacement for a gabled roof whose peg holes remained. The woman carved there, holding a staff in her right hand, was blurred with centuries of weather and simple to the point of naivety. And yet her blind face, by its very existence, had dignity.

He said, as gently as he could, "Siân, trust me."

Her fingers moved clumsily, pathetically. He knew she was crying but at the touch of his hand on her shoulder she sprang up, almost shaking him off.

"What do you want me to say!"

"I don't know. It's your secret. You have to live with it."

"I don't have to tell you."

He considered her tear-streaked, averted face. "No. But I'm not sure I can live with it unless you tell me what it is."

"That's an ultimatum, is it?" Her voice was harsh. "You tell me about your lovers and I tell you about mine! Oh, Madoc, it isn't that easy."

He said encouragingly, "I know he hurt you. Talk about it, please."

She looked at him then. "It'll hurt you too. You know him — it was Justin. You might have guessed. You know what he's like. I know, it was stupid! I knew it was stupid then, when I agreed to go out with him, but I couldn't, I don't know, not do it. He dazzled me.

Deep down I didn't like him. I kept finding myself fighting him off and asking myself why and not knowing the answer."

"Didn't you talk about it to anyone?"

She gave a short laugh. "You know me, the more I hurt, the less I say. Anyway who could I talk to? All the other girls were watching me to see how I coped in my turn, and the lads were running a book to see how long I'd last. None of them knew I hadn't even gone to bed with him, and how could I talk about that?"

He said, "But you did go to bed with him."

She screamed, "I didn't! I didn't! Listen to me! It only happened — just that one time — the day he rode Canterbury in the McAlpine, the day Double Jump first raced. Helen told me about moving her to Claybrooke, I went down to the house to give my notice and then I thought, well, they're all having a party, I'll go in and see the horse, what the hell, they can't sack me now, can they!" Tears poured disregarded down her face. "Oh God, it was all so stupid. I heard his car come back and I shut myself in the box — I thought he wouldn't find me — but he checked in the hostel and everybody was out, so he came looking..." She was quivering with the effort of controlling her voice. "He was drunk. We'd had a row already and I'd said we were finished — they'd told me he had another girlfriend — I thought it was over — but he just kept on and on, and he took no notice when I said no — and in the end I had to fight him, really fight him, and he was so strong I couldn't — I couldn't stop him, Madoc, oh God, I couldn't stop him..." Her voice trailed away in a long keening wail, and her hands held her body, crossing, fumbling, before they went up to hide her face.

He slowly took her into his arms and she lay there howling, letting out all the anger and fear that her foolishness had brought upon her. And he heard it and welcomed it, painful as it was, because now he knew, and although his eyes were closed with the bitterness of her grief, he could hold her tight, knowing that he must never let her go.

How long they stood there he was never sure. A small child came running to play on the swings and he was back in the present, aware of the young mother looking curiously at himself and Siân, so desperately embraced. He did not move. He was not embarrassed. He made a slight, protective gesture, and smiled. The mother turned to lift her child on to a swing, and he remained on watch.

When Siân's sobbing died to a mere catch of the breath, she stirred at last and looked at him. "That's all it was," she said.

"More than enough. No wonder you ran away."

"I was afraid. I thought I might be pregnant." Her eyes followed the child on the swing. "I couldn't have coped with that."

"Weren't you on the pill?"

"That was a panic reaction, afterwards."

"Something else you didn't tell me."

"It all got so complicated," she said, rubbing her wet face. "It was like a shield in my hand that I couldn't put down."

"And now?"

She managed a smile. "Maybe I'm not afraid any more."

* * *

They meandered peacefully back over the wide flood of the Dee where, under the narrow bridge, the tide had turned and the river once more ran seawards. Madoc dropped the rubbish into the first bin they passed and walked blithely on, his arm round Siân now, his doubts dispelled.

"We may as well go back on to the Wall," he said. "I need to call into a shop by Eastgate."

She guessed from the suppressed chuckle that there was some surprise waiting but she couldn't be sure of its nature so she didn't quite have the courage to ask, nor the self-confidence to assume, what it might be. She was not entirely surprised that he descended to street level, but she stood open-mouthed when he led her past the colonnaded front of the Grosvenor Hotel and towards the brightly fabulous windows of the jewelers. And then he simply left her there, saying with a smile, "Don't come in with me — I'll be back in a minute."

He was gone before she had time to say more than, "But... !"

And of course he took longer than the bare minute he had promised. Why on earth did he have to keep her in suspense out here, in this Aladdin's cave, with its marble columns and smoothly tiled floor? In her drained state she could do no more than stand mesmerised by the brilliance of the window displays where diamond, emerald and sapphire broke and reflected light into her eyes like a sword. *He must not buy me anything,* she resolved. *Here I am in my wax jacket and jodhpurs, stained and tawdry and tear-splattered — no wonder he didn't want to take me in with him. I don't deserve stones like these; he ought to give me jet, or those dark, cheap sapphires that never glow again after you take them from the window but sulk dully on your finger. I could never wear such a blue as these. They look too much like eyes...*

Before she knew it, Madoc was at her shoulder.

Awkwardly, without saying anything, he offered her a small box, not the modern mock-velvet she had expected, but an old, battered brown thing with a little gilt button which sprang the catch. She was embarrassed, partly because years of feeling undeserving had made her shy of accepting presents, and partly because this was so different from her imaginings. She fumbled in picking it off his palm, and the dive they both made to save it broke the ice.

"Sorry..."

"Sorry..."

They both laughed and Madoc said, "I brought this in to have it cleaned. I've been in twice for it already and it hasn't been back from the workshop... It was my mother's but if that bothers you, we can get something else."

She looked at him uncertainly for a moment, then opened the box.

Inside lay a gold ring set with a ruby and two diamonds.

Against the magnificence in the displays, the stones seemed small, but the window lighting struck them into fire and treacherously revealed an imperfection, a flickering water drop like a small tear at the centre of the red stone. Siân studied it tenderly.

"How beautiful," she said.

He watched her absorption and was satisfied. His hands hovered near hers, softly and with caution, as though guarding a wounded bird.

"Shall I put it on for you?"

She looked up at him, weighing what he was asking of her and what giving in return. After a long pause she said carefully, "I am not marrying Afonwen. If I marry you the two must be distinct."

"Agreed," he said slowly. "Afonwen is only part of it, a touchstone if you like. You're solitary, like me. You're happy in your privacy. How many other people have been inside the caravan? You don't burn to introduce me to your family, you don't rush off to anyone's protective bosom when things get rough. Afonwen won't demand total isolation but it was important that you liked it, that you were in tune with it. Otherwise I shouldn't have spoken."

"Love me, love my farm," she said, softly mocking.

His eyes pleaded with her. "Is it such a responsibility?"

"I'm scared of being tied to things rather than people. I had such a lot of that with Dad's shop."

"I'll do my best to avoid it." His fingers closed warmly on hers.

She gave him the ring then and he placed it carefully, down to the knuckle. Neither of them quite knew why she should capitulate at that moment; perhaps it was a spark of bravery, a gesture of determination about the future. He kissed her briefly, aware of the curiosity of passers-by, and set off quietly into the city, holding the newly captured hand with assurance.

"I can't promise you total freedom," he said. "There's going to be a lot of work to do. Do you know anything about VAT? Unless the government changes its mind we're going to have to register, and there'll be a lot of paperwork besides that. Will you be able to cope?"

"I can try," she said. "I'll do some courses." But she clung to her independence as if to a straw in the flood. "We must have some help though. I don't want to be totally bound up in Afonwen or in you. That would bore us both."

"Never be afraid of that," he said. "You'll always have friends, just because you can manage without them... I know, because I'm the same. I know I enjoy company, but other people, mostly, are like wine, pleasant in small quantities. They aren't the water of life to me. And you are."

She was speechless.

She looked down at the ruby on her hand, the flawed yet beautiful stone still glowing in the afternoon sunshine. She looked up at the glory of the city and it swam before her, richly exuberant, black and white buildings tottering on their ancient foundations, gaily coloured shop windows shining in the shadowed galleries of the Rows, gables, turrets and oriels soaring dizzily up four storeys into the sky. There were spring flowers in the street and outside the cathedral an early busker optimistically played "Jesu, Joy of Man's Desiring" as a dance. It was a busy, cheerful world, fantastic but with its feet on the ground. *I have built my foundations today,* she thought, and closed her eyes in sheer wonder.

She knew by the little pressure of his hand that he had appreciated her mood but his remark on it took her by surprise.

"I think we should start by getting you a driving licence."

She hung back for a moment, uncertainly, until the implications sank in. Then, weakly at first, she began to laugh. It was astonishing to be so understood and provided for, to be loved so practically as well as with passion, to be offered both a retreat and the freedom to escape.

"Aren't you afraid," she said, falling into step once more and taking his arm, "that I'll drive off into the blue one day and you won't be able to catch me?"

He shook his head. "I shall make sure any car you have is much slower than mine."

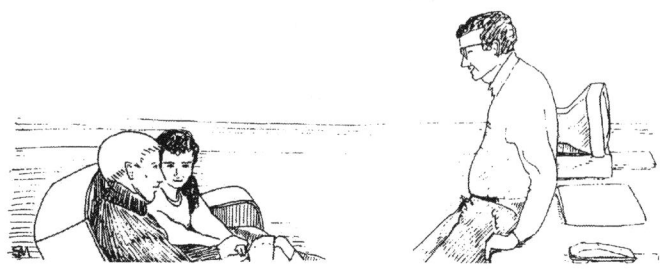

TWENTY-SIX

If anyone had asked Siân how the stable would react to the engagement, she would have guessed that Ken would be delighted and ribald, John Paddy uninterested, and Ted ostentatiously indifferent in order to hide his hurt feelings; that Dava would be the only one who did not notice, and Grace coldly disapproving. She was surprised how wrong she was. She made no particular show of the ruby ring, indeed, on the Saturday she reluctantly obeyed the voice of common sense which told her to keep it safely in its box during the endangering hard work of the yard. But it pained her strangely to leave it off and wear it only at night, and by Monday, when the full staff once more assembled, she could not bear to be parted from the public symbol of her commitment. The presence of Bill Houghton, driving everyone on, kept initial reactions to a minimum, but Siân, hypersensitive, knew there would be more said.

Her first encounter was with Ken after first lot. As usual he was already in the tackroom brewing up. She was completely unprepared for the huge hug and kiss he gave her, but her delighted laughter turned quickly to regret when she realised he had tears in his eyes as he let her go. She had no time to talk about it because John Paddy came in immediately and went through such a similar performance that she was sure they had rehearsed it, only he was less exuberant, simply pleased for her, without any undertones. Ted, when he arrived, settled into his usual corner with a curious, worried air and jumped when she spoke to him. He did not appear to be conscious of the outside world at all, let alone the engagement.

From Dava and from Grace, there was no immediate reaction. Claybrooke had horses to race and work to do, its sights firmly on the Liverpool meeting and the McTay in particular. Madoc reported absent nods from Dava and a smile from Grace, and seemed to think these indications sufficient. He, too, was more interested in the list of acceptances for the Trophy than in the comments of outsiders on what was, after all, a private affair. Siân had her first taste of playing second fiddle to Cymru and told herself it was only fair, after her involvement with Double Jump, to be in this position for once.

Three other Claybrooke horses, including Aholibah, were runners on the Friday of the National meeting, and in the preparations Siân began to lose the sense of being merely an accessory.

When Dava appointed her to look after Cymru at Liverpool, she grew an inch with unmixed pride.

"Jack won't be capable of handling him — it would be unfair to ask him to try — and John Paddy didn't have much success with him at Uttoxeter. You'll have time to turn him out properly because Hollie's race is later. Ask Ted to teach you how to plait tails and that — there's a prize for the best presented horse." She did not think to ask how much the prize might be. Dava seemed for the first time to notice the addition to her left hand and, after a moment, he said, "Come in the house. There's something I must discuss with Madoc and you'd better hear it, I suppose."

He led straight through the kitchen to the office, but as Madoc was washing his hands she joined him instead. "What's going on? Any idea?" she asked.

Madoc pulled a face, and Grace said, "Brace yourselves. This has been brewing for over a week."

"Do you know what it is?"

Grace tucked her mouth into a disapproving line.

"Yes, but I'll let the old fool do his own dirty work. If it's any help, I'm on your side." More than that she would not say, merely settling herself to a stack of paperwork with a displeased expression. They dried their hands and went into the office.

Dava was perched on the edge of his desk, his back to the computer screen. He offered Madoc and Siân a place on the sagging settee.

"I wanted a word," he began without introduction, "about next Friday. The McTay in particular, and Cymru's future from then on."

"In other words, money," said Madoc.

"Yes and no. I've had to make one or two decisions recently and it's only fair I should tell you about them because they directly concern you. I'm making the assumption that you still intend taking Cymru to Afonwen. Eventually."

Siân was a little surprised that there should be any doubt about it but Madoc leaned back, crossed his knees, and said calmly, "Of course. I assume you're trying to decide on a price."

"In a way." Even Siân could see that Dava, normally so brusque, was finding it hard to get started, and she wondered with a sinking heart just how far Madoc was going to be pushed financially.

Madoc said, "Well, we've got to talk about it sometime. I can't expect to be given Cymru on a plate. But I hope I am going to be given credit for the work I've put in on him."

"Yes, that is one of the things I've taken into consideration." Dava looked down at them from his perch and Siân felt the settee was more than just physically uncomfortable. "Cymru was bought with your future in mind... "

"And your past," said Madoc. He had no doubt that Dava was working up to a dubious proposal and he had also no intention of making the job easy for him. Dava, surprisingly, flushed.

"Which would be a very good reason for me to retain part ownership and the right to send you some good mares every season."

"Assuming the Arabs haven't bought them all by then and taken them to the continent," said Madoc. "Come on, Dava, why the stage management? What's going on? You're as embarrassed as hell about something. You might as well tell us what."

"You can make up your mind right now," said Dava with sudden energy, "that the horse is not going to be yours and yours alone. If you haven't calculated it already, do it now — he's got a reputation, he's favourite for the McTay since Bartholomew Boy beat Musketeer in the Gold Cup and if he wins you won't be able to afford him."

"Thanks very much," said Madoc. "So what do I do, join a syndicate? How many shares do you 'calculate' I'll be able to afford?"

Dava, already sharpened to argument, did not noticeably react to Madoc's sarcastic tone. "You're going to need some help, boy — partners, if not a full syndicate. I'm not a big enough fool to give you the horse, not even for the five thousand he cost me."

"Isn't it funny how putting a price on things to members of your family stirs up the emotions?" said Madoc conversationally to Siân. She sat very quiet, not knowing how to help. "Put a price on it, Dava."

There was a brief pause. "Well, to start with, I had an offer. A very good offer. From Mrs Selwyn-Hughes."

"Surprise, surprise. I hope you refused."

"As it happens, I did."

"But it forms a base line — a floor in the market?" said Siân. Dava looked at her as though the cat had spoken and she stared him out, wondering whether her intuitive mistrust of his generosity was going to be proved correct.

"Of course. I don't see why he can't struggle a bit for his success like the rest of us. Anna put forty thousand on the table immediately after the race at Carlisle where Cymru fell. No doubt Peter Walbrook advised her that I'd be more likely to bite when things weren't looking too rosy."

Siân sat aghast at this careless tossing of figures, even though the sum was less than Madoc's estimate that day on the windy hillside of Tal-y-fan.

"If you insist, I'll match that," said Madoc. "A mortgage, or one of Gwylim's business contacts... if you want more I'm prepared to look for it."

Dava scratched among his grizzled hair. "You must remember that you'll need some capital to live off. House to fix up. Wife to keep." He nodded at Siân, conceding her rights, and went on to explain, "Anna had it all ways. She didn't buy Baner, she inherited him from her father and she had the financial nous to marry a man who could afford to pay training fees while the horse made his name. Now, bearing in mind that Baner, like Cymru, was a staying horse, not classically bred for the mile and a half, his stud fees were not astronomical. But in the course of a reasonably long stud career, he must have netted Anna *at the least* half a million pounds. I want you to understand that we're not talking peanuts. I can't give away a share in that kind of money, not when the horse is mine to start with."

Siân was speechless at the sheer weight of money involved.

Madoc said acidly, "We're both well aware that Cymru belongs to you. Also that Anna wants him. You said she offered forty 'to start with'. What else has she offered? What were you up to in that little corner at the Gold Cup party?"

"Not so much as you," snapped back Dava, "and I'll thank you not to imply anything sordid was going on."

Madoc took Siân's hand. "You had better explain to us then, hadn't you, from your superior moral stance."

Dava glared at him. "All right! This isn't easy for me, you know. I came off worst on all counts when Anna took Baner away twenty years ago. You might expect me to be sore about it! But you don't know everything, so listen.

"Anna has never held any particular grudge. I often thought if Alistair hadn't had all the cards — in the form of cash and land — she wouldn't have taken Baner away. She might not even have married him."

"He never struck me as a passionate man," agreed Madoc dryly, "but then I don't assess racehorse owners in those terms."

Dava blinked. "There was only ever Anna that I looked at that way, and you know it. If I haven't been able to face talking to her — about what happened then, about racing or any other thing — it wasn't through hatred. We could be in the same paddock, the same winning enclosure and I daren't speak. I didn't trust myself not to grovel, to make a fool of myself all over again. And anyway she was married, wasn't she?"

Siân had tight hold of Madoc's hand.

"She found me — in that quiet corner you mentioned — at the party," went on Dava. "I was trying not to be too near her. That was easy enough, it was a biggish do if you recall and there were plenty of people I knew to talk to other than her. I couldn't believe it when she came up and said she wanted to discuss Cymru."

"Doesn't beat about the bush, then," said Madoc.

"No, you don't understand. She — no, I can't tell you what she said... She caught me off balance, that's all I can say." He took off his glasses and rubbed his eyes, just an ordinary tormented mortal. He cleaned the glasses with his handkerchief, blew his nose rather hard, and put the glasses back on. He caught Siân looking at him wonderingly, and said, "I haven't sold Cymru. I haven't sold him to you, I haven't sold him to Anna. I told her he was your future. She said I mustn't forget that neither of us was old and that we had a future too that had to be provided for."

He remembered her sweet, slightly accented voice saying, "My dear Dafydd, I was fond of Alistair but I can't bring him back. No amount of public disapproval will make me live in a vault to his memory. I'm going to go on living the way he would have wanted, holding parties, going racing, backing my horses. Jerry Monk can wear a black cap instead of a white one, but Musketeer will run, and wherever he runs I'll be there to cheer him on, and I imagine you won't be able to resist running Cymru against him, so you'll be there too, won't you?" The challenge of her eyes! He could see them still, echoed by the more innocent gaze of the Davies girl. Himself and Anna. Madoc and Siân. Which of them would he have to betray? Would the compromise he had found be enough?

He saw how Madoc held Siân's hand and waited. "Well," said Dava, "she wanted to buy Cymru outright. He is the only entire grey descendant of Baner that we know of, and the amount she offered made my mouth water. But I said I couldn't let you down. I offered her a part share instead, which she wasn't so keen on, so we got Peter Walbrook to come over and help thrash out the details."

Madoc sighed sharply. A third party knowing the deal would make it hard to retract. Dava managed a chuckle.

"It was getting pretty late by the time we agreed and I had had one or two glasses of champagne..."

"I wondered," said Madoc.

"Not that many. We arranged a wager. All sporting and above aboard. Nothing applies until after the horses finally pass the post in the McTay Trophy."

"Dava, I will personally nail you to the ground behind a hurdle in the next schooling session if you don't come to the point!"

"Anna Selwyn-Hughes has offered me," said Dava with deliberation, "one hundred thousand pounds."

Siân felt the jolt of Madoc's tension, and her mouth went dry.

"I'll sell her a percentage for that, and that percentage depends on the result of the race. If Cymru wins, or even if he finishes ahead of Musketeer, I retain control and she receives forty per cent. If Musketeer wins or finishes in front of Cymru, she takes sixty per cent and stands him at her stud, Aiketgate, in Shropshire."

The stunned silence was so deep that Siân could hear Ken and John Paddy talking as they went down the drive on the motorbike, while next door a clock ticked with a slow, hoarse stroke. Madoc's grip on her fingers was painful.

"And the day you relinquish your licence, I'll transfer my share to your name, free of charge."

"But if we lose!" burst out Madoc. "Forty per cent! Anna having the controlling share and the right to take him to Shropshire! What do I do with Afonwen? Where do we go then?"

Siân said tentatively, "We'll still have Afonwen. And won't there be some income from stud fees?"

"Forty per cent!"

"You wouldn't have to struggle on with Afonwen," pointed out Dava. "Anna's well organised and the stud is already established. She thinks she could guarantee a full service book for the first three years and that would give you a share amounting to around sixteen thousand each year. You could sell Afonwen and live quite comfortably almost anywhere."

Madoc had to struggle to get up out of the depths of the settee and Dava was on his feet first so the blow was never offered, but nobody had any doubt that violence had been intended. Siân, too, got up, frightened by all the dark emotions around her.

Madoc said, "What if I make sure Cymru can't run at Aintree?"

"You wouldn't!" said Siân and was ignored.

"Peter said you'd think of that. I hoped he might be wrong. If either horse doesn't go to post, the other is deemed to have won the wager."

"I hope he's putting a security guard on Musketeer then," said Madoc bitterly. The little room suddenly seemed much too small to hold the two men.

"I think that's all," said Dava coldly. "I'd like you to go now. Grace has some paperwork to put into the computer."

Madoc went straight through the kitchen and out into the blustery sunshine of the yard and he did not stop until he reached Cymru's box. He stood with his head against the door jamb, more defeated than Siân had ever seen him.

"Don't be so angry," she said, putting her arms round him. He was rigid.

"How could he?" he said tightly. "I've ridden for him all these years and he never even spoke to her, and now, with one stroke, he does this to me. How could he do it!"

She shook her head, and rubbed his back, carefully, remembering that there were still bruises from a fall two days ago. "I understand it," she said. "I thought perhaps you did too, because of us... He loves her. Whether she loves him or not doesn't matter. Maybe it is just a clever ploy, maybe he has been taken in, it doesn't matter. The arrangement gives him an honourable way of pleasing her, without cutting you out."

He said, "I see a newly widowed woman throwing herself at Dava to get what she wants, and Dava being totally irrational. She can offer far more money than I can and there's nothing I can do about it. Except perhaps get him drunk," he added bitterly.

Siân said, "She's offered him so much money that he feels he can give Cymru to you."

"Yes — a percentage!"

"And an incentive to win." Cymru turned his head briefly from his manger, but did not consider it worth while to leave his oats.

Siân shook Madoc slightly. "Don't you think he can?"

He began at last to relax and turned to put his arms around her.

"I wanted to give you Afonwen," he said, "and a bright, busy world all to ourselves, where we could succeed by our own efforts and count the gains our own. Dava has spoiled all that."

Siân said robustly, "He hasn't. It's up to you now. You told me Cymru could beat Musketeer at level weights and isn't that what you've got? A good field, the kind of fences he likes and a fair test? You mustn't give up because Dava has a bet with Mrs S-H. It doesn't say much for your faith in him if you don't think you can ride Cymru to win."

He smiled slightly. "Perhaps we ought to put you up instead, if you're that confident."

"I'm only telling you to get things in perspective."

"All right, Minerva." He managed a better smile.

Ted Gray, wheeling his motorbike out on to the yard, slanted a look at the lovers, blatantly twined together at the door. Madoc's head was bowed and he clung to Siân as though he might fall, but she caught Ted's dark, distracted stare and she trembled.

TWENTY-SEVEN

Friday, April the second, dawned bright and clear, the sort of morning that made your blood run faster, even without the tingle of excitement supplied by the running of the McTay Trophy, a day to be up and about early, as Siân was, or cheerful about the end of a spell of duty, like the security man finishing his night watch and chatting to her as she collected the morning feeds for Aholibah, Did Ya See Me and Carola.

"I got curious about this racing lark," he said. "Went over to Aintree with me brother yesterday to have a look. Huge, isn' it? If it wasn' for the telly screens you wouldn' have a clue what goes on down the far end."

Siân, never having been to Liverpool, agreed politely.

"Did you have any luck? Any winners, I mean?"

"Yeah, matter of fact I did. Funny thing, it come from the opposition — Walbrook's. I only backed it 'cos of its name. Night Watch — well, I couldn' pass that up, now could I? No offence, like!"

Siân congratulated him and went to feed her horses, reflecting ruefully that the bookies must love people whose money went on such illogical hunches. It would be wonderful to picture all the supporters of the entries for the McTay Trophy: the whole of Wales would back Cymru, while Canterbury would attract its citizens and the Archbishop, Musketeer the Sealed Knot society, and Black Letter every antiquarian bookseller in the country. Each of them might seem the ideal bet for these people but there were still four other horses, any of which could win this afternoon. Siân, fitting Aholibah's manger into its holder, wished she could share these cheerful fancies with Madoc, but he was tensely concentrated on the horses and she respected his single-mindedness.

Dava sent his runners off good and early. He personally inspected the bandaging of each horse's legs, muttering to himself about travelling being as much strain as racing, and insulted Jack by reminding him to drive carefully, no matter how horrendous the traffic might be on Scotland Road. Jack, his face twisted with suppressed pain, climbed into the cab and, when the ramps had been put up, dourly informed Dava that he had no option, did he? He would drive with the grace of a ballerina.

As the horsebox grumbled down the Tunnel, John Paddy produced a sheaf of newspapers and, holding them up one by one to the ghastly light coming in through the window, began to read out the racing headlines. Siân groaned at the terrible puns which the writers seemed to find necessary: Black Letter Day, Musketeer on Target, McTay Plaid for Cymru?, Canterbury to Trot Up. John Paddy found them funny but Ted broke in restlessly to ask how the betting forecasts looked.

"Jackie boy's in the first, isn't he? Hmph. They're only quoting tens. Somebody know something we don't? After that win at Cheltenham? What d'you say, Ted?"

Ted shrugged awkwardly. "Some good horses in there, after all. What about the McTay?"

"I thought you didn't like 'that grey bastard'? All right, all right, I'll look. It's too dark for you to read it over there." John Paddy held the papers out of Ted's reach and read the forecasts with maddening deliberation. "Cymru's favourite — just. He's seven-to-two, and Musketeer and Canterbury are on threes.

Black Letter and Ordnance at sevens and eights, Gambling Queen tens but might go out — there's a query, she's missed a workout last week with heat in a joint. That enough for you? Where's your money gone?"

Ted flapped a hand. "I don't back 'em, not unless it's one of mine."

"You'll have a bit on Jackie, I s'pose."

"Mm." Ted turned, with an air of gathering his courage, and asked Siân if she was going to plait Cymru for the McTay parade.

"I expect so. I've been practising on Hollie since you showed me. I'm going to start with his mane and leave the tail till last, then, even if I don't get it right, some of it will be done and he'll still look quite tidy."

"I'll come and check him over for you," said Ted, "and see that everything's stitched good and firm."

Siân admitted, "I was going to use rubber bands."

"No, not on the tail. Spoils the look of that long plait completely."

"Oh well, I'll just leave it; brush it out and leave well alone."

"I'll lend you a needle and thread. D'you want black or white?"

Siân, cornered by this persistence, decided on black, and Ted brought out a card of linen thread and a blunt-ended needle, which she put away in Cymru's tack box.

"Scissors?" he went on.

"No... wait a minute, yes. They were in the corner."

"Fine." Ted sat back with an odd air of relief.

John Paddy, without lowering the Racing Post, said, "If you two are that keen, you can tart up Ledgy as well, save me having to do it."

"There isn't a turnout prize for that race," said Ted, so sharply that Siân looked at him in surprise. He was pale and twitchy, but then he never looked very well and perhaps travelling in the living area of the wagon didn't suit him. Siân was nervous herself at the prospect of attending Cymru and taking part in the parade, so she dismissed Ted's behaviour as worry and thought instead about her own forthcoming duties.

* * *

Madoc, too, was at Aintree in good time, but there were others ahead of him. Close by the changing room door, almost among the conditional jockeys, was Justin, nattering and jibing with the force of nerves. Madoc barked his shin on a bench and corrected himself hurriedly, dismayed by the upsurge of hatred he felt. *I must control this,* he thought — *there's no place for distractions today.* He itched to flatten the too-handsome face but there were more important things to be done before he could give himself that pleasure. He found his place and changed, slowly, trying to keep his emotions in balance. It was easier said than done. The edgy Lancashire voice cut through the surrounding chat as though intended for his ears alone. Madoc reminded himself that, around the time of the Bangor spring meeting, Pick had been away for a week, reportedly beaten up by an angry husband, and the jocks had been highly amused and not at all sympathetic. None the less, he found it hard to distance himself as he usually did before important races and he was short with Jerry, who, by contrast, was relaxed and inclined to chat.

"Cock o' the North seems in good voice."

"Yeah."

"I hope he hasn't got some stupid practical joke up his sleeve. He's in the mood for it."

"Mmh."

"What's up with you? You sound like an amateur waiting for his first ride."

Madoc pulled himself together. "Sorry. Miles away."

"It's not that big a deal, you know."

"What!"

"This bet between your Guv'nor and Mrs S-H. Lot of publicity, I suppose — have you had to put watchdogs on, like we have? — but God knows, Madoc, we ought to be able to cope with that sort of thing by now."

"We are getting long in the tooth," agreed Madoc with a slight smile. "I suppose that's why the result bothers me."

"That was all you were thinking of, was it?" asked Jerry curiously. "I thought your mind was somewhere else. No? Well, I don't think you need to worry. I don't think she's planning to take this one away from old Dava, not like she did with Baner. The Hon. Alistair isn't breathing down her neck any more, is he?"

"I'm more bothered about them both taking him away from me," said Madoc.

"Agh, sorry, chum, I forgot — your sheep farm. Yes, I can see she might just throw a spanner in the works. Still, at least this way you have a chance of influencing the results. They might have decided the balance of the partnership by tossing a coin!"

"Very true," said Madoc with a reluctant grin. "You don't know how true that is."

"There now. Haven't I made you feel better? Give me a putty medal and a halo out of that top drawer."

Madoc sat beside Jerry, relishing the sound common sense he exuded, from his balding, wrinkled head to the tips of his prehensile toes. Justin's voice was still carping on at the far side of the dressing room but for the moment it had ceased to be an irritant.

Listening, Jerry suppressed a laugh. "You know he's never ridden round Aintree, don't you?"

"How'd he manage to avoid that?"

"Oh, I don't know, but I'm sure he hasn't. That's why Colin and his assistants have stuck him over there by the door."

"Getting their own back, perhaps, for the opinions he doesn't keep to himself about the valet service?"

"I wouldn't know," grinned Jerry and dived into his first set of colours as if for time to think. "What I do know is that I owe him one for cutting the toes off a perfectly good pair of socks when I beat him by a short head at Sandown last week... I've got an idea."

Madoc, normally too easy-going to indulge in pranks, couldn't help grinning as Jerry outlined a well-worn routine. "Suits me," he said.

"Get Kev, then — he can be the one with the cup of tea."

Madoc strolled over to canvass Kevin and Jerry rolled up the Racing Post and squinted through it at them. Kevin's face creased with amusement.

Madoc came back. "All set."

Jerry looked at the clock. "Plenty of time before the first. Don't want the stewards complaining we've made the little bugger late. OK, Kevin, come and sit here." He raised his voice. "Pick! Pickering! What're you doing over there?"

"These awkward devils have put me here."

"What? They've punched your ear?"

"They — oh hell, I'll come over."

Jerry winked at Madoc. "Seconds out," he said.

"Just because I haven't been here before," Justin was saying as he made his way across. "They've got a down on me, you know. Two years I've had my licence and I think I've earned a better place than that."

"There are so many of us elderly has-beens here today," said Jerry comfortingly, "there simply isn't room for the young and talented in the first-class compartment."

"Ah, come on, Jerry, nobody's suggesting they should kick you out. I'd just like a better perch than the one I've been given."

"Maybe they think you should ride round the National fences before you qualify for that," said Kevin. "No, mind my tea! I've no idea what they think really."

"Haven't you been round before?" asked Jerry, in carefully faked surprise.

"Well, as a matter of fact, no, I — " Justin was about to launch into explanations, but Kevin spluttered noisily into his tea and drew everyone's attention to himself.

"Ugh! No sugar! Madoc, be a duck and fetch the sugar. You don't want to hear how Pick has avoided Becher's Brook up till now, do you."

"I don't know how you can drink tea before you ride," said Madoc, wandering off to bring a sugar bowl.

"How can you drink tea with sugar in it?" asked Justin.

"Well, you put your lips to the cup, like this — mind I'd rather have whisky, but it's too early in the day. Ta," he added, as Madoc came back. "You don't take sugar, do you Madoc? No? Somebody did tell me it was muscle... If you're not careful there won't be enough slack in your breeks for you to bend over. What'll you do if they split going over Becher's and you on the telly and all?"

Madoc, still holding the sugar bowl, said, "I'll just have to smile and blush prettily."

Jerry grabbed Madoc's waistband and stuffed the rolled-up Racing Post inside. "Not a lot of room there!" he chided, and retrieved the paper in order to turn on Justin, who backed a little, warily. "What about you? You've had a bit of time off recently. Manage to keep the weight off OK?"

"He has a harem to do that for him," said Kevin. It was somewhere around then that the other jockeys began to cock an ear to the conversation. Madoc noticed a subtle change in the background level of noise and eased closer to Jerry and Justin.

"Well," said Jerry, "they'd better be keeping him fit. It's a long walk home from Becher's."

"Thanks for the vote of confidence," said Justin. "I don't have to fall just because it's my first ride here."

"That young horse you've got in the McTay isn't all that bold a jumper, though, is he? You see the size of the Chair? You'll have to sit tight."

"He was OK at Haydock," said Justin uneasily. He had unnerved himself by walking the course on Thursday, originally in order to familiarise himself with the confusion of crossings where the Mildmay course and the National course converged, but, in effect, he had been overwhelmed by the sheer size of the fences and the immense width and flatness of the course.

"Ah, Haydock!" Kevin was scornful. "Nothing like Becher's at Haydock."

Justin, out of bravado, had taken up his father's challenge that he would not dare to stand on the far lip of the Brook and look up at the spot where he and Canterbury would be jumping. Now he looked faintly sick. He said, "They've levelled the landing. And the Guv'nor says the Chair is easier."

"Still need to sit ready for them," said Jerry, shaking his head. "There's only one fence doesn't have a drop behind it. All the others — well, watch me." He stood up, crouched a little and pushed the rolled-up Racing Post down the back of his breeches. "The trick is, keep your back straight, see, like this, keep your spine straight, so you're balanced over the drop. You have to sit behind the movement — just a little bit." He put his feet apart, bent his knees and demonstrated. "Try it. Keep the newspaper touching your spine — here, I'll put it in for you." He whipped the roll out and stuck it down the back of Justin's breeches, and Justin, although he shook out his hair, made no attempt to stop him. "Now, go on, get your feet apart. Bend your knees — that's it... Now... !"

And Madoc tipped half a pound of sugar down the tempting gap.

The roar of laughter that went up proved that everyone knew what was going on, but Justin's steam-whistle shriek cut through it. For a moment he was stuck, completely immobile, and Kevin and Jerry used the instant to step prudently backward. Then he lunged furiously at Madoc and, with laughter, Madoc ran. Everyone knew it was no contest. Madoc's legs were too long and Justin was hampered by the exquisite grittiness of the sugar working its leisurely way to his boots. A lot of the dodging jockeys carefully got in his way. On the second circuit Madoc pushed the sugar bowl into Jerry's hands. On the third he eased up, one wary eye on Justin, keeping near the other two pranksters but fairly certain there wasn't going to be an explosion.

Justin was bowlegged by this time and the changing room was hysterical.

"What d'you think you're trying to do, cripple me?"

"Now, now," soothed Kevin in nursemaid accents, "the little boy only meant it as a joke."

"Stupid bugger, what's he trying to prove?" He shook the slack of his breeches, futilely. "Gor bloody hell, this is agony." For some reason the valets laughing annoyed him more than anyone else and, shutting both eyes, he shoved Madoc hard in the chest. Madoc only gave way gracefully and laughed.

"Leave off, Pick," said Jerry placatingly.

"Smirking bastard, think you're God Almighty... "

"As a matter of fact it was my idea," said Jerry, catching Justin's arm before he could push Madoc again.

"Was it now?" Justin stood balanced, his anger momentarily blocked by the respect the whole room felt for the champion. He flicked the hair off his face with an insolent gesture. "Yes. Well. Ha ha, very funny. So old Madoc was just the stooge. He likes things secondhand, don't you, Madoc? Cars, jokes, women, they're all the same, hey, Madoc?" He shook off Jerry's hand and headed towards his distant place. But he turned back to face Madoc before he had gone more than a couple of paces. "She must be due her MOT test by now. Got her booked in yet?"

He paused fractionally too long and Madoc caught him an unscientific but immensely satisfying blow on the left side of the jaw.

Everyone jumped in then. Kevin pinned Madoc's elbows, Johnny Robson and Derek hauled Justin to his feet, Jerry got between the two factions and faced them down.

"Enough's enough."

Somebody asked plaintively, "What did he say, for Christ's sake?"

"Let go," panted Madoc, jerking in Kevin's grip.

"Not on your nellie," said Kevin, hanging on grimly, as Justin showed signs of reviving temper.

"All right, calm down," said the senior master valet, moving in carefully. "Take off those breeches, Pick, and we'll have them inside out and shaken clean in no time. There's no need to make all this fuss over a joke."

"Tell him that," said Justin, thickly. "God, I bit my tongue too... Him and his high standards... Have you had *her* turned inside out and shaken clean? Pressure washed and hoovered?"

Kevin gasped as Madoc struggled towards Justin, but Jerry got in his way — slow, deliberate, and unmoved — and Madoc's rage died down.

The grouped figures spread a little, warily. The brief hush that the fight had caused swelled into noise again and the jockeys who had climbed on to benches to see better jumped down, not fully understanding the exchange, but realising the fun was over. Johnny and Derek cautiously let go of Justin.

"I'm all right," he said crossly. "For God's sake, I can stand by myself. I'm not going to the doctor, he'll ground me."

Kevin released Madoc's arms. "Look out now," he said, "Any more shenanigans and we'll have the stewards chasing our tails."

The noises of the changing room gradually reasserted themselves: the trial scales began to quiver under booted feet, small curses punctuated the bustle. Justin turned carefully and walked away, crunching sugar underfoot and saying, loudly enough to be heard, "You must be bloody desperate."

Madoc turned his back, clenching his jaw on the anger that surged up again. He pulled on his colours, savagely, snapping the bands round his wrists, hardly able to see straight. Kevin and Jerry looked at each other and quietly went on getting ready for the first race.

When there was no more to do — saddles, weights and numbercloths all handed over to trainers or travelling lads — Jerry said quietly to Madoc, "Sorry."

"For what? You weren't to know."

"I never thought it would spark all that off. What's up with you two? I know he niggles you, but he niggles everybody."

Madoc drew a long, calming breath. "Some day, Jerry, I'll tell you, but at the moment I ask myself, do I really want everyone to know? And the answer is, no." He couldn't discuss Siân. It was nobody's business but hers, and to make it public was to reduce himself to Justin's level. "It's just bad luck that I haven't seen him till today and we're all that much more wound up than usual." He achieved a smile. "And the real business of the day has hardly started."

"Jockeys out," said a voice, and Jerry stood up, punching Madoc sympathetically on the shoulder. Kevin stepped delicately over the heaps of spilt sugar and the undrunk milky puddle of his tea.

"Oh dear," he said in a female voice, "just look at the mess you boys have made." Then dropping to his normal tones, "And I never could stand tea with sugar in it."

TWENTY-EIGHT

Siân was in Cymru's box in the Aintree stables, busily wiping the last specks of dust from his gleaming, marbled black coat. She had plaited his mane, wrapping the pale ends of each plait in a rubber band and doubling them under out of sight, and now he looked strangely cold and aristocratic. Siân rubbed his nose, impressed with the transformation.

"You're starting to fade," she said, tracing the faint stripe that was forming down the bone of his face. "What colour will you be by midsummer, hm?"

Cymru put his ears back and avoided her hand. He was feeling mean, he was hungry and thirsty and his mouth was dry, and he was not inclined to endure much fuss. Siân popped a wet sponge into his mouth for a moment, then slipped his bridle on, and he champed sharply at the cold metal of the bit while she put his headcollar back on and tied him up again. He fidgeted, shifting his racing plates with little clicks on the bare floor as he tried to peer out of the doorway at other horses going by. *The first hurdle race must be over,* thought Siân, *I'm about on time. But is he going to co-operate while I plait his tail?* She threaded the needle Ted had given her, and poked it through her collar for safe keeping, then damped a water brush and applied it to the top of his tail. Cymru sidled, crossly. She moved her grooming box round in order to stand on it and prodded him firmly.

"We haven't got time for your daftness."

He stood, to her relief, but with an air of suppressed impatience, eyeing her over his shoulder, while still flickering his ears at the open half-door.

There were enough long hairs at the top of his tail to draw into the plait, but she must get it right first time, firm enough to stay tidy, not so tight that it would upset him; there would not be time to have a second try, even if Cymru's patience lasted that long. She worked as rapidly as she could, hoping he would continue to watch the outside world and disregard her fingers creating the fine plait down the bone of his dock, tidying all the stray hairs into a regular pattern. Ignoring the ache which was settling in her upper arms

345

she plaited on doggedly, right down to the pale hairs at the free end of his tail. Then she caught the end of the plait with her knotted thread, stitching it tight, and doubled it up underneath itself just below the end of the bone, where she fastened it off, forming a loop as Ted had shown her. "If you were hunting," he'd said, "you'd stitch the halves of the loop together so it couldn't get caught on anything, but that won't be a problem on a racecourse, so leave it." Siân, glancing at her watch, saw that there wouldn't be time anyway for a second lot of stitching. "You stay right there. I need the scissors." She got off the box, dug them out of their corner, and snipped at the dangling thread.

"Now I remember why I thought I hadn't got any scissors," she said to Cymru. "These are as blunt as your backside. Come *on.*" The last fibres parted, raggedly, and she poked the needle into its card of thread and put it back in the box. "There now — all set. Nobody's going to peer under there to see if the ends are cleanly cut, are they? There's just your rug to put on, then we're ready to go."

She tucked his reins under the roller, buckled on the leading rein and led him out, turning him quietly so she could push the door shut. As she clicked the padlock into place she was assailed by the usual momentary panic that she hadn't got the key but it was there, safe in her trouser pocket. It was her constant dread that she would have to ask the stable manager to open a box on her horse's return from a race. Dava, safety conscious, always supplied an extra padlock, the key kept by Jack Brindley, but Siân left that in her pocket. Jack was still not too mobile and might be hard to find with a tired horse in tow.

She saw Ted Gray approaching and stifled irritation. She hoped he wouldn't nitpick, because there was no time to correct trifling flaws in turnout.

He nodded approval of the plaited mane, surveyed the trim legs, the oiled feet, the set of the rug and roller. Then he moved to the rear. Siân held Cymru watchfully; his ears said he didn't approve of Ted.

"You haven't pulled his tail out over the fillet string."

Ted fussed over it and Cymru flinched and kicked out with one hind leg. "Stand up! Siân, look, you haven't fixed the end of this plait."

"I have!" she wailed.

"Well it's loose — look." He came to Cymru's head, and the horse sidled, eyeing him. "Stand, stupid. I'll hold him if you want to get your thread."

Siân hesitated, but she allowed Ted to take Cymru's rein while she, too, checked his tail. Sure enough, the long plait hung free. She gave a cry of frustration. "I swear I fastened that properly!" Then she reached for the key and went through the time-consuming process of unlocking and opening the door, finding needle and thread, coming out and restitching the plait. Cymru stamped impatiently and began to scrape with a forefoot. Ted checked him and Siân bent over the plait.

Her fingers grew still. She had been certain that her stitching was firm and here was proof: the loose end of thread was short, with no trailing length, no kinks, no fuzzy chewed fibres where her blunt scissors had struggled through. It was cut short and clean. Her brain began to fizz. She very nearly said something and then she shut her mouth abruptly because only Ted could have cut it. But why? She could see no reason. Ken or John Paddy might, on a less-important occasion, have played a practical joke on her, but not Ted, the humourless, unoriginal one. She thought furiously. If he had done it, it was to distract her attention for a minute or two. From what? He had a sharp knife. What was he doing?

She controlled herself, finished her stitching and put away the needle and thread. She snapped the padlock on again and pretended her agitation was sheer hurry.

"Phew, what a rush! Ta. I must go now or I'll be late for saddling."

"Jack gave me the key to Hollie's box," he said. "D'you want it now, or later?" He gave it to her, keeping her attention on his hands, preventing her from looking at Cymru. "Better dash on now. They're going into the prelim ring already."

Siân crushed down her anger at being rushed when it was Ted who had delayed her. She just nodded and set off at a brisk walk. Cymru, impatient, tucked in his nose and pranced, but the lead rein held him and she was thankful — a loose horse now would be the final straw! Above all she must get him to post in one piece. The security men watched her go out, observant but uncurious, but she looked back under cover of the turn through the gate and her suspicions were confirmed. Ted was following, head up, unusually alert, his eyes on the stallion. She would have to keep going and resist the temptation to check the horse over until he was no longer watching her, but not until she reached the ring, with its audience of critical eyes, was she free of him. He peeled off towards the nearest bar and she heaved a sigh of relief.

Round and round the paddock with the seven other runners. Was the horse all right? He was doing his usual dancing but there was nothing odd about it — he felt normal, he walked sound. The maroon rug flapped in the breeze and he kicked out once, but she growled at him and he subsided with a playful shake of the head. The horse was all right. So what was wrong?

The only thing he was wearing which could affect his race was the bridle — the bridle which Ted had had to himself for two or three minutes while she fiddled with needle and thread and Cymru's tail.

The pace was too quick for her to be able to check anything thoroughly, even on the nearest side to her, and with so many people watching she was unwilling to turn out of the trackway and draw attention. So she kept on walking and worried. When Dava appeared with saddle and weightcloth, she was tremendously relieved.

He was alone and that, too, was a help. Mrs Selwyn-Hughes was with Peter Walbrook as he saddled Musketeer further down the line. Siân turned Cymru briskly and pushed him into place without ceremony. Dava glanced at her.

"Go easy. Just hold him quietly." His attention was centred on the horse as he stripped off the rug and put on Madoc's good saddle. The weightcloth contained nearly half a stone of lead strips and required exact placing so that it would lie free of Cymru's shoulders yet close to his centre of gravity at a gallop. Siân curbed her impatience, but as soon as Dava replaced the rug she spoke urgently.

"Dava!"

She never, ever, forgot to call him 'Mister' and he stared.

"What?"

"Will you check the bridle? I — there's something wrong."

He hesitated. What could be wrong? Siân had cleaned and saddle-soaped that bridle endlessly over the past couple of days and it gleamed. He cast an eye over the straps, held the bit out level, checked the total fit, and nodded satisfaction.

"Perfectly OK."

He refastened the roller, dismissing her worries, but Siân was fretting still. She ran her fingers over the familiar leather, pulling, picking at the stitching she had done so painstakingly under Bill Houghton's eagle eye. There was nothing, nothing...

"Come on," said Dava, tucking the reins under the roller.

"The reins — Dava, look, look here — "

At the authority in her voice he was instantly alert.

"What is it?"

"Look. Someone's taken a sharp knife and slit all these stitches." She had hold of the right rein. "See? From the bit ring, here, nearly to the end of the billet."

Dava pushed his finger into the slack of the loop and the remaining stitches parted.

"Duw," he said, "that would just about have held until he got over the first fence." He looked at Siân. "How did you know about this? What's going on?"

"I don't know, but the only person who could have done it is Ted Gray. The bridle was OK until he came to check us over."

"Would you swear to that?" His eyes were piercing. "I have to tell security, and the police... Even if there isn't a legal prosecution there's bound to be a Jockey Club enquiry. If you're right, it means a trip to Portman Square. You'll have to be prepared to face the stewards. Would you?"

"Of course," she said sharply. "Why not?"

"Give me the lead then," he said. "I'll take him into the ring while you run after John Paddy and get the bridle off Irish Legend. Shift!"

She was gone like a rabbit.

* * *

Madoc perched very steadily over Cymru's withers as he cantered to the start. He did his best to ignore Musketeer and Black Letter, ahead, and Canterbury following, and to persuade the stallion to do the same, but it was not easy. Cymru was excited by the changing of his bridle in the ring, and by the parade in front of packed stands and crowded rails; even at Chester there had not been such a charged atmosphere. Periodically he bored down on the bit, trying to get hold, to take command from Madoc, who foiled him each time and blessed Siân's observation, knowing that the horse was so wound up he was going to go off like a bomb once the race started. The brakes held all right when he reached the start but Madoc wondered whether Cymru still had enough sense to tackle the big fences intelligently. He wondered, too, who was behind the sabotage: Anna Selwyn-Hughes? Surely she would not want Cymru so much she was prepared to endanger him? Justin? But how could he have arranged it so quickly? He walked Cymru round, assessing the opposition, distracted by the possibilities. Jerry rode by on Musketeer, keeping out of range. The bay horse had been on the light side at Christmas, unfurnished and green-looking, but three weeks ago at Cheltenham he had come out a picture of health, packed with hard muscle and ready to run for his life. Although the going had been too deep for him and the older horses too experienced, knowledgeable opinion had said that, next year, with another season's stamina, it would be a different story. Madoc looked critically at him: he was slender, he looked like a flat racer. If the last three weeks had been wet, Cymru would have galloped all over him. But the weather had been dry and the flat Aintree course was riding fast, so only the wide, extraordinary fences would be in Cymru's favour.

When all the other horses had cantered to the start, Madoc walked the stallion back to inspect the first fence. Jerry followed him and they both rode their horses up to the spruce for them to feel the height of the obstacle. Cymru was intrigued by the smell for a moment but then turned towards Musketeer, flattening his ears crossly, so Madoc growled at him and turned him away. A physical attack on the opposition would almost certainly lose him the wager. They cantered back to the start and the tapes were wound down.

Madoc had never known the routine of the start seem so long-winded. It must be his own nerves which so strung time out; certainly the stallion was on edge, so that tightening girth and surcingle was a delicate operation. At last they were all checked off the starter's list. He mounted his rostrum, the white flag went up, the eight runners began to move into a disciplined bunch and the tapes finally flew.

Cymru bounded forward, ears pricked intently at the big green obstacle ahead. There were horses alongside him and he bounced and fought Madoc's restraining hands. There was Canterbury on his inside, Lavender Blue on his outside, neither hurrying but both crowding him, knowing how easy it was to upset him and to force a mistake over these big and unfamiliar fences. Cymru snapped his ears flat and Madoc heard Justin shout, "I'm watching you, you big sod!" while Mark White, grinning on his other side, held an unswerving line towards the first fence. Cymru tilted his head, trying to slide the bit into his teeth and not succeeding, but each time winning a little more rein and pushing his head in front. And each time Justin let out a notch on Canterbury so that he came alongside once more. *Steady, you fool,* thought Madoc, trying to send out calming emotions. *There's nearly three miles to go before you need to feel like this.*

Cymru's only response was another impatient bounce.

Why is Canterbury up front so soon! — *He usually runs best when he's waited with* — *it can't be a serious attempt to win! Maybe they're trying to crack Cymru*

— make the race for Musketeer... It doesn't make sense.

As the first fence loomed up, Justin kicked on and Cymru surged forward angrily, determined not to let the bay head him. Madoc had to let him go this time or be pitched off. All three rose together and although Cymru jumped clear, the startled flicker of his ears at the rattle of spruce following Lavender Blue and Canterbury warned Madoc that there would be a surge of panic as he landed. He managed to sit tight and stay with the horse but by the time he was fully in control again he was a length ahead. Then Justin and Mark reappeared on either side of him, grim and determined. Just for a moment Madoc was back at Bangor, with Kevin deputising for Justin, riding upsides in the same way and trying to half-length him. It hadn't worked then because Diaghilev was not a good enough horse, but now it was Canterbury who was hustling him, with Justin his determined pilot. The speed was creeping up once more as each looked for the advantage.

They came to the second fence three abreast and again Cymru rose clear while the other two scattered branches. This time the stallion did not startle, and when Canterbury came alongside, almost dangerously close, he swung his head jealously.

"Give me room, damn you!" shouted Madoc. Justin only bared his teeth in a grin.

They were galloping hard towards the Chair, the biggest open ditch in the country, hugely tall, yawningly deep, right under the buzzing stands. It was not a wide fence, which made its height all the more enormous. Madoc was sure Cymru would jump it if only he wasn't distracted, but what satisfaction it would give Justin if he did fall here... And it was here that it must happen. It was now, going in under that looming green wall, that Canterbury must be pushed forward into a half length lead. Madoc waited for the telltale movement of Justin's hands, heels, whip, but there was nothing, no attempt to push on, no sense of attack. He sat tight and drove the stallion at the fence.

"Gaaarn!"

The violence of the leap took them clear. As the great fence swung away beneath them and the horse landed, bunched, thrust forward again, there was a rattling, sickening crunch behind. Madoc looked back, thinking that Canterbury must gave gone, but no, he was still there — lurching a bit, but upright —it must have been Mark White's Lavender Blue who had fallen. Madoc spared him no sympathy. He shouldn't have ridden up to force the pace, not over fences like these.

Then Canterbury inched alongside again and they jumped the water together.

Justin was still letting Canterbury lean into Cymru so round the first turn, Madoc had to take a wider course than he might ordinarily have done. As they galloped side by side across the Melling Road and out on to the firm turf of the country, Madoc looked across at Justin, wondering just how far he was prepared to go in this duel. There wasn't much of his face to be seen under the disguising cap and goggles but there was a pinched look to his cheeks as he looked ahead at the long run to the next — the fence that was always the first to meet the cavalry charge in the National, huge, green and astonishingly wide, a great barrier right across the course. In a rare flash of insight, Madoc knew that Justin's nerve had failed him, back at the Chair.

He drove the stallion on.

Again Cymru rose, soared and landed, secure in his power, revelling in the challenge. Madoc looked back at Justin and saw Canterbury sprawl and shake him as he landed. The rest of the field rose to the fence. Madoc let out a yell of triumph and rode on.

Cymru was alone now, his long stride eating up the ground. Madoc switched him to the right lead and let him bowl on and the outward stretch below the railway banking flowed beneath and behind him, a great silent green rollercoaster. Anywhere else these monsters would be masterpieces in their own right. Here they were only preludes to Becher's.

Madoc held his usual route down the centre of the course, and Cymru, facing at last a challenge large enough for his abilities, came back obediently to the left lead and took the fence straight and true, lifting into a bold leap at the perfect take-off point and soaring over the spruce and the steep-banked Brook. Then he thumped down, gathered himself, and slid away neatly to the rails and the turn.

Madoc risked a look behind him. Canterbury was landing over Becher's, stickily, Justin sitting at the full length of the reins. Musketeer was rising to it. *More than enough,* Madoc thought, *if Musketeer's still there.* He rode onwards with determination. There was no drop beyond the next fence where, years ago, Popham Down had refused, bringing carnage to a National and lasting fame to Foinavon. If Cymru did not stand back to jump this one, their joint career would be over. But he did, jauntily as ever, as though to say, "Me? Get too close to a fence? Never!"

"Good lad," said Madoc and looked ahead for the Canal Turn.

The Turn would never be allowed past the design stage of a modern racecourse. It is a right angle, demanding skills more often practised by three-day eventers. Madoc felt the bit delicately, lightly suggesting that Cymru should come over to the right and tackle the fence in a left-handed swing. Not long ago he would have got a stubborn "no" for an answer and they would have charged straight ahead for the Canal, wasting lengths and lengths turning wide, but now Cymru had learnt that this course demanded respect and that his rider knew its pitfalls and was guiding him for his own good. He obeyed and the awkward fence wheeled neatly beneath them.

It was impossible, though, to moderate the pace as the stallion pounded down to Valentine's Brook. He surged over it and set sail for home, happy to accept Madoc's instruction to change legs once more but giving him to understand that from now on he was to be no more than an educated passenger. Madoc went along with that, balancing through the swift, soaring jumps and blessing his luck that, after all, this horse had come to Aintree and proved that his talents were made for its unique challenge. The three fences beside the Canal fled away beneath the reaching black feet and Cymru galloped on, over the Melling Road once more, obediently seeking out the home turn among the confusing entrances of the Mildmay course.

As they met again the fence which had been Cymru's first experience of Aintree, Madoc felt a little mulish pause in his stride which said, "But I've done this!" He kicked on determinedly and the habit of obedience held. Again the bold leap, solidly balanced and neat. Madoc gathered the reins and risked another look behind.

Three horses abreast were jumping in his wake: Musketeer, Gambling Queen and Ordnance. They were near enough for Musketeer's famous finishing speed to be a danger. Madoc straightened and drove Cymru into the last.

The stallion responded bravely, flying the fence, touching down cleanly, galloping on as Madoc steered him right, off the chase course and onto the hard grass of the racecourse, clearing the Elbow and running into the wall of sound from the stands. Back went his ears. This was when horses came up to catch him. He could hear them behind. He half thought of swerving but Madoc kept him straight, spoke to him and drove him for the finish. Who was behind him? Gambling Queen? Musketeer? It didn't matter. Madoc drew his whip and swung it into Cymru's line of sight.

The black ears flattened tight to Cymru's head. He heard nothing of the crowd any more, no longer heard the hooves behind him, nor even the words that Madoc shouted as he urged him on. He abandoned everything but the need to out-distance any rival. No-one, no one was going to pass him. He would battle them off though the effort burst his heart. The crazy human on his back would have no need to strike if only he would remain in balance and abet his own madness, to let him run for his life up that endless, roaring run-in...

He did not know when he had passed the post. He only felt Madoc's balance alter and the urgency slacken. As his centre of gravity came back towards his quarters, he fell back to a canter, then a trot and finally a walk.

Two police horses closed in on him, rounded and stolid, their riders decked with flowing-plumed helmets, but by now he was conscious of the racing and the rivalry being over and he did not object to this honour. Madoc flung an arm down and round his sweating neck in an abandonment of gratitude.

The placed horses wheeled after him, pulling up, necks lowered and nostrils red, their ears pointing wearily outward. Jerry Monk grinned at Madoc and shook his fist in the air from beyond the flanking police horses.

Madoc only laughed and looked about to take stock of the horses who had finished behind him. Jerry with Musketeer; Johnny with Gambling Queen; Tom Firth on Ordnance; Kevin on Black Letter. Three missing.

He shouted, "Was Mark all right? I saw him go at the Chair."

One of the sergeants said, "He walked away OK."

Madoc nodded. It was as much as you could ask. The runners walked, surrounded by hot breath and steam, back towards the crowded enclosures and the excited faces lining the horse walk. Jerry shouted something that Madoc didn't catch.

"Sixty per cent!" he shouted back, but Jerry shook his head and rode closer, and shouted again.

"You forgot to tell Pick there's no drop at Foinavon's."

Madoc saw Jerry's grin and felt his own face split in answer. "Really! Dear, dear, I wonder how it came to slip my mind."

"That'll be worth more than a cup of cocoa from the missus tonight." Jerry had to fall back to let the police horses escort Cymru up the horse walk, but they were both laughing. The stallion began to jog-trot towards the shining glass of the winner's enclosure.

THE END

About This Book

This story is set in the world of National Hunt racing and therefore uses the names and geography of existing racecourses. All the places mentioned, except Afonwen, Claybrooke and Green Bank, are real. All the characters and most of the incidents are fictional.

I am grateful for the help given to me in 1994/5 by Mrs Margaret Kendall, who rode and trained, by Helen Louise Bevan who had recently obtained her conditional licence, and by Mr Stephen Pollard of the Jockey Club. They all patiently answered questions about procedure both on and off the racecourse. I realise that some of the technical details are now, inevitably, out of date, but they were accurate at the time so I have left them in period to support the sequel, *Scratch*

Sue Millard 2018

Other books by Sue Millard

SCRATCH

Sequel to Against the Odds.

A Woman. A Family. A Farm.

Siân and Madoc have borrowed heavily to buy a neglected farm, Stone Side, in Cumbria. They are land-rich now but short of cash and indebted not only to the bank but to members of their family.

Racehorses and Fell Ponies

Madoc has reluctantly had to give up his ambition to breed thoroughbreds, and instead runs the sheep farm and pre-trains young horses for National Hunt racing. Siân is a fierce mother of their three teenage children, Robbie, Cerys and Jack. In what free time she has, she buys and trains Fell ponies.

Although it will be a long haul before Stone Side begins to pay, it just might work. But...

Someone is Out to Destroy Them

When Madoc's brother calls-in a big loan, the tensions begin to mount... and on the wild fellside, for someone the stakes are as high as murder.

GENRE: Fiction, family saga / thriller, sporting, equestrian

ISBN 9780957361294 (Paperback) £ 12.99

Coachman

Good-looking and ambitious George Davenport travels to London with his bride Lucy, determined to make the most of his skill in driving a four-in-hand of horses. It's 1838. Queen Victoria is crowned and England is at peace, but it isn't a good time to be a coachman.

As George finds employment with William Chaplin, the "Napoleon of coaching", the first railways are about to open across the country. Their competition will kill off the road-coaching trade. George has a lot to come to terms with... even before the boss's daughter starts to stalk him.

GENRE: Historical fiction, romance, sporting, equestrian, transport.

Published: 2012.

ISBN: 978-0-9573612-5-6 (Paperback) £9.99

Kindle ASIN: B009DORFOI.

Hoofprints in Eden

Winner of the Saint and Company Prize at the Lake District Book of the Year Awards, 20 June 2006. Based on a 2-year-long series of interviews with established breeders, this book explores the Fell pony breed and its traditions at the start of the new millennium.

Read about the Fell pony's Cumbrian background, the events of a typical year, its life on the fell, its traditional keeping and its links with hill farming, its characteristics and the work it can do.

Fully illustrated, and complete with a dictionary of Cumbrian farming expressions.

GENRE: Non-fiction, equestrian, history, farm & working animals

Published by Hayloft, 2005.

ISBN 978-1-9045243-4-2 (Paperback) £17.00

Hoofprints in Eden

4-part digital edition for Kindle

The 2005 text is revised and additional photographs are included. Each part is roughly 25% of the whole book, though because some chapters are longer or shorter the number of chapters does vary.

Parts 1, 2, 3 and 4 (November-December 2013) are available on Kindle.

Kindle ASINs:

B00GB84MWC

B00GFW78L6

B00GWPCTD8

B00H8XMYMY

One Fell Swoop

This is where it all started, with humour, history and horses.

Norman Thelwell was Sue's hero (they both hailed from the Wirral) so when Sue moved to Cumbria and bought a Fell pony this "fellwell" book was the inevitable result.

A series of affectionate cartoons, poking gentle fun at the Fell breed and its history.

GENRE: Cartoon humour, farm & working animals.

ISBN 978-0-9573612-7-0 (Paperback) £5.00

Kindle ASIN B008ZBPB14

The Forthright Saga

Nothing ever happens in a small country town ... does it?

Nora Forthright and her grandson Wayne stumble through the fictional Cumbrian towns of Dangleby and Pullet St Mary, putting things right entirely by accident.

GENRE: Comedy thriller / cosy crime.

Published: 2012.

ISBN: 978-0-9573612-3-2 (Paperback) £6.99

Kindle ASIN: B0099RQNLU

For Children

Dragon Bait

Princess Andra volunteers to act as bait for the dragon ravaging her father's lands, on condition that she is released from an arrangement to marry a foreign prince.

Unfortunately the Knight Rescuer who turns up is not the trusty old retainer she expects, but an unknown conservationist who wants the dragon, not the lady. After that very little goes according to plan.

GENRE: Comic fantasy (age 9-12).

Published: 2012.

ISBN: 978-0-9573612-1-8 (Paperback) £6.99

Kindle ASIN: B008K8SDWG

Fell Fun and Fell Facts

Two activity books for children relating to ponies, and Fell ponies in particular.

Fell Fun

for ages 4 to 7 years

Puzzles, counting, colouring, spot the difference, spot the same, matching, rhyming, starting letters, mazes and dot to dot, cutting and sticking – all about ponies.

GENRE: Activity book. 20 pages. £2.00

Fell Facts

for 7 years and upwards

Description of the Fell pony breed, what the ponies can do,, where they live, crosswords, wordsearches, picture quiz, a story and lots of pictures, plus a list of other books and DVDs about Fell ponies.

GENRE: Activity book. 20 pages. £2.00

Both books can go in one mailing for the same postage cost.

Fell Fun and **Fell Facts** were produced at the request of the Fell Pony Society and may also be purchased from the FPS office in Appleby, Cumbria, and at shows and events run by the Society.

Printed in Poland
by Amazon Fulfillment
Poland Sp. z o.o., Wrocław